I0692921

SYLVIA MERCEDES

THE VENATRIX CHRONICLES BOOK 2

For Una

THE VENATRIX

Drauval Borough

Skada Mountains

Aalis River

Castra Brecat

Wodechran

Sang River

Tchanor City

CHRONICLES

Aldreda Borough

The Great Barrier

Dulimurian

The Witchwood

Sang River

KINGDOM
OF
PERRINION

THE VENATRIX

Aalis River

Rivanduru

Caiduru

Hollen

Elsinoe

Dunloch Castle

Milisendis

Cabralet

WODECHRAN
BOROUGH

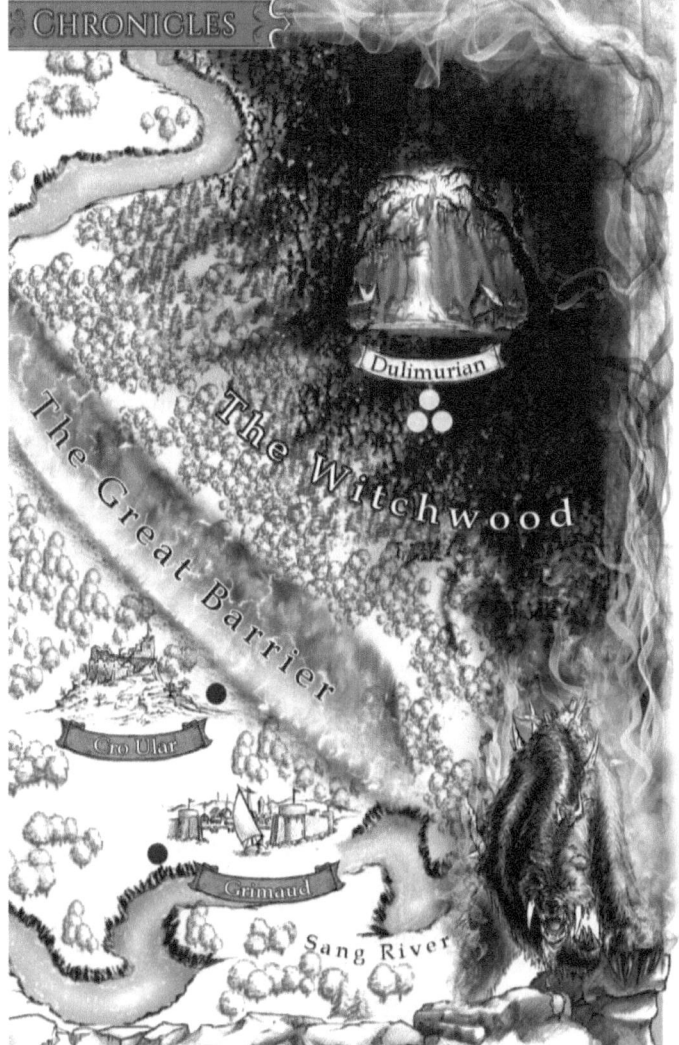

Dulimurian

The Witchwood

The Great Barrier

Cro Ular

Grimaud

Sang River

GLOSSARY OF SHADES

Shades: Disembodied spirit-beings who have escaped from their hellish dimension—the Haunts—and entered the mortal world. They cannot exist in a physical reality without mortal hosts, whom they possess and endow with unnatural powers. If left unchecked, they will gain ascendancy within a host-body and oust the original soul, taking full possession.

The following are the known varieties of shades as catalogued by the Order of Saint Evander:

ANATHEMAS
Abilities pertain to blood and curse-casting.

APPARITIONS
Abilities pertain to mind control and manipulation.

ARCANES
Mysterious entities with abilities not fully understood, but which seem to pertain to energies such as heat, motion, light, magnetism, and electricity.

ELEMENTALS
Abilities pertain to the natural elements of wind, fire, water, earth.

EVANESCERS
Abilities pertain to *evanescing*, or instantaneous distance-travel.

FERALS
Abilities pertain to heightened senses, augmented strength and agility.

LURES
Abilities pertain to enchanting voices and siren calls.

SEERS
Abilities pertain to visions, foretelling, and predictions. May also look into the past.

SHIFTERS
Abilities pertain to temporary transformation of host-bodies.

TRANSMUTERS
Abilities pertain to the transformation and manipulation of material substances.

PROLOGUE

HE KNEW THEY WERE DEAD. HE COULD SEE THE UGLY death wounds, still bleeding.

But they walked on either side of him, silent and strangely graceful in their motions, forcing the little boy to keep to the center of the paved road as he trailed behind the other prisoners.

The man on his right . . . his name was, or had been, Bryat. He was a footman in the princess's service, tall, slim, handsome in his palace uniform. The boy had liked him, for Bryat would sometimes sneak him salted nuts from the kitchen when no one was looking. He'd been killed by a blow to the head, his skull crushed. All the blood had drained out of his face, leaving him ghastly as he glided along the edge of the road.

The man on his left was unfamiliar to the boy. A lord of Talmain, part of the princess's entourage, clad in gaudy red and boasting a gold chain and medallion, donned that morning in preparation for the royal banquet he'd expected to enjoy that night. He'd been killed by a knife to the throat. The boy could see its hilt still protruding from his neck.

There were others as well—other dead on all sides, before and behind the prisoners. All perfectly silent beneath the overcast sky, the brisk spring wind whistling through their hair, blowing in their lifeless faces. Thirteen in all, unless the boy had counted wrong. He was quite young, after all, and not yet confident in numbers beyond what he could count on his fingers.

The road dipped down a steep incline into a valley far below. The boy stumbled and fell hard to his hands and knees, scraping his palms and then his chin on the black paving stones. He didn't cry at the pain. He was much too frightened to cry. But he remained where he fell, squeezing his eyes shut and trying to pretend he didn't exist. Perhaps the dead would glide on by without noticing him. Perhaps the tall figure on horseback behind them would simply steer his horse around him and go on his way.

Instead, a pair of hands gripped him under his arms, pulling him up onto his feet in a single powerful motion.

"Come on, Terryn," a deep voice whispered close to his ear. "Keep up your courage. That's my brave boy."

Terryn wiped at his smarting chin, leaving a smear of blood on the back of his hand. He looked up into a pair of pale gray eyes set in a dark face. Blood ran from a gash at the man's hairline, and an ugly bruise purpled one eye. But Terryn's father still managed to give him an encouraging smile.

"Come on," he said again. "We're not out of this yet. I need you to be strong, Terryn. The Goddess is with us—"

A sudden pound of hooves behind them startled Terryn into pressing against his father's legs. Then a harsh voice called out, "Move your feet, or I'll take the boy and see that he does not slow you again."

Terryn gazed up over his father's shoulder at that figure on horseback. At that deep crimson cowl pulled low, obscuring the face. But not the eyes. The eyes glittered down through the shadows of the cowl, bright disks through which deadly spirits gazed.

His father instantly set off in a long-legged stride, dragging Terryn behind him by the shoulder of his garment—such a fine velvet garment, which the princess herself had dressed him in that morning, telling him she needed him to look smart for when they met the Chosen King. She had smiled at him so tenderly and kissed his cheek before wiping away her own stray tears.

Terryn hadn't understood why she cried. He'd cupped her face in his small hands and said, "Don't be sad, Princess. I won't leave you."

This must not have been the right thing to say. Her tears only came harder, and the princess had risen quickly from her knees, calling to her lady-in-waiting. "Please, Mylla," she'd said, "take him away. I can't . . . I can't bear it just now. Not today of all days."

Lady Mylla had led him from the princess's pavilion

and finished preparing him for the day's travel. They'd been journeying for two weeks now along these lonely roads. A large party of courtly lords and ladies, priestesses and holy sisters, servants and soldiers. And, of course, the princess's personal guard, captained by Terryn's father.

Also, five Red Hoods, meant to escort them across the Witch Queen's territory.

What had become of the princess? Terryn hadn't seen her since the attack began. Had she died along with so many others? But Terryn didn't see her among the dead walking on either side of him. He hoped she'd gotten away.

His father dragged him along so fast now, he often lost his footing and only stayed upright due to that strong grasp on his shoulder. His little feet could not keep up the pace, and the terror pulsing through his veins was not enough to drive him faster. He was too small. But his father wouldn't let go.

Terryn saw Lady Mylla up ahead at the front of the procession. She did not seem to be dead. She stumbled along with her head bowed. Her wimple and veil had been torn away, and her lovely golden hair trailed loose down her back. Her lavender gown was stained with mud and blood, and sometimes Terryn heard her weeping. The dead could not cry, so surely she must be alive.

A tower rose on the landscape like a wild animal's fang jutting from the soil. It was quite tall, taller even than the highest turrets of Venerandon, Terryn's palace home. A huge stone wall surrounded the tower, with only a single gate, open like a hungry mouth to receive the prisoners and the dead alike. Terryn balked at the sight of that gate and tried to pull from his father's grasp.

"Don't," his father whispered. "They'll kill you. Do as you're told. I'll . . . I'll find a way out of this."

It was a lie. Young as he was, Terryn knew when he heard a lie, even spoken from his father's lips. There would be no last-minute burst of strength, no daring getaway, no sudden reversal of their fortunes. But he clung to his father's words, clung to his voice. Clung to that lie as his only hope.

They passed through the open mouth of the gate, staggering into the courtyard beneath the looming tower. The dead, moving at the command of their master, pushed and prodded the living into a line—Lady Mylla at one end, and Terryn and his father at the other. Eight others stood between them, including a few faces Terryn recognized. Ambassador du Jyne, who held himself tall and proud. And Lord Lulas, who slumped and wept where he stood.

Terryn couldn't bear to look at Lord Lulas. He stared down at his boots instead. Even so, he was aware when the door to the tower opened and a woman stepped out. He cast a furtive look up at her from beneath his tangle of dark curls. She wasn't old, but she moved stiffly, limping with every step. Each breath she took hissed through her teeth as though it gave her pain, but she advanced anyway, her pace determined. Her face might have been beautiful once. Not as beautiful as the princess, no, but quite lovely in its way, with delicate features and creamy skin. Now it was too twisted by pain for beauty.

A black sigil tattooed her forehead, stark above her fair brows.

"Gillotin," she called out, "what is this you've brought through my gates?"

The witch in the crimson cowl dismounted and approached the woman. He pushed back his hood, revealing a broad, handsome face with thick black brows and strong features. His forehead bore a sigil the exact match of the woman's—a horizontal slash from which rose five vertical slashes, like a child's drawing of a crown.

"A little present for you, Ylaire," he said. "I found them on the south patrol, a large party from Talmain. Half of them escaped—there were Evanderians in their number, more than I could manage on my own. But I thought you might enjoy this little sampling of mortal flesh. The pretty girl at the end may be of particular interest to you."

The tattooed woman said nothing in response. She stepped between two of the dead, jostling them aside. They parted without resistance, and the witch approached the prisoners. She kept one hand pressed to her hip, grimacing as she moved down the line, looking at each of them in turn. Her gaze rested for a few long moments on Lady Mylla, who sobbed uncontrollably. But the witch moved on from her, studying each face she came to.

At last, she reached the end of the line and looked down at Terryn. She paused.

"My, my." A smile drove back the pain in her face,

making her features once more beautiful. And much more terrible. "My, what a sweet little creature you are."

The witch man stepped to her side, crossing his arms over his chest. "He's too young to be of any use. But I thought you and Inren might enjoy a pet. Something to brighten up this gloomy tower of yours."

"Inren doesn't care for such things," the woman said with a dismissive toss of her head. "I, on the other hand . . ."

She reached out and touched Terryn's cheek with the tip of a long, claw-curved fingernail.

A lunging movement at Terryn's side, and his father stepped between him and the woman. He shoved her away, roaring like a lion: "Don't touch him!" Terryn had never heard such a voice coming from his father's mouth. It frightened him even more than the witches.

The woman staggered back, cursing, her face contorted with pain. "Gillotin!" she snarled without taking her eyes off the tall captain. "Get your puppets under control."

"Terribly sorry, Ylaire." The witch man raised a hand and twisted it sharply at the wrist.

Terryn's father cried out and fell to his knees. His arms were pinned to his sides, his back arched, and his eyes stared out from his head. The cords of his neck protruded starkly, and his jaw clenched tight.

"Dada!" Terryn cried and flung himself at his father, grabbing his shoulder, pulling at his arm, trying to make him stand up. His father's eyes swiveled in their sockets to look at him. But otherwise, he could not move.

The witch woman pulled herself upright, sneering at her attacker. "He looks strong enough," she said. "Are you planning to take his body?"

"Yes," Gillotin replied. "Soon . . . not yet. This host I'm wearing is still in good condition, but I thought it wise to have a spare on hand."

The witch woman sniffed. "Very well. Just keep a grip on him. And get him out of my sight. Take all of these," she added with a sweep of her hand at the line of prisoners, "Except the girl at the end. And this child."

"I thought you would like them." Gillotin flashed a smile. "Enjoy your presents, Ylaire."

So saying, he motioned with his hand again. Terryn's father stood so abruptly, the action knocked Terryn to the ground. Without a word or look at Terryn, he faced to the right, standing at perfect attention. Then he and the other prisoners set off marching briskly, as though in time to some drumbeat heard by their ears alone.

"No!" Terryn cried and tried to run after his father, tried to catch his hand.

"Stay where you are, boy."

At the witch's bark, he stopped short. There was no compulsion other than fear to force his obedience, but fear was more than enough. He stood as though frozen, watching his father and the others vanish into a windowless building within the fortifying walls. The cowled witch man trailed after them, leading his silent dead in his wake.

The witch woman stepped to Terryn's side again. He saw her in his peripheral vision but couldn't bear to look at her. Instead, he stared down at his boots. The beautiful, brand-new boots the princess had given him just before they set out on this journey. Now stained with mud. And blood.

A hand rested on his head, gentle at first. Then fingers gripped his curls and pulled his face up, forcing him to gaze into that pain-seared face.

"It's all right, sweet child," the witch crooned. "All your fears will soon be gone. But first, I must claim you."

Her long nails flashed before his vision. Then one of those nails pierced his skin, and he screamed and screamed as the witch carved a perfect circular pattern into his face.

CHAPTER I

TWENTY YEARS LATER

THE WATCHTOWER OF MILISENDIS OUTPOST APPEARED stark against the orange-streaked sky. The sun sinking beyond the horizon cast a glare in Ayleth's face, but she pulled her hood lower to shade her eyes and urged her horse on at a trot. She was ready to put an end to this day.

"Has it really been a single day?" she whispered. The brisk autumn wind whipped at her face and carried her voice off into the darkening twilight. She shuddered, her body suddenly so bone-weary, she feared she'd topple from the saddle there on the narrow trail long before reaching the outpost.

If she'd had any idea what her first full day serving in Wodechran Borough would entail, she never would have run away from home, never would have disobeyed Hollis. She never would have dared present herself to the Golden Prince.

What lunacy ever made her think she wanted this Haunts-damned job?

Hoofbeats pounded the trail behind her— Terryn, Venator du Balafre, also returning from their little adventure beyond the Great Barrier. Ayleth sat straighter in her saddle, not wanting any bowing of her shoulders or hanging of her head to betray her exhaustion. No reason to let Terryn think he held any more advantage over her than he already did. The two of them may have survived the venomous Witchwood by working together, but that didn't mean they were friends or even comrades. They were competitors. Next door to enemies.

At the end of the three-month trial period, the Golden Prince would choose only one of them to fill Venator du Vincent's vacant place in Milisendis. The other would be sent packing.

Ayleth dared not fail. The very idea made her shiver straight down to her soul. Venator Terryn merely faced returning to Castra Breçar, where he would soon receive another assignment somewhere in Perrinion or one of the other Gaulian kingdoms. But Ayleth . . . she had nowhere else to go. They did not know her at the castra, for she had never been officially presented. She couldn't expect to find a place for herself there.

What other option did she have? Would she crawl back, shamefaced, to Hollis's feet and beg forgiveness, beg for her old job back? And then return to the menial apprentice work she had long since outgrown. No more responsibility. No more adventure. No more hunts.

All the while knowing that Hollis was manipulating her mind, her memories . . .

No. No, she couldn't go back. Though the thought caused a twist of pain in her heart, she knew that door was shut. Forever.

She returned her focused to the outpost tower ahead while resolve grew inside her like a tree, its roots plunging deep. She would finish this competition, and she would prove herself to the prince. She would take her place at Milisendis. She had already faced the Witchwood and survived. She'd done battle with Crimson Devils and walked away in one piece. What worse misadventure could the borough possibly throw her way?

Did she really want to ask that question? Much less discover the answer . . .

Ayleth shook her head beneath her hood. Now was the time to strive toward one goal and one goal alone: a bath. She stank, positively reeked, of blood and rot and pus and infection. Even worse than that, she stank of *oblivis*—the air of the Haunts. It permeated her skin, her hair. It seemed to breathe out from her pores and coat her teeth in a layer of gritty slime. She was covered in it from head to toe, and she'd breathed it deep into her lungs. It felt as if she wore evil itself in a thick crust all over her skin.

So, yes. First things first. A bath. And if she was quick, if she made it through the outpost gate and into the blockhouse first, she could claim the big copper tub ahead of Venator Terryn. He was equally as disgusting, following their escape from the Witchwood, but he could just stand out on the doorstep and wait his turn until she'd scrubbed herself clean in front of the fire.

She hurried her horse into the rocky valley where Milisendis Outpost stood. The outpost looked and felt somewhat familiar to her eye, built as it was in the same style as Gillanluòc, where she had spent the years of her apprenticeship. The tower loomed three stories above the surrounding landscape, and a tall wooden wall surrounded the squat blockhouse and a few other buildings. It was a small but efficient fortress, intended to house no more than four or five Evanderians at a time. Only two these days, following the depredations of the war and the severe depletion of Evanderian ranks.

A troubling intuition pricked at the back of Ayleth's brain as she approached the gate. When she'd arrived, only the night before, the outpost had been rigged with any number of curse traps. Some of these had been deadly, while others were merely inconvenient. Having found and dismantled nearly half a dozen of them, Ayleth knew better than to ignore any uneasy feeling.

Something about Milisendis felt . . . *expectant*, somehow.

"*Laranta*," she spoke inside her head. Only the distant hum of a song spell responded, and she winced with remembrance. She'd suppressed her shade following the extreme use of its powers throughout the day. Should she summon her powers back up now? Did the uneasiness trickling down her spine warrant pulling out her Vocos pipes to unwind the suppressing spell and call Laranta to higher ascendancy?

An exhausting prospect. Besides, she realized with a sudden dull thud of her heart, she didn't have a Vocos anymore. The Windwitch had stolen both of her bone pipes from her while she lay paralyzed on the altar in the ruined shrine house. She had no pipes, no poisons, and no scorpiona.

What kind of a venatrix was she?

Venator Terryn approached swiftly behind her. She heard the shift of his horse's hooves thudding on stone rather than dirt as he began his descent into the rocky valley. She would have to hurry if she wanted to get that bath before him.

Setting her jaw, Ayleth nudged her horse on toward the gate. No curses lashed out at her, and all was quiet on the far side of the wall. The sensation of expectancy did not lessen, however. She dismounted, her hand moving by habit to the empty knife sheath on her belt, and approached that place in the wall where she knew the secret mechanism to open the gate from the outside was hidden. Her searching fingers, after some fumbling in the deepening evening shadows, found the pin and switch at last. The gate swung open with eerie silence.

She'd have felt more comfortable if it had creaked. At least a little.

Her eyes alert and her right hand still reaching for a knife that wasn't there, she led her horse through the gate—and came to an abrupt halt.

A poisoned dart, poised in the air not an inch from her right ear, was gently pushing back the edge of her red hood.

"Dear lady, I should very much like to assume that you are a sister of my Order," a smooth-as-honey voice spoke from the dark space just beyond that dart. "Indeed, it would give me untold pleasure to welcome you with open arms and a most brotherly salute. But I cannot discern the color of your hood beneath all that muck, so you're going to have to convince me."

Ayleth's eyes swiveled as far right as they could go. In the dark and without Laranta's senses, she couldn't see or smell what kind of poison it was that hovered so very near to her skin. Something sinister underlying those too-sweet words told her it was the Gentle Death.

Her throat thickened, and she held perfectly still, hardly daring to breathe. "I-I am Ayleth, Venatrix di Ferosa," she gasped. "I am an Evanderian, one of the Order. You . . . you can believe me—"

"Oh, relax, lovely." The dart whisked away, allowing her hood to fall back into place. The figure on her right moved to stand in front of her, lowering the scorpiona affixed to his right arm and snapping it out of firing mode. "I can *hear* the song spells playing inside you. If you're not a venatrix, the Order is getting quite lax with its secret-keeping. Which means we're all doomed anyway, so you might as well come in."

Ayleth stared. Standing before her with a strange and not-exactly-welcoming smile stretched across his face was a man of some thirty-odd years, square and strongly built, and not quite as tall as she. A ragged goatee ringed his chin and lip, and a pale stubble sprinkled across his cheeks, presumably after some days on the open road.

"Venator . . . Venator du Tam?" Ayleth ventured. Her heart thudded as though preparing for battle. But she wasn't in danger. Or . . . or was she?

"Yes, yes, that's me," the man answered with a nod, even as his gaze ran up and down her uniform. "Dear Goddess love me, you look as though you dived face-first into the pigsty. And you smell worse. Were you chasing shade-taken swine while I was away? Better you than me, I must say." He shivered, his mouth twisting as though he feared he'd be ill. "Still, the Golden Prince apparently considers you something of a wonder, at least according to the message I found waiting for me on my desk. I confess, I was expecting someone quite different, according to a recent letter from the Venator Dominus."

Terryn. He was expecting Terryn, of course. The Venator Dominus's own protégé, hand-selected to take over the empty post at Milisendis. Ayleth's stomach cinched up at the thought. But it wasn't the Venator Dominus's appointment to make. Only the Golden Prince could determine the final outcome of this competition. The prince whose life she had saved not two days ago.

She still had a shot. A long shot, but . . . she was a skilled markswoman.

Just then, Ayleth heard the approach of Terryn's horse at her back. She drew herself up straight and tall, assuming a stern expression beneath the caked mud on her face. "I don't know about any message from the Dominus," she said, determined to regain her footing in this conversation. "I am Ayleth di Ferosa, and it is my—"

"We've covered that. What we have not covered is why *you* are covered from the top of your pretty little head to the soles of your rather impressively large feet in what appears to be some repulsive combination of blood, mud, and manure. There's a story here, I would imagine. Whether or not it's worth hearing, I hardly dare guess."

Ayleth swallowed. "I went beyond—"

"Ah, wait. Who is this?" Venator du Tam sidestepped around Ayleth and once more lifted his scorpiona, snapping it into firing mode and sighting along his upraised arm. "Stand and declare yourself!" he called into the night.

"Is that thing even armed?" Terryn's voice rumbled.

Ayleth blinked. It wasn't the answer she would have given to such a command. Venator du Tam, however, merely sniffed, lowering his arm and once more disengaging the firing mechanism. "Of course it's armed. I know better than to aim an empty weapon at a potential foe looming from the shadows."

"What's it armed with?"

"A little something of my own invention. If it pricks you, you'll sneeze uncontrollably for two hours straight. I'd like to see anyone try to fight me off then!"

Ayleth, frowning, stared at the side of the strange venator's square face, trying to decide whether or not he was joking. It was impossible to tell. The perpetual lift of his eyebrow and twist of his lip might denote sarcasm but might just as easily denote a truly dangerous individual with perhaps a dash of madness mixed in. She caught a gleam in the eye closest to her, but that might very well be a trace of the venator's shade and not a glimpse of good humor at all.

Venator du Tam stepped back from the gate, allowing Terryn to ride through and dismount in the yard, then closed the gate behind him. As Terryn swung down from his horse, his cloak swirling, the older venator cried out and flung up a hand to cover his nose. "Haunts damn us all to oblivion! You reek as bad as di Ferosa here. Were the two of you brawling in the muck together? Some rite of passage or initiation? I'll have none of that sort of thing here, my boy! You're not castra pips any more, and you'd do well to remember it. Now, what are you doing here?"

Terryn glowered from under the shadow of his hood. "I came to present my candidacy to the Golden Prince."

"I had been given to understand that the post was as good as yours," du Tam replied. "But I find you in company with di Ferosa here, and according to the letter from the Golden Prince—left on my desk by one of you, I gather—you are to compete for the position over the next three months. Is that indeed the situation?"

Terryn shot Ayleth a quick glance and, lifted his chin coldly. "Yes."

The venator looked closely at Ayleth, then back at Terryn again. "Interesting. Who among us can predict the whims of our royals, eh?" He shook his head and waved a dismissive hand. "But no matter all that. Explain to me the reason behind your current befoulment."

"We went beyond the Great Barrier," Terryn answered without preamble.

Even in the deepening gloom, Ayleth could see the blood drain from Venator du Tam's face. His other eyebrow rose, and his lip lost its distinctive curl as his mouth gaped slightly open. "Beyond the Barrier?" he breathed. A muscle in his cheek twitched oddly, and he shook his head, turning his gaze to study Ayleth as well. "Both of you?"

She nodded. "Prince Gerard requested that we put our efforts into discovering what happened to Venator du Vincent. It's been some time since his disappearance and—"

"Six weeks."

Ayleth stopped, uncertain how to proceed. The venator's eyes did not stray from hers, holding her gaze with an intensity too great for comfort.

"Six weeks," he said again. "To the day. Since Nane vanished. And the prince, you tell me, did not think I had done my sufficient duty in trying to locate my lost hunt brother? He believes I'm not bearing up as I should?"

"Not at all," Terryn put in at once. "He is merely concerned that you are overwhelmed with the many duties involved in maintaining a borough so large as Wodechran. He meant it as a—"

Du Tam held up a silencing hand. "Whatever our esteemed Golden Prince meant," he said, his face sliding back into that expression most familiar to his features, sardonic and a little hard, "he certainly did not intend for you two yearlings to go galloping off beyond the Great Barrier." His gaze flicked up and down both their persons, one after the other. "Though, apparently, enormous fun was had by all."

With that, the older venator strode swiftly forward, causing Ayleth and Terryn to step back swiftly so that he might pass between them. "*Faugh!*" he grunted as he went, waving his hand before his face. "Neither of you is stepping foot into my blockhouse. There's a well across the yard, and a bucket. I'll toss some soap out the window, and you do what you can before you come anywhere near that front door. Do I make myself clear, children?"

So saying, he crossed the outpost yard to the blockhouse, leaving Terryn and Ayleth to stare after him until he had pushed the door open, stepped inside, and slammed it shut. A few moments later, a projectile flew through an open window. The promised soap, presumably.

Ayleth turned to Terryn. He did not look at her. "We have a bucket," she said. He did not answer. "And an open yard," she added.

She watched the muscles in his throat constrict.

Ayleth crossed her arms. "So, what do you propose, Venator du Balafre?"

"I'll . . ." Terryn swallowed again, then reached out and snatched her horse's reins from her hands. "I'll see to the horses." Without so much as a glance in her direction, he pulled both his red mare and her brown gelding after him toward the stable.

CHAPTER 2

THE HARD BLOCK OF SOAP GRIPPED IN ONE HAND, Ayleth stood a long moment beside the well. Forlorn thoughts of the large copper basin in the blockhouse flitted through her brain, along with those fond imaginings of a luxurious bath before a roaring fire.

Instead, she had a bucket. And a trough, currently full of rather scummy rainwater. And the whole open sky above her, slowly filling with stars, and a brisk autumn wind whistling through the small gaps in the wall to freeze her skin.

Just how badly did she want Venator du Tam to let her inside?

Ayleth drew a breath, inhaling once again the horrible reek of her garments and body. Motivation enough, right there.

Setting the soap bar aside on the trough lip, she set to work, tossing the bucket down the well and hauling it up again, full and dripping. Then she stripped off her hood, her cloak, and her outer jerkin. Undressing took less time than usual without her weapons. The Windwitch hadn't even spared her two arm bracers. Goddess above, she'd better hope some spare equipment was kept at this outpost, or her part in this competition would come to an abrupt halt! She couldn't even summon up her shade again unless someone loaned her a Vocos.

Gritting her teeth, she tossed all of her outer garments into the trough and whirled them vigorously until the water was black with Witchwood grime. She made a few half-hearted scrubs with the lump of soap, but ultimately gave up and simply draped her sopping garments around the lip of the well to drip-dry and hopefully catch some sunlight in the morning. At least she had a spare uniform inside, which she could use until she found opportunity to give these items a proper wash. Meanwhile, she was cold, hungry, tired . . . and still disgusting.

Her skin prickled beneath the thin fabric of her light, blousy shift, and her bare feet felt like lumps of ice. Her arms, wet to the elbows from dunking her outer garments, trembled when the wind blew against them. But she knew she was nowhere near clean enough to get past Venator du Tam and gain access to the hearth.

Firming her jaw, Ayleth lifted the heavy bucket and dumped it over her head and shoulders, soaking herself to the bone. She gasped, the breath stolen from her lungs. Her long hair, still partially tied back in a braid, plastered to her face and neck, and her undershirt stuck to her bosom and stomach. Streams of blackened water rolled down her body, her trousers, and pooled around her dancing bare feet.

"Haunts damn, Haunts damn, Haunts *damn!*" she ground out viciously. Snatching up the soap block again, she scrubbed at her arms, her neck, her face. She pulled the shirt away from her body and stuck the soap right down the front, scrubbing it so hard she would probably have bruises in the morning. The burning stink of lye started to replace the stench of the Witchwood, and though her eyes stung, she welcomed the change.

Pulling the bar out from under her shirt, Ayleth squeezed too hard, and it shot out of her hand. She whirled, grabbing for it, but not fast enough, and watched it hit the ground and skid across the stone pavement, trailing slimy bubbles as it went.

It came to a stop, gently pressed beneath a boot.

Ayleth, wet hair dripping in her face, looked up into a pair of eyes so cold they seemed to freeze the water into icicles across her skin.

Venator Terryn stared at her, his gaze fixed on her face. Carefully not sliding down her wet body, carefully not taking in how her thin linen shift molded to her figure, preserving no modesty whatsoever.

Somehow, the care with which he did *not* look made Ayleth feel much more exposed.

She crossed her arms over her breast. Then, hissing another curse through her chattering teeth, she turned her back on the venator, snatched up her soaked red hood for modesty, and, leaving the rest of her garments draped around the well and her boots standing to one side, ran across the outpost yard as fast as she could go.

"Venator du Tam!" she barked, clutching her hood across her chest with one arm to free one fist to pound at the door. A sudden icy wind renewed her shudders. "V-Venator, luh-leh-let me in! P-p-please!"

The door cracked open, and the venator's eye appeared in the narrow opening. He looked her up and down critically. Then, with a longsuffering sigh, he stepped back, pulling the door wide. "Pathetic," he said as she tottered over the threshold into the firelit main room of the blockhouse. "There, di Ferosa, have a seat by the fire before you catch a chill."

The solicitude in his voice did nothing to relieve the hardness in his face, but Ayleth wasn't about to complain. She hastened across the room, stepping around the long table that took up the bulk of the floor space, and collapsed on a low wooden stool pulled up close to the fire. Venator du Tam had stoked up the blaze to a roaring heat, and the fire's glow against her skin felt like heaven. Ayleth dropped her sopping hood on the back of a chair and held out both hands to the flames as though she'd like to hug them to her.

"Don't burn yourself," du Tam said, stepping to her side. He held out a wooly blanket, which Ayleth reached for, intending to drape it around her shoulders. "Hold on!" The venator withdrew a step. "Strip off your shirt and those trousers and hang them on that peg there. No point in wrapping yourself up all wet."

Ayleth, with the first flush of the fire's comfort past, frowned at the venator, withdrawing her reaching hand from the folds of the blanket. He took in her expression and laughed a single, scoffing snort of a laugh.

"Does the lady's modesty tremble? Some venatrix you make, little girl. If you think I've not seen my share of female flesh over the years, think again. It's of no more interest to me now than it ever has been. Nevertheless, to spare your maidenly blushes . . ."

He tossed the blanket into her arms and pointedly strode to the middle of the room, turning his back on her, arms akimbo. Her brows drawing into a tight knot, Ayleth watched the venator closely. She wasn't sure she trusted him, but . . . if she ventured up to her own tower chamber, she risked freezing to death before ever managing to get the wet clothes off her body.

So, keeping a wary eye on du Tam, she undid the topmost ties on her shirt and pulled it off over her head. Her bare skin prickled with pure relief to be free of the cold garment.

"I noticed several of my hunt brother's protection curses unraveling when I returned," du Tam said, his back still firmly to her. He studied his fingernails before buffing them disinterestedly against his shoulder. "I trust neither you nor Venator du Balafre fell prey to any of the nastier ones? They were not meant to affect fellow Evanderians, you know. Only outpost invaders."

Standing up to slide free of her trousers, Ayleth snorted softly. "We encountered a few. We managed." She started to loosen the fastenings around her waist.

The door opened. Terryn, bare-chested and dripping, stepped through.

Ayleth shrieked and whirled to face the fire, dropping to her knees and grabbing for the blanket, her wet braid slapping against her bare shoulder. A second later, the door slammed shut again, and Venator du Tam gave a huge shout of laughter. Glaring over her shoulder and pulling the blanket tight around her body, Ayleth watched the venator stagger across the room to the door, pausing a moment to lean against the wall in an effort to compose himself.

"Terryn, my dear boy!" he cried, pulling the door open again. "You can't stand there sopping on the doorstep all night long! Come in, come in. Hunt brothers and hunt sisters must not be shy with one another. No, don't bolt for the stables! You're not spending the night with your horse. Di Ferosa is perfectly decent now"—this with a glance back over his shoulder at Ayleth, who stood bundled in folds of itchy wool—"and I'd hate to have to write to the Dominus and explain to him how it happened that his protégé died of embarrassment shortly after his arrival. Come in, I say!"

By the time Venator du Tam managed to collar Terryn and drag him back inside, Ayleth was creeping for the stairwell to her tower room above. Du Tam spotted her, however, and sprang across the room, catching her by the blanket and tugging so hard that if she resisted, she would lose it entirely. Unwilling to expose herself again, Ayleth followed the venator as he led both her and Terryn back to the fire.

"Sit, both of you," he said, pushing Ayleth onto her stool and Terryn onto another one beside her. Ayleth's skin flushed so hot, she rather thought she'd dry herself off in a matter of moments, fire or no fire. If Venator Terryn had found it difficult to look at her before, she might as well be invisible now. He fixed his icy gaze on the hearth flames with such concentration, she feared he'd freeze the heat right out of the room. The fire's glow contoured the tense muscles of his bare chest and arms, and though the darkness of his skin disguised any blush, Ayleth was almost certain the venator was as warm as she.

Ayleth shifted on her stool, her damp trousers squishing uncomfortably. No way under heaven would she try to remove them now!

Venator du Tam, still chuckling, draped a blanket over Terryn's shoulders. "My friends, thank you." He backed away from them and pulled out the square chair at the desk a few feet away. He took a seat and leaned back, wiping at his eyes with his thumb. "I needed that laugh more than you can know. Oh, to be young and stupid again! You don't realize what a blessing youthful stupidity is until it's gone. Mature stupidity is simply not the same."

Ayleth scowled harder. Terryn's face did not move, not even a flicker. He might have been turned to stone. The only sign of reaction was a slight whitening of his knuckles as his fingers clenched his knees.

Shifting on her stool, Ayleth faced Venator du Tam. He had turned away from the hearth, his attention now fixed on the papers spread across the desk's surface. Papers which Ayleth herself had shuffled through earlier that morning. She remembered the notes made in du Tam's hand concerning what appeared to be a body-shifting shade—inexplicable deaths, apparently by suicide, of both animal and human hosts, always followed by a new shade-taken appearance within a few miles' radius. Death of a host body ordinarily left a possessing shade vulnerable to the draw of the Haunts, but a violent death could empower the indwelling shade with such force that it would be able to escape the Haunts' pull and, if fortunate, find a new host body.

Venator du Tam's notes had indicated the successive violent deaths of a shade-taken old man, a cat, and a cow.

Ayleth wondered if the venator had succeeded in tracking down the shade and ousting it from this world. She had almost worked up the nerve to ask him when the venator looked up and met her gaze.

"All right," he said, all traces of mirth gone from his voice, though that one sardonic eyebrow slid back into position. "We've all had our little laugh. It's time to get down to business. So, the two of you ventured into the Witchwood in your search for my hunt brother. Did you find him?"

Ayleth nodded, not waiting for Terryn to offer his side of the story. "We discovered his body just on the far side of the Great Barrier. There was an opening in the spell, as though he had tried to get back out, but it had been poorly repaired by someone who did not know the variations of the song spell. We thought perhaps you had . . ."

Her voice trailed away. Venator du Tam was not hearing what she said anymore. The moment she spoke the word *body,* all the blood drained from his face, leaving him ashen. One elbow propped on the edge of the desk, he lifted a trembling hand, supporting his head with it as though he found it suddenly too heavy for his neck. His gaze drifted off into some distant place over Ayleth's shoulder, so focused that she half turned to see if there was something of interest on the fireplace mantel. There was nothing, and she looked back toward the venator, frowning.

Then realization struck.

"Oh," she whispered. Some of the things du Tam had said earlier now came back to her in a new light. The way he'd known to the day the date of Nane's disappearance. His expressed frustration that the prince thought he wasn't "bearing up" under his hunt brother's loss. Even his glib remark about his lack of interest in female flesh.

Ayleth closed her mouth and dropped her eyes before Venator du Tam might catch her staring. The Order, she knew, did not look kindly on romantic relationships between hunt brothers and hunt sisters. If the bond of the hunt strengthened into a deeper passion, there was always the risk of a child being born of that passion. Any child born of a shade-taken mother or sired of a shade-taken father would carry in its mortal body a newly spawned shade. From the moment of conception, such unholy progeny were doomed to the eternal suffering of the Haunts, for the mortal soul was too entwined with the inborn shade for ordinary means of separation to work.

The only hope for such children was a violent death: death by fire.

No venator, however devout, relished the prospect of burning children alive. It was a merciful necessity, but nonetheless a horror. Therefore, it was against all the laws and teachings of Evander for a venator and venatrix to engage in the natural pleasures born of passion, and such romantic bonds were punishable by death.

But a bond between two hunt brothers? Such a love, though not officially sanctioned by the Order, was never expressly forbidden by Saint Evander himself. There was, after all, no risk of inborn children being produced. In most cases, the castra simply turned a blind eye.

Venator du Vincent and Venator du Tam had served together in Wodechran Borough for many years. How deep of an attachment had formed between them? Judging from the look on du Tam's face, a profound attachment indeed.

"I knew he was dead." Kephan spoke at last in a voice

that seemed too small, almost drowned out by the crackle of the fire. "I knew it. He would have contacted me otherwise, would have found a way . . . But no. No, he is gone. Gone and—"

The venator's voice choked, and he dropped his face into his hand. Ayleth could almost hear the thought which he dared not speak. Nane had died in the field. Alone. Without a fellow venator on hand to separate his soul from that of his shade. No one had saved him from the evil possessing him. His soul had not flown on to the Goddess's Light.

Ayleth glanced at Terryn, who had twisted in his seat to look, not at du Tam, but at her. His gaze was hard, warning. He knew about the two venators then, had known all along. He'd probably been briefed by the Venator Dominus on all the various secrets and intricacies of Wodechran Borough. And he obviously knew du Tam rather well, based on their easy rapport.

Yet another advantage he had over her in this little competition, Goddess blight him.

Du Tam recovered himself at last, sitting up straight in the chair. He shook his head as though he could somehow shake the heartbreak out from behind his eyes, and fixed a firm gaze not on Ayleth but on Terryn. "So, you found him in the Witchwood. And what, if I may ask, was my esteemed colleague doing in that Goddess-forsaken place?"

"I don't know," Terryn answered.

"*We* don't know," Ayleth put in.

Du Tam continued to address himself to Terryn. "If that is the case, what were you doing all that time beyond the Barrier? Besides mud bathing, of course."

"We located and investigated the body," Terryn said. "While we were about this task, Venatrix di Ferosa was . . . taken."

"Taken?" At this, the older venator's gaze finally slid from Terryn back to Ayleth, and his brow puckered. "What does he mean by *taken?*"

Something sick and horrible slithered in Ayleth's gut, the memory of those venomous vines gripping her limbs and dragging her into the forest of wounded trees. She shivered and tried to shrug off the sensation, to present a stalwart face to the venator. Why did Terryn have to phrase it like that? It wasn't her fault. She didn't control the Witchwood, and she'd certainly never asked Terryn to come tramping in after her!

Granted, if he hadn't, she would almost certainly be dead by now.

She opened her mouth to try to explain. But for some reason, the words wouldn't quite come. How could she begin to tell him that the Witchwood itself had captured her? Had strung her up in the branches of a tree like some sort of holy-day ornament? The Witchwood was a curse, not a sentient being. Wasn't it?

There were too many things she didn't understand. So she said only, "The witches. Zilla d'Utrehd and her brother, Zarc. I was captured by them. Venator du Balafre found me, and we fought our way out again."

"Wait." Du Tam raised one hand palm out, his eyes rounding hugely. "You encountered *two* Crimson Devils? And you *survived?*"

Ayleth nodded.

The venator shook his head slowly, sitting forward in his chair and resting his elbows on his knees. "I'm not saying I believe it, but . . . do, please, go on. This *is* a story worth hearing."

Ayleth caught Terryn's sidelong glance. Then the two of them launched into a piecemeal depiction of their adventure, often interrupting each other along the way. Ayleth got the impression that Terryn was also finding it difficult to explain his experiences with the forest itself, and Ayleth left out more than she told. She described how she recognized the two witches—how they still bore the tattoo mark of Dread Odile on their foreheads. She described their decrepit state after having lived and breathed the poisonous air of the Witchwood all these years.

But she did not try to describe the conversation she had overheard between Zarc and Zilla—how Zarc argued for her death while his sister insisted that they must keep her alive. She did not try to describe the twins' obsession with taking and preserving her blood.

She did not try to say that name she'd heard them utter with such dread. That name spoken both with mortal lips and spirit tongue: *Oromor.*

Realizing that she'd lapsed into a long silence, leaving Terryn to dominate the telling of their tale, she pulled her mind back into the present and fixed her gaze on the side of his face. He glanced her away again, aware of her sudden return of attention. Then his gaze flicked down, just briefly. Her blanket had begun to slip away from her shoulders. Ayleth quickly wrapped it tighter. The damp and itchy wool was starting to get uncomfortable so close to the fire, but she was nonetheless grateful for the covering.

Terryn turned to Venator du Tam again. "I repaired the problematic portion of the Barrier song spell. But someone had tried already to fill in the gap and not woven the spell correctly. I . . . I assumed that was you."

"I'm flattered," du Tam said, his lip curling once more. "But no, it wasn't me. I've not been near the Great Barrier in months. That was Nane's job, not mine. I know the theory of the song spell, but not well enough to implement it myself. I could scarcely raise a barrier around this outpost."

"But . . . but someone closed the gap," Ayleth inserted. "If it wasn't you, then who?"

The older venator shrugged, his expression dismissive, but a gleam in his eye betrayed a much deeper, darker concern. "Whoever it was, we owe him our gratitude.

Even a poorly mended Barrier is better than a Barrier with a gaping hole in it. Who knows what might have gotten through otherwise?"

"Who knows what got through before the repair," Terryn added darkly, and Ayleth shuddered.

"And amid all these other questions, you still do not know what exactly killed Nane?"

"A blow to the back of the head," Ayleth said.

Du Tam's eyes flashed to hers, slicing like two sharp blades. "But delivered by whom?"

To this, Ayleth had no answer.

"What of the logbook?" he continued, sitting back in his chair. "Nane always kept a faithful if somewhat abbreviated log on his person. What did it tell you?"

"We never found it," Terryn said. "We searched his body, but he either didn't have it with him, or it was taken off him at the time of his death."

"Interesting." Du Tam's voice was thick in his throat, as though he struggled to suppress some strong feeling. But, like any trained venator, he pushed emotion back, concentrating on the information he'd been given.

Ayleth chewed the inside of her cheek. She'd not

stopped to consider the mystery of the logbook's absence. Amid everything else, it had not struck her as particularly important. But it was significant, for the log might offer a clue as to Nane's most recent hunts. It might even offer insight into his motivation to cross the Great Barrier into the Witchwood.

"It seems to me," Venator du Tam said, rising from his chair and folding his arms across his square chest, "that your next task is simple. Return to the fringe forest, back to the location where you found the gap in the Barrier. See if you can find a trace of Nane's log. If what I'm sensing in di Ferosa is correct, she is possessed of a powerful Feral shade. Is it powerful enough to pick up a trace of Nane this many weeks after . . . after he crossed the Barrier? Strong enough to catch a scent of the book, even?"

Ayleth hesitated before answering. "Perhaps," she said. "If you have something of Nane's I can use to start. A . . . a lock of hair, perhaps?"

Du Tam met her eye, his face a mask. "I might. I'll see what I can find."

Ayleth swallowed and nodded. "In that case, I might

be able to trace the logbook. Anything he touched with his bare hands."

"It's a start. I'll also see to the replacement of your pipes and your poisons," du Tam added. "I know we have a spare Detrudos around here somewhere, and I believe there is a Vocos tucked away as well. Both are old and possibly a little sour, but I trust you can make them serve."

"Yes," Ayleth said, relieved. "And thank you."

The venator shrugged, then dismissed both Ayleth and Terryn with a sweep of his hand. "Get some sleep tonight. Tomorrow, retrace your steps to where Nane crossed the Barrier and see if you can't bring that logbook back to Milisendis."

"What, both of us?" Terryn scrambled up from his own stool and towered over both Ayleth and du Tam. He dropped his blanket in the process, and Ayleth's vision was filled once more with the sight of his bare chest and the hard muscles of his abdomen. She blushed and lowered her gaze to her lap, her eyes wide.

"We don't both need to cover the same ground," Terryn persisted. "There are other leads I could follow."

"What other leads?" du Tam demanded, tilting his head slightly to one side.

Though Terryn opened his mouth and his lips moved, no answer came.

"That's what I thought." The older venator's lip twisted again, this time in the facsimile of a smile. "Remember, Venator, according to the will of our prince, you and di Ferosa here are mere candidates for this post. Neither one of you is appointed, which makes both of you my subordinates. Not my hunt brother or hunt sister. You are my, for want of a better term, lackeys. So, you will do as you are told. Ride out tomorrow and find me that log. In the meantime, allow me to wish you well, and I shall retire to my room. I've just come from a long and fruitless hunt myself, and I'm fairly certain I hear my pillow singing my name. Di Ferosa, I'll see about that lock of hair. Good night!"

With these words, he offered a lazy salute and crossed the room to the narrow stairwell, his boots clomping on each tread as he climbed to his room above. Terryn remained standing, his fists curled so tight that the knuckles stood out pale from his dark skin. The pink, circular scar covering his right cheek seemed to glow red in the firelight.

His gaze shot suddenly down to meet Ayleth's, catching her watching him. A flash of pure, hot wrath seared across his face.

"This is your fault," he said, his deep voice rumbling low and tense in her gut.

Ayleth opened her mouth to answer, to protest. But before she could decide on a response to spit back, Terryn whirled on his heel and stomped across the room to the stairwell. A few moments later, Ayleth distinctly heard the door to Nane's old room slam shut.

CHAPTER 3

ALONE IN THE LOWER LEVEL OF THE BLOCKHOUSE, Ayleth left the warmth by the fire just long enough to hunt up some barley cakes from the storerooms. Three of these clutched to her chest, she scurried back to her stool and perched there, nibbling and dropping crumbs on the hearth. The cakes were bone dry and a little hard to swallow, but she was so hungry she hardly cared. Terryn, she realized, had forgotten to eat before making his sulky getaway. Ayleth grinned around another dusty mouthful.

Hopefully he'd wake up in the middle of the night absolutely *starving*.

Forcing down the last few swallows, she stood and tested the dampness of her shirt hung on the peg. It was only half dry, so she decided to leave it. One hand clutching the blanket around her shoulders, she banked the fire, then hurried up the stairwell in the dark.

She paused on the second-story landing just outside the two shut chamber doors. Behind one door, she could hear Terryn's aggressive stride. Despite the exhaustion of their day, he was still up and pacing the room. Maybe waiting to hear her ascend the tower stairs before he ventured back down to scrounge up a meal for himself. More likely concocting some cunning scheme to get rid of his competition. Ayleth sneered in the general direction of his door.

By contrast, in Venator Kephan's room, she felt nothing but . . . stillness.

She took a step closer, held her breath, and tipped her ear. Even without Laranta's senses ascendant, she perceived a sort of strange, wakeful restlessness about that silence, even more restless than Terryn's thudding footsteps. Ayleth could remember hearing a silence like that only once before—three years ago, when she stood outside her mistress's room, putting her ear to the door, afraid to knock.

The absolute, stricken silence of a broken heart.

Ayleth hunched her shoulders under the sheltering folds of her blanket and hurried on up the steep stairs.

A cold, unwelcoming room awaited her at the top of the tower. Intended as a lookout, not as a bedchamber, it contained no furniture whatsoever. Ayleth's own travel bags lay on the floor along one wall where she'd dumped them the night before. Her bedroll spread out next to the chimney bricks, and when she put her hand to them, Ayleth found they were still warm from the blaze below. It wouldn't last. Too bad she didn't dare leave the fire going all night.

Instead, she took her spare shirt from one of her bags and pulled it on over her prickling skin. She wrapped up both in her own blanket and Venator Kephan's wool blanket, wishing she could add her cloak as well. But it was still soaking wet and dripping around the lip of the well outside, and she didn't own a spare. Hopefully it would dry out by morning.

Settling down on the bedroll, she laid her head on the thin pillow and closed her eyes. Instinctively, she looked around in the darkness behind her eyelids and whispered, "*Laranta?*"

Only the hum of the Suppression spell song answered her.

Ayleth squeezed her eyes tight and waited for sleep to claim her. But the moment her eyes closed, images played through her mind. Images of the day, of terror-filled moments, of so many horrors she longed to unsee but which she knew would be with her for the rest of her life. Nane's corpse lying broken in the mud with vines crawling through the eye sockets and mouth. The tumorous growths covering the faces of the two witches, and the stark tattoos slashed across their foreheads. The vaulted ceiling of a shrine house high above her while she lay paralyzed on an altar stone.

And another image . . . an image faint in her memory, like the phantom remnants of a dream. The image of a woman's face she both knew and didn't know, and the crown on her head. The burning crown, blue and liquid and living.

Possessed.

She rolled onto her side, tucking the blanket closer, and shivered, not from cold this time, but from the chill down in her core. But it was only a dream. It couldn't be anything else. Shades could not possess inanimate objects. They required living hosts to exist in this world. So, whatever she'd seen, it was just a dream, a frantic image conjured by her unconscious in a moment of extreme stress.

But why could she not shake the feeling that it had . . . looked at her?

That it had known her.

Her lips moved in the darkness, sounding a word that could not be fully spoken by a human tongue. But she whispered it, or an approximation of it, and her breath whirled in cold vapors before her face.

"*Oromor.*"

A bolt of terror shot through her heart. Ayleth sat upright as though waking suddenly from a dream. Her breath hitched painfully, and she stared around the tower room, her eyes wild, searching for devils in the shadows.

But there was nothing. Only her bags and belongings. Only the chimney at her back. Only the lonely watch windows with their battered shutters through which she glimpsed a starry sky.

Had she fallen asleep? Dreamed again?

Laranta stirred, down beneath the suppression spells. *Mistress?* she growled.

"Quiet, Laranta," Ayleth snapped at once. She lay back down again, curling onto her side in a tight ball. She closed her eyes tight and willed herself to sleep.

A relentless pounding on the door woke Ayleth after what felt like mere moments of rest. She popped upright, scrambling free of her mound of blankets, and crawled off her bedroll. She was halfway across the floor before managing to get herself to her feet, her hair wild, her eyes crusted. She fell against the door, fumbled for the latch, and pulled it open to glare up into a pair of ice-pick eyes.

Terryn's upraised hand dropped to his side. "Five minutes," he said, his voice a deep growl in her sleep-numbed ears, "or I'm leaving without you." His eyes narrowed slightly. "I won't wait around for you to polish your buckles."

Ayleth's lip curled at these last words, an echo of her own spoken the day before, when it was she who woke Terryn from a deep sleep. A deeper sleep than hers . . . and, to be honest, a ruder awakening. Her sneer shifted into a half smile before she could stop it, and she stood there in the doorway of her room, her linen shirt untucked, her hair hanging in limp snarls on either side of her face, grinning.

Terryn's face hardened. He pivoted on the heel of his boot and marched down the narrow stairwell without another word, ducking to get his head under the door arch. Feeling as though she'd won a round despite not speaking a word, Ayleth turned back to her room. Her smirk melted away.

Haunts damn it, there was no chance she could be ready to ride in five minutes!

She rushed through what would have to pass for a morning routine, yanked the ties of her shirt tight, braided her hair to hide the tangles, and stomped barefoot down to the main room below. The air was biting cold in the stairwell, but someone had revived the fire on the hearth. Venator du Tam sat at the long table, a selection of fletched darts fanned out before him, and a series of clay pots all within reach. He was carefully removing the tip of a dart from one of these pots when Ayleth made her appearance, and he did not lift his gaze from his work when he called out, "Your boots and jerkin are by the fire. They're going to be tight."

Ayleth grunted. Someone had carried her garments in from where she'd left them draped around the well and hung them up to catch the heat from the blaze. Venator du Tam, presumably, as Terryn would no doubt prefer to see her struggle into cold, wet boots on this chilly autumn morning. As it was, her boots were dry, although, as du Tam had warned, rather tight. She struggled to get them on her feet, bracing one foot up on the wall and pushing all her weight into it. Her heel finally popped into place, and she almost fell over at the suddenness of it.

She glanced du Tam's way, wondering if he had watched her undignified display. He was, however, absorbed in his work, delicately placing a newly tipped dart to one side and reaching for another. He dipped its end into one of the pots and held it as his lips moved in a silent count. Then he withdrew it, shook off the excess, and dipped it in a second pot for another count.

Ayleth set about forcing her second boot on, eyeing the venator while she did so. This was her first time observing him by daylight. He sat with his back to the window, so his face was still partly shadowed. Even so, Ayleth saw that he was painfully pale. His cheeks, scraped clean of the scraggly growth of the night before, were hollow in his square face, and his eyes were ringed in purple smudges. He looked as though his soul had been wrung out, leaving him empty. He looked . . .

Ayleth paused mid-tug, frowning. Laranta was still too deeply suppressed to call upon her shadow vision. Still, Ayleth had worked with spirits and souls long enough to detect a sense of *wrongness*, even without ascendant powers. Her first thought on seeing the venator's rough appearance was that his heartbreak was getting the best of him. But this feeling, this *almost* feeling, was something else.

Was she simply picking up a trace of du Tam's own shade? Or was it—

The venator's eyes swiveled to meet hers. Catching her staring at him, he turned in his chair and faced her full on. "My dear di Ferosa, while the fascination I seem to have inspired in you is undeniably flattering, I trust you have better things to do with your time than sit there one-booted with your mouth ajar. You make a man a bit nervous, I won't lie."

Ayleth blushed furiously and shoved her foot the rest of the way into her boot. "I'm sorry, Venator, it's just . . . I'm only . . . Never mind." Snatching up her jerkin, she slid it on over her shoulders and fastened the distinctly unpolished buckles. Her fingers trembled, for now Venator du Tam watched her with a mocking sort of attention that made it suddenly difficult to perform simple tasks.

"I've prepared a selection of poisons for you," the venator said, once Ayleth finished pulling herself together. "Only two of each variety—you'll have to prepare more yourself as time allows. But these should get you through the day."

Gratitude warmed Ayleth's heart. In her exhaustion, she'd not even thought about readying darts before her ride this morning. Not that she anticipated encountering any shade-taken this morning, but a venatrix ought never to ride out unprepared.

Venator du Tam slid each pair of darts into their appropriate quiver before passing them to Ayleth to sling across her chest. He then moved to the armoire across the room, opening it to retrieve a somewhat outdated scorpiona and bracer. While Ayleth affixed the bracer to her arm and strapped the holster to her leg, Kephan rooted deeper into the armoire to retrieve a yellowed Vocos, a cracked Detrudos, a knife, sheaths, and another bracer, this one with a rusted iron spike. Each of these items he handed Ayleth's way.

"Take care with that scorpiona now," he said as Ayleth checked the stiff firing mechanism. "It shoots to the left. Not a current model, so don't expect the same range."

Ayleth nodded. "I'll manage."

"That Detrudos may not play as you expect either," du Tam continued, indicating the crack near the mouthpiece. "Take care with your variations. The Vocos is true at least, just old."

Old, battered, bent—it hardly mattered. Pure relief

flooded Ayleth as she donned each weapon in turn. She felt like a real venatrix again.

More than five minutes had certainly passed by the time she finished strapping the second arm bracer in place. She could only hope Terryn had made good on his threat and ridden on without her. But when she glanced toward the door, du Tam seemed to read her mind. "Don't worry," he said. "The young colt is still out there champing at his bit. Now, before you go . . ."

He closed the armoire doors, then turned to face Ayleth, reaching his hand into the front of his jerkin. With a strange quirk to his lips, he withdrew a small pouch and held it out to her. It was still warm from having been close to his skin. Over his heart.

"Inside is a lock of . . . of his hair," du Tam said. He didn't speak Nane's name, and though his faintly mocking expression remained in place, he didn't meet Ayleth's gaze either. "Use it well."

Ayleth accepted the pouch, tucking it into the front of her own jerkin. "Don't worry, sir," she said, securing the front of her jerkin to be certain the pouch remained in place. "We'll find whoever killed Venator du Vincent."

Kephan's gaze met hers for an instant before he looked away again. One eyebrow quirked, and he drew a long breath through his nose. "Be off with you, di Ferosa," he growled and returned to his poisons.

Ayleth ducked out of the blockhouse and into the cold morning outside.

CHAPTER 4

THE RIDE BACK TO THE FRINGE FOREST WAS A SILENT affair. The overcast sky spattered condensation, which was somehow worse than an actual downpour, soaking into hood and cloak and trousers with a slowly freezing dampness. Ayleth huddled miserably in the depths of her hood, watching Terryn's back as he rode ahead of her.

He had waited for her, despite his threats. When she finally emerged from the blockhouse and stumbled across the yard to retrieve her horse, Terryn had regarded her much as one might gaze upon a natural disaster made flesh, saying nothing. He, of course, looked as polished and put together as though freshly minted from Castra Breçar.

Just how many extra uniforms did the man own that he could turn himself out so impeccably following yesterday's ordeal? Haunts damn him.

They hadn't spoken as they led their horses out from Milisendis and shut the gate. They continued not speaking as they mounted, as they rode through the stony valley, as they entered the open countryside beyond. Terryn took the lead, and Ayleth let him, happy not to have his disapproving gaze fixed on her back for the long hours of this ride. Judging from the set of his shoulders, he intended to get through this entire day without saying another word to her.

Well, fine, then. It wasn't as though saving each other's lives in the Witchwood should have bonded them in any way. It wasn't as though there should be any camaraderie between them, any hunt-brother and hunt-sister bond. He was her competition, nothing more. If he wanted to sink into a sulk, he could help himself. She wouldn't let him get to her.

And, Goddess help her, she wouldn't let herself dwell on the memory of his walking in on her last night. That instant of eyes meeting, widening, that rush of hideous embarrassment and heat. Him, bare-chested beside her at the fire, the warm glow of the blaze playing across his tightly muscled frame, water dripping from his dark curls to spatter on his broad shoulders . . .

Intolerable man.

She adjusted her grip on Chestibor's reins, and once more she longed for Laranta's presence. Part of her was tempted to take out her Vocos pipes and summon up her shade, just to feel that comforting familiarity. But . . . Ayleth huffed a cold breath through her lips. Terryn would only challenge her on it. A good Evanderian did not tap her shade's power without cause.

The fringe forest loomed into view. Terryn entered ahead of her, vanishing into the gray branches still thick with soggy brown leaves. Ayleth followed soon after. Though one stretch of forest tended to look much like any other, she believed she recognized their location. They had crossed the landscape in a nearly straight line, not bothering with roads or trails, just as Laranta had led Ayleth the day before when pursuing the curse thread.

All too soon, the trees thinned around them. Ayleth's bones shuddered, struck by the vibration of music from the Great Barrier, the massive song spell that kept the Witchwood at bay. A few more minutes of riding, and Ayleth gazed upon a stretch of clear ground where the fringe forests had pulled back several yards from the Barrier, as though afraid to touch it, afraid to draw too near the darkness on its far side. Without access to her shadow senses, Ayleth couldn't see the spell itself. It manifested to her mortal vision as an obscuring mist.

And unseen beyond that mist, crouched on the landscape like a vast predator waiting for the right moment to attack its prey, was the Witchwood. The final curse of Dread Odile.

Ayleth shuddered. Just a glimpse of those shadowy depths made her throat thicken as though she breathed in a lungful of *oblivis*. Her icy bath of the night before hadn't fully washed away the stink of infection and rot that had permeated her skin down to her bones.

Terryn swung down from his saddle and stepped to

the edge of that clear land. A gray pallor stained his dark cheeks, and the tension in his jaw and neck told Ayleth he experienced much the same sense of revulsion that even now told her to ride away, to turn her back to the Witchwood and run. But they had a job to do.

Ayleth dismounted and secured Chestibor's reins to a nearby tree. Unless she was mistaken, it was the same tree she'd tied him to the day before. The grass and under-growth hereabouts looked thoroughly grazed. Terryn had led them to the right spot even without Feral powers to guide him. Ayleth was impressed despite herself.

But no amount of natural woodcraft was going to help them find Nane's logbook. This task required something stronger. Something supernatural.

Keeping an eye on Terryn as he slowly approached the Barrier, Ayleth slipped the yellowed Vocos pipes from their sheath on her belt. Though the shape was the same as her old pipes, they felt oddly unfamiliar in her hands as she snapped them into position. Nonetheless, she lifted the mouthpiece to her lips, preparing to call up her shade.

But rather than begin the Song of Summoning, she instead found herself watching her fellow venator as he paced closer to the Barrier. Something in the set of his shoulders worried her. Did he see something on the far side? Why did he draw so near? Personally, she'd prefer to never peer through that spell again.

Why in the Goddess's three holy names had Nane chosen to cross the Barrier? The question struck her again, even as it had multiple times since she first glimpsed the venator's poor, broken body just on the far side of the barrier spell. It was the act of a desperate man. Could he have been captured and carried across? Or was he chased?

Answers wouldn't spring out of thin air. And Terryn, no matter how closely he watched through the spell mist, wasn't going to spy them out either. They needed to find that logbook.

Taking the Vocos mouthpiece between her lips, Ayleth called the Summoning song spell to life. First, the deep rumble of the drone spilled into the air around her, reverberating into the ground beneath her feet. Perhaps it was pitched a little deeper than her former instrument, but its tone formed a solid foundation on which to build the complex melody. This melody lilted from the pipe's second head, the complex notes trilling hesitantly at first as she adjusted to the new instrument, but swiftly gaining speed.

The music itself was unlike any music of the mortal world. It was far more complex and inaudible to mortal ears. When she played well, Ayleth knew that her song spells were the closest she'd ever come to speaking the language of the shades themselves. The phrases she played, if shaped correctly, worked powerful influence over spirits.

She closed her eyes, throwing herself into the spell. In the darkness behind her eyelids, the tall pine forest of her mental landscape took shape. She saw the spell song like a silver thread streaming out from her into the forest. It caught something, tensed, and began to pull. She felt the weight of Laranta, who offered only token resistance as the spell drew her to the forefront of Ayleth's mind.

The shade manifested to Ayleth's awareness in her giant wolf form, shaking her head with relief as the suppressions binding her relaxed. Her eyes flashed at Ayleth. *We hunt, Mistress?* she asked eagerly.

Ayleth nodded. She finished the variation she played,

then modulated the melody into the Song of Command. *"I need you to find a mortal trace and follow it. The man we seek is dead, but he had a book on his person, and we must find it."*

Laranta shrugged, but by the light in her eye, Ayleth knew she was intrigued. Her shade never could resist the lure of the hunt, though she preferred living prey.

Ayleth resolved the song spell, allowing the drone to linger a little longer after the melody itself was complete. Then she sheathed her pipes and said, *"Come out, Laranta."* Her wolf shade poured from her mind to appear in the mortal world beside her. She was a being of pure spirit, invisible to all other eyes, but to Ayleth she looked almost solid, like a real wolf.

Ayleth pulled the silk pouch Kephan had given her from the front of her jerkin. Loosening the tie, she peered inside, noting a thick curl of gray-streaked brown hair, tied with a leather thong. A love token, perhaps. A useful one under the circumstances. She plucked the hair out and held it out for Laranta to sniff. As a being of spirit, Laranta was not limited to mortal senses such as sight, sound, or smell. Her perceptions were much more complex. But to Ayleth, she looked like nothing more than a large black wolf sniffing an interesting scent.

Dead, Laranta declared almost at once. *I found this one already. Dead.*

"*Yes, I know,*" Ayleth replied. "*But now we are searching for his book. We believe someone may have carried it out of the Witchwood. He would have touched it with his bare hands. Can you find it?*"

Laranta's lip curled, not in a snarl so much as a wolfish grin. *I can find anything,* she declared. Ayleth smiled at the enthusiasm and watched her shade bound away, nose to the dirt, searching. In her zeal, she lost most of her wolf shape and became an inky, writhing cloud of spirit stuff, wafting like a shadow several inches above the ground.

Ayleth glanced Terryn's way. He was some distance from her now, still looking at the Barrier. Had he summoned up his own shade? Looking at him with shadow vision, she could detect no trace of a second spirit. Remembering the power she'd witnessed from his shade the day before, she hardly blamed him. She wouldn't want to try to control such an intense spirit herself. Laranta was shade enough for her.

Laranta's exploration took her right up to the Great

Barrier. Unless Ayleth was much mistaken, she concentrated on the same patch of spell Terryn had worked to repair yesterday, following their adventure—the opening Nane had made when trying to escape, which someone else had closed behind him.

Ayleth frowned. It made sense that Venator du Tam had closed the break in the Barrier. And yet he denied it absolutely. But if not him, then who? There were no other venators or venatrices in Wodechran Borough, were there?

A chill crept along the edges of Ayleth's soul. She remembered again lying on that stone altar slab at the mercy of witches. The Windwitch had used one of Ayleth's own poisons to paralyze her. All seven of the surviving Crimson Devils had once been members of Saint Evander's Order, and they knew how to wield the pipes as well as the poisons.

Could it be that one of them had escaped and closed the Great Barrier behind them? But using what instrument? Not Nane's. Ayleth and Terryn had found both his Vocos and his Detrudos pipes on his body in the Witchwood.

It was a puzzle—a dark, dangerous puzzle, one which would no doubt grow more complex before it began to make sense.

Suddenly the dark mass that was Laranta sprang up into wolf form and barked excitedly, *The hunt! The hunt!*

Ayleth sprang into motion. Without bothering to call out to Terryn or waiting to see if he would follow her, she fell into step behind her shade, following the soul tether which always bound them together. Laranta led her away from the barrier spell back into the forest, heading north. Ayleth's heart beat a thrilling rhythm, and her soul lifted from the mire of confusion and exhaustion that had held it captive these last twenty-four hours. The thrill of the chase coursed through her blood. This was her calling, her purpose. All other mysteries, all other duties could wait. For now, there was only the hunt.

Laranta bounded through the trees, and Ayleth bounded after her, further and faster until suddenly . . . both came to a halt. Laranta, several paces ahead, lowered her head, growling softly. Ayleth reached out, perceiving what she could through her shade's senses.

She smelled death. And decay.

I found the dead man's trace, Laranta said, turning to look back at Ayleth. *It ends here.*

Ayleth approached, carefully placing one foot at a time. Beneath the browning autumn foliage, she saw an outstretched skeletal arm, a hand. The bony fingers still clasped the leather binding of a venator's logbook.

Whoever had stolen Nane's records had already met a gruesome end.

CHAPTER 5

TERRYN'S EYES GLEAMED WITH SHADOW-LIGHT AS HE peered into the misty wall, studying the complex weaving of the impressive song spell.

While all members of Saint Evander's Order learned to play the same basic spells on their instruments, the variations of those spells were unique to each individual venator and his shade. Terryn had no trouble recognizing his former master's work. Fendrel carried an Anathema shade, which he controlled with impeccable skill. The song spell he had woven bore all the earmarks of an Anathema variation.

But that gap—that place in the spell where Nane had made an opening when trying to escape back through the Barrier—that gap bore traces of two other shade varieties. Arcane, of course: Terryn's own shade, which he'd used to repair the gap yesterday. But underneath lay the poorly woven spell worked by a third shade-taken.

Terryn frowned, his eyes narrowing as he concentrated his gaze. He could swear that spell was created using Feral power. Like the spirit housed within Venator du Tam.

Why would Kephan deny making the repair? There was no fault here, no wrongdoing. He was not properly trained for the maintenance of the Great Barrier, true, but any venator discovering a gaping opening should do whatever he could to fill it until one better equipped came along. And yet Kephan refused to acknowledge his role. Furthermore, he appeared sincere in his denial.

Which meant some other Feral shade-taken trained in the use of the Evanderian pipes had come along and filled the gap . . .

Terryn didn't look back over his shoulder. He'd heard

the venatrix playing her Vocos, summoning up her shade. Was it possible she had come to this spot before yesterday? She'd acted as though her shade had led her here, following a broken curse thread. Terryn had been impressed by this—it took a powerful shade and, more than that, a powerful venatrix controlling such a shade, to follow a curse thread once it was broken.

Perhaps things weren't as they seemed. Perhaps the venatrix had known to come to this exact spot because she'd been here before.

Maybe she'd found and mended the gap.

She had allegedly arrived in the borough two days ago, but who could say if that story was true? She might have been riding the back roads of Wodechran for days, even weeks.

A chill ran down Terryn's spine as he studied the nearly vanished Feral magic in the song spell. A number of questions arose in his head. Why, in all his years of training and apprenticeship, had he never once set eyes on this Ayleth di Ferosa before? Where had she been during that time? Training under Venatrix di Theldry as she claimed? Surely she would travel with her mistress to

Castra Breçar for her yearly inspection with the phasmators. Terryn knew all the brethren near his age by sight, and he should have seen Ayleth at some point. He certainly would remember a face like hers—

No. No! He was *not* thinking *that*. Not now. Not ever.

He stepped closer to the Great Barrier, concentrating on those winding threads, those three variations of song spell woven together. He shouldn't have been so quick to correct the spell yesterday. If he'd left it, he might able to get a better sense of it today, to verify whether it belonged to Kephan or to the venatrix. Haunts damn his short-sightedness!

Something moved.

Terryn's heart leapt to his throat and lodged there. His eyes shifted of their own volition from shadow sight back to mortal vision, peering into the mist. But that was useless. His mortal gaze could not penetrate that dense obstruction. He blinked back to shadow sight, staring through the shimmering song threads.

The shadows of the Witchwood took on solid form. Though he'd spent hours walking beneath those fleshy, pussing trees, Terryn was in no way desensitized to the horror. The very air on the other side of the Barrier was thick with foulness, a foulness he still felt coating the inside of his lungs.

He ought to back away. He was here on a mission after all. The song spell was repaired, and whatever lurked beyond could not escape. And yet, Terryn drew closer still, staring between the webbing spell threads, struggling to penetrate the darkness beneath those trees.

A man stepped away from the trunk of a tree. A soul gleamed bright to Terryn's shadow sight, a human soul bound inextricably to another, stranger being—a fully ascendant and yet fully controlled Anathema shade. The man approached the Barrier spell, leaving the shelter of the trees behind.

Pale gray eyes locked with Terryn's gaze, holding his attention as thoroughly as though his very heart had been caught in a snare.

He knew this figure. He knew this face. The tall, broad, powerful host body was hardly affected by the poisonous air he breathed, despite his long years of imprisonment. His hair hung long and loose down his back, a black curtain stranded with glints of silver. His dark skin nearly blended into the shadows, but his soul shone too bright to hide from shadow sight. The wrong soul for that body.

The man strode straight up to the Great Barrier and smiled at Terryn. Smiled using his father's mouth.

But it was the Corpsewitch's soul that looked out through his father's eyes.

Terryn took a step. He did not even realize he was doing it. His hand went to his knife, drawing it from its sheath, and his feet carried him straight into the Barrier spell. Another step, and he would pass through into the Witchwood, swinging his blade straight for his father's throat.

He started, however, at the sensation of magic wrapped around him. Reason returned with a jolt, and he staggered backward several paces, his knife glinting in the sunlight.

The Corpsewitch threw back his head and laughed.

Terryn could not hear the sound through the humming of the spell, but the gesture cut him to the heart. That was how his father used to laugh—that same tossing of his head, that same flash of his teeth, that same full-bodied mirth. He turned away, his head bowed, shoulders hunched, the knife gripped tightly in his fist. His eyes stared at the ground, but his vision seemed to fly back years. He saw himself again, a small child, scarcely four years of age, watching as his father was led away with a string of prisoners, his body not his own to command . . .

Terryn landed hard on his hands, the impact jolting through his bones. He managed to catch himself before he fell to his face. He gasped, spat, shook his head as though he could shake free every instant of that hideous memory.

His face burned beneath the circling scars ringing his cheek. Burned as though a red-hot knife even now carved into his flesh.

Closing his eyes, Terryn concentrated on his breathing. One long breath, held and released, followed by another and another. Slowly his heart calmed. Those memories . . . they were many years in the past now. He was free. Fendrel had found him. Fendrel had saved him. He was free.

The heat of his father's eyes nearly seared the back of

his head as Terryn stood and straightened his jerkin and cloak, as he sheathed his knife. He refused to look back. Vengeance was not his mission today. No matter how his heart fought within him, he must maintain control. Gillotin du Visgarus was a prisoner of the Witchwood. He would never escape. And someday, eventually, the poisonous air would kill his host body, leaving his soul and that of his shade vulnerable to the draw of the Haunts. This was the Goddess's justice.

Giving his head one last vigorous shake, Terryn turned to where the venatrix's horse stood tied to a tree. Where had the venatrix herself gone off to without her mount? His own horse, still loose, nibbled disinterestedly at a patch of brown scrubgrass nearby. Terryn fetched and secured her beside the brown gelding, all the while telling himself that he did not feel the Corpsewitch's gaze following his every move.

He was just turning to study the forest floor, to search for some sign of where the venatrix may have gone, when he heard a shout—almost but not quite a scream. His head shot up, and he threw his shadow sight ahead of him, as deep into the fringe forest as it could go. Was that a gleam of Feral soul he detected?

Another shout . . . followed by a roar, deep as rolling thunder.

Terryn lifted his scorpiona arm, snapping the weapon into firing mode. He set off at a run into the forest, leaving the Great Barrier behind.

The Corpsewitch, still smiling his father's smile, watched him go.

Ayleth watched Laranta circle the body, sniffing carefully and sometimes lifting her muzzle to stare off in various directions. After some moments of this, the wolf shade sat, tilting her head at Ayleth.

"*What?*" Ayleth demanded.

Shade, Laranta answered. *I smell shade.*

"*What, here?*"

But Laranta shook her head. *Gone now. Ousted.*

Despite this reassurance, Ayleth's pulse quickened. She snapped her scorpiona into firing mode as she moved toward the body. Reaching out with Laranta's senses, she tried to get some impression of the corpse. A woman's corpse, she thought, though this was merely a guess. Decay had already done its work, and little remained but the skeleton. *"Was this body shade-taken?"* she asked her shade.

Laranta growled in affirmation.

Interesting. So, this mysterious shade-taken had stolen Nane's logbook. Had she killed Nane in the process? Ayleth crouched beside the outstretched arm, her hand reaching for the book. She paused, however, her eyes widening as she took in more of the situation.

The skull was crushed. A single blow from behind, just at the base of the neck. A violent wound, no doubt the cause of death. And, unless she was much mistaken, the same wound she'd found on Nane's body.

What could this mean? Had this person, this shade-taken woman, stolen Nane's logbook only to be killed by Nane's killer? Why? Not for the logbook, presumably, as that had been left behind. Was she working with Nane in some way? After six weeks of exposure, all of her clothing had rotted away, leaving behind nothing for Ayleth to study.

No, wait. Something gleamed on the woman's finger.

Lowering herself to look more closely without actually touching the skeletal hand, Ayleth inspected the gold signet ring. Dirt smeared its surface, but Ayleth could just discern the shape of a . . . Was that a bull?

Ayleth drew back slowly, her brows drawing together in a tight line. She wasn't well versed in the various crests of the great houses of Gaulia, but the five royal families she knew: the eagle-and-crown of Perrinion, the dolphin-and-lily of Campionarre, the lion-and-ax of Nion, the dragon-and-tree of Linorne, and the bull-and-star of . . .

"Talmain," she whispered. "The royal house di Taureau du Talmain."

How had a signet ring from the di Taureau family ended up on the finger of a dead shade-taken woman here, of all places? In the Goddess-forsaken fringe forests of Wodechran Borough?

Ayleth's eyes lingered on that death wound. A death so violent had no doubt propelled the indwelling shade far from this spot. Had it found a new host body before the Haunts caught and dragged it back into its chaotic depths? Was the shade still active in this world?

And if so, was it still keen to find this logbook?

Shade, Laranta growled. *Shade, shade.*

"*I know, I know,*" Ayleth murmured, shushing her wolf with a look. She reached for Nane's log, carefully sliding it out from under that fragile hand. The bones broke at even the slightest movement, and the gold ring flashed in the light. Ayleth hesitated, then plucked the ring up too. There must be a connection somewhere, somehow—

Shade! Shade, shade, shade!

Ayleth's senses exploded. With a shout, she surged to her feet, stuffing Nane's logbook into the front of her jerkin as she did so. "*Show me!*" she commanded, allowing Laranta to shift her gaze where it needed to go. A powerful spirit moved through the trees, gaining speed as it came. A shade. A fully ascendant shade. But in what sort of host?

Ayleth took a step back, then another.

She was taking a third when the bear burst through the underbrush, roaring with magic and rage.

CHAPTER 6

"LARANTA, GIVE ME YOUR STRENGTH!" AYLETH CRIED. Immediately, Laranta leapt to her, flowing into her head, her powers coursing through Ayleth's limbs, her veins, down to her core.

The bear, sensing the influx of magic, swallowed its roar and turned its heavy head her way. A terrible gleam of unnatural intelligence flashed across that dumb animal face, and the small dark eyes flared with shadow-light. She felt the soul contained within that bear's frame reaching out, studying her, sizing her up. Determining exactly what kind of a threat she posed.

For an instant, Ayleth was so overcome by the sheer force of that spirit that she froze. Spirit bind overcame her body and soul until she couldn't move, couldn't breathe. Distantly, she felt the dull thud of her heart and the pulsing power of Laranta burn through her veins, but it seemed to belong to someone else.

Then the bear charged.

With a jolt of terror, the spirit bind shattered. There was no time to think or plan, only to react. Ayleth sprang straight up, putting all the shade strength she possessed into her legs. Her head and shoulders struck small branches overhead, but she burst through these, rising ten feet into the air.

The bear passed underneath her at incredible speed, massive jaws gaping. Its huge paws crushed the skeletal remains of the Talmain woman as it went.

Coming down again hard, Ayleth fell, rolled, and shot up into a defensive crouch, one hand on her knife. She needed to use her scorpiona, but until she knew what sort of shade crouched inside that bear, she dared not take a shot. Using the wrong poison would not only fail to bring the shade-taken down, it would also serve to further enrage the shade within, driving it to greater violence.

The bear, having missed its target, lumbered to a stop and turned its head around, searching for Ayleth. Its gaze landed on her, and Ayleth prepared to leap again. Was Laranta's strength a match for such a foe? She couldn't know for certain, not when she'd left so many suppression spells in place. Even an ordinary bear would pose a threat she didn't want to face, and shade-taken was another story altogether. She needed to determine the variety or else—

"Haunts *damn!*" she cried.

The bear changed before her eyes. With a scream that sounded like a woman's voice, it rose up on its hind legs and threw back its head. Its bones shifted beneath the thick coat of fur. Ayleth could see them bending and breaking, could see the muscles twisting, warping. Magic, dark and malicious, poured from the beast's mouth, nostrils, and eyes, but Ayleth still could not discern what kind of shade could do this, *would* do this to its own host body. The bear shrieked and shrieked again.

Then it fell onto all fours, roaring once again, an explosion of sound that blasted Ayleth off her balance. She landed on her elbows, gazing up at the monster. It was not a bear anymore. The basic frame of bear remained, but from its spine protruded huge spikes dripping with the beast's own blood. Its jaw distended, unhinged to accommodate an enormous cage of razor fangs.

Ayleth sprang up and ran. Not away, as her good sense told her to do. Not for the nearest tree, which she doubted would do much good against such a foe anyway.

She ran at the monster, straight into that opening maw.

The bear flinched. For a moment, the shadow-light wavered in its gaze, as though it could not believe what it saw, could not believe that this small human would dare something so incredibly stupid. It recovered itself just enough to take a swipe with a paw tipped in huge curving claws. Trusting to Laranta's powers inside her, Ayleth jumped, not high, but just enough to avoid that blow. One claw caught and tore through the edge of her cloak, much too close to catching her leg.

She came down hard, but immediately braced her feet and, putting everything Laranta could give her into her arm, she hauled off and punched the bear right in the nose.

The monster crashed back onto its haunches. The earth shook. It blinked, all the shadow-light flitting from its round eyes. For the space of three heartbeats, it looked like an ordinary bear, despite the demonic warping of its frame. It turned its head slightly to one side as though contemplating some difficult problem.

Ayleth didn't wait for it to reach a conclusion. She punched again, this time hitting the bear in the ear. Laranta's power bolted through her arm, delivering a blow like a hundred-pound mace.

The bear fell to its side. But the spirit inside that monstrous frame leapt back to full ascendancy. Ayleth's shadow sight exploded in her brain at the sudden flare of magic and power and wrath. She sprang back just in time as claws ripped through the air mere inches from her face.

She landed on her back and pushed herself into a roll. She kept rolling as the bear's claws tore into the ground where her head had been a moment ago, three times over.

On the fourth rotation, she hit a tree trunk and stuck there, staring up into a dizzy whirlwind of branches and shafts of sunlight and the towering shadow of the spine-backed bear. She saw her death in a cage of yellow teeth.

A knife thunked into the bear's right eye.

It appeared out of nowhere like a miracle, quivering where it struck. The spirit flaring within the bear shuddered, dulled.

Ayleth wrapped her arms over her face before the burst of shade power erupted above her. The lifeless body of the bear fell, one great paw landing next to her head, jostling her arm, claws tearing into the ground a mere breath from her skin. Her mind reverberated with the screeching storm of a shade violently torn from its host. She felt a flash and a burn—not like fire or any other natural heat, but the unnatural blast of a sundered spirit—rip across her own soul.

All went terribly still.

The next thing she heard was footsteps pounding through the crisp leaves. "Venatrix! Venatrix!" a voice cried as though from far, far away. "Are you alive?"

She didn't bother to answer, but lowered her arms

from her face just as Terryn reached her. He grabbed her by the elbow, pulling her up before she was ready. With a snarl, she shook his hand away, using rather more of Laranta's strength than necessary. Her head whirled, and she struggled to catch her breath.

A shudder, a reaction to the violence of its death, convulsed through the bear's body. Ayleth recoiled, even though she knew the beast was certainly dead, the spirit inside gone. She scrambled to her feet, using the tree for support, and stared down at the hideous thing. Those bloody spines! The stench of shadow blight filled the air.

Dully, she realized that Terryn's hand was on her elbow again, that he was speaking. "Venatrix, are you hurt?"

She shook her head, not bothering to shake him off this time. Instead, she tore her gaze away from the bear, glaring at him. "What in the *festering* Haunts were you thinking?"

His brows drew together, and his hand released her elbow. "I beg your pardon?"

"A *violent* death? *Really?*" Ayleth shook her head, huffing an angry breath through her teeth.

"You were about to be gutted."

"Then you should have *shot* it with something!"

"I could not discern the shade variety."

"Then you should have *guessed!*" Her whole body quaked, both with the continued pulsing of Laranta's power in her veins and with pure human shock. She tried to take another step back from the bear, from Terryn, but ended up falling against the tree again, hitting her shoulder hard on the trunk as she leaned in heavily to stay upright. "Now it'll find some other host. It'll take some innocent, destroy some other body and soul."

"And when it slaughtered you? What would happen then?" Terryn's voice rumbled low, much too even, too controlled. "Your violently loosed shade would have found, possessed, and damned some other host body just as easily. So, I chose to save your life. Use it wisely and save many more in turn."

Ayleth lifted her still-spinning gaze to watch the venator as he stepped away from her and stood over the bear, studying it, his face an unreadable mask. He was right, haunts damn him. Choosing to save her gave them a stronger chance of bringing down and ousting this deadly shade later, whereas if he'd let her die—let Laranta loose into the world—he would still have to face the bear alone. And possibly die as well.

Yes, he'd made the right decision. But, Goddess love her, she wasn't about to admit it.

Ayleth hung onto the tree trunk until the world stopped spinning, watching Terryn as he inspected the bear. His eyes widened more and more as he took in the breadth of the monster, the extreme horrors of its distortion. Something flickered across his face, some emotion that came and went too quickly for her to discern.

"What is it?" she demanded at once. "Do you know something? About this shade?"

Terryn's eyes flicked to meet hers for an instant. Then he backed away from the bear several paces, his feelings once more hidden behind that mask of emotionless control. "I may have seen this kind of magic before. This mutation of the host body."

"*May* have? You don't know?"

He crossed his arms. "It was a long time ago." Facing her again, he said, "What brought you out here?"

Ayleth's hand went to the front of her jerkin. Her heart skipped a beat when she realized the logbook had fallen out, but a cursory glance of the surrounding area revealed it lying close by. Still unsteady on her feet, Ayleth tottered to where the book lay open, pages moving softly in the wind. Snapping it shut, she plucked it up and handed it to Terryn.

"Nane's logbook," she said, watching his eyebrow rise slowly. "And this," she added, reaching into a pocket. To her relief, the signet ring still nestled there. She pulled it out and dropped it into Terryn's palm. He held it up to his face, turning it slowly.

This time, he was not quick enough to disguise the expression flashing across his face. Ayleth saw surprise written there, coupled with something much stronger, much deeper. She jumped in at once. "You know it? You know this ring?"

"It's the royal insignia of di Taureau—"

"Yes, of course, but you *know* it. You know something about it."

All the blood had drained from his face, leaving his dark cheeks a sickly gray. The ugly circular scar stood out like a raw wound. "The bull-and-star," he said, speaking softly as though to himself. "And the rose."

"The rose?" Ayleth took a step and tried to snatch the ring back. It had been smeared with dirt when she looked at it, and she'd not noticed anything added to the royal crest. Terryn was too quick for her, pulling the ring away before she could catch it. "What does it mean?" she persisted. "Why a rose?"

"This insignia was especially made in honor of Princess Leurona di Taureau. The Chosen King's bride. When the marriage agreement was finalized, King Guardin commissioned this ring from a Campionarre artisan and sent it to the princess as a gift."

Ayleth gaped at him, then slowly turned her gaze to the mass of bones trampled beneath the bear's feet. Terryn followed her gaze and, seeing the remains, moved quickly over to them, demanding, "What is this? What did you find?"

"She was holding Nane's logbook in one hand," Ayleth said, following him and standing close as he crouched over the remains, trying to make sense of the disaster. "She wore that ring on her finger."

Terryn put down a hand to steady himself. The muscles in his cheek, beneath the scar, ticked oddly. "I know who this is," he whispered. "I know . . ."

With shadow sight bright in her eyes, Ayleth watched the dark cast of horror that fell across Terryn's soul. It was terrible to look at, so she blinked quickly back to mortal vision. "It . . . it can't be Leurona. Can it?" she said. "The princess married King Guardin and died a few years later."

"Princess Leurona gave the king's gift to her waiting lady, Mylla di Hersent, in gratitude for the services Mylla loyally performed for her mistress."

"What? How do you know this?"

Terryn turned to look at her over his shoulder, dark curls spilling back from his forehead. "Because I was there," he said.

Ayleth stared at the venator. "You . . . you're saying you saw the princess give this lady the ring. You were there. Present. In the room at the time."

Terryn nodded.

She blinked. "I don't . . . That is . . . How?"

The venator drew a deep breath. He stood above the

ruins of the corpse, looking everywhere but at Ayleth. "Lady Mylla claimed me as her son," he said at last.

"She was your mother?"

"I didn't say that."

He certainly didn't look like a man who had just discovered the mortal remains of his mother. But then, he was Terryn du Balafre. Perhaps evasive and taciturn was his way of manifesting profound grief. Ayleth didn't buy it. Still, by the set of his jaw and the warning gleam in his eye, she knew better than to push.

"So . . . Lady Mylla," she said instead. "What became of her? Was she a shade-taken when you knew her?"

"No," he answered. He turned then and faced her squarely, looking her right in the eye, his feet braced as though prepared for battle. "Lady Mylla was possessed by Ylaire di Jocosa. I watched it happen."

Ayleth knew that name. She'd seen it not very long ago, written down by her mistress's hand in the pages of a skin-bound book. There were seven names listed. That name had been at the very top . . . and beside it, a title.

"The Warpwitch," she whispered. Then she shook her head so sharply that her long braid swung over her shoulder. "You're telling me this woman carried inside her the spirit of the Warpwitch. Dread Odile's chief lieutenant, mistress of the Crimson Devils."

Terryn nodded once. His eyes flared with shadow-light. "And now her spirit is loose somewhere in Wodechran Borough."

CHAPTER 7

NEITHER OF THEM SPOKE DURING THE WHOLE OF the long ride back to Milisendis Outpost. Huddled deep in their cloaks against the cold blast of wind and the occasional spitting of rain, they retraced the path they had forged across the rolling landscape. At some point, Ayleth realized that this was the first time they'd really ridden together, side by side. Her mouth quirked at the thought. After their recent experiences, perhaps they were beginning to form some sort of a bond.

A sideways glance at the venator's face partially hidden beneath his hood . . . and she changed her mind. No, this was not a man with whom anyone could bond. Except, perhaps, Prince Gerard. But he was a better man than most, being the prophesied fulfillment of the Goddess's will and all that. It would take divine intervention to foster warm feeling for someone like Terryn du Balafre!

And if what she now gathered about the cold venator was true, there might be a stronger bond between him and the Golden Prince than mere friendship.

Through Ayleth's memory flashed a recent image—the glimpse she'd had of Queen Leurona, depicted in an idealized portrait hung in the gallery of Dunloch Castle. She'd been struck at the time by the intensity of rage in the queen's eyes. The queen's ice-cold eyes . . .

Ayleth shifted in her saddle. The speculations crowding in her head were uncomfortable, and she couldn't guess where they might lead. Better not to dwell on it at all. Better to focus on the many tasks at hand.

The afternoon was well advanced by the time they reentered Milisendis. Venator Kephan appeared in the doorway of the blockhouse to greet them, peering out into the drizzling yard. His face was pale, his eyes red-rimmed. Had he been weeping in those few hours of privacy while Ayleth and Terryn were away? His expression was so hard, so stern that Ayleth found it hard to imagine him giving way to tears.

They led their horses to the stable, leaving both saddled, but looping feedbags over their noses. At least someone would get a proper meal today. Ayleth rubbed Chestibor's cheek, then hurried to catch up with Terryn as he exited the stable, crossing the damp yard to the blockhouse.

Venator Kephan leaned against the door frame, watching their approach. "Did you find it?" he called to them.

Ayleth produced the logbook and held it out to the venator. Neither she nor Terryn had read it yet. Her mind was still reeling with the revelations Terryn had so reluctantly made. Still, she watched with great interest as Kephan flipped the book open, paging to the last few entries, his eyes darting back and forth as he took in his former hunt brother's writing.

"An inborn," he murmured.

Ayleth's heart plummeted. Yesterday morning, while shuffling through the stray notes on the desk in the blockhouse main room, she'd come upon a message from Castra Breçar—a confirmation that a sample Nane had sent to the castra had come back positively identified as belonging to an inborn shade-taken. An inborn child.

According to Saint Evander's teachings, there was only one way to save an inborn shade-taken's soul.

Sickness thickened her throat. Ayleth swallowed with some difficulty. Apparently Nane's last hunt, his last entry in his logbook, had been on the trail of the inborn. Had he found the child? Had he . . . done what was required by law?

Kephan looked up at Ayleth and Terryn. His face was stricken. "Did you read this?"

"No, sir," Ayleth said as Terryn shook his head. Kephan shoved the book into Terryn's hands and crossed his arms. Terryn began to scan the page, and Ayleth leaned into his arm to read as well:

Elsinoe Shrinehouse, south of Hollen Village. Mother Vesta sent word. Child came for sanctuary. Sees visions. Possibly the missing inborn, Jerlo du Bucheron's daughter. Riding out to investigate.

This was the last entry in the logbook, dated six weeks earlier, almost to the day. Ayleth looked up from the page, trying to catch Kephan's eye. "Did you know where Nane rode on his last hunt?"

"I was on the west circuit at the time." Kephan shook his head and rubbed a hand down his face. "He never mentioned an inborn child to me. Probably didn't want me to know."

Terryn shut the book with a snap. "It may be connected to Nane's death, or it may not. But there is something else you need to know, Venator. This book was found with the remains of a dead woman, and I have reason to believe she was Ylaire di Jocosa's host body."

"What?" Kephan's eyes flashed with horror, and he took a step back into the blockhouse. "The Warpwitch?"

"The very same."

"I thought you said the Crimson Devils were still held behind the Great Barrier," Kephan stated, his tone an accusation. "You told me you found the opening repaired, if badly, and that you yourself have since strengthened that repairing."

"This woman was killed around the same time as Nane," Ayleth put in. "I saw the body. It wasn't far from where Nane entered the Witchwood. I saw the death wound. It was the same blow dealt to Nane. I could only discern so much from a corpse so far decomposed, but I would wager they were murdered around the same time by the same person."

"What are you implying?" Kephan spat. "That Nane was somehow in league with the Warpwitch? That they were working together?"

"They need not have been working together to share a common enemy," Terryn answered quickly. "We don't know what links the two deaths. We have only the information we've given you."

"And what proof?" Kephan persisted. "How can you be certain that it was the Warpwitch's body you found?"

Terryn fished the signet ring Ayleth had given him out the front pocket of his jerkin. "I myself witnessed Princess Leurona di Taureau gifting this ring to one Lady Mylla of Talmain. Twenty years ago. A mere two weeks later, I watched as the witch Ylaire cut the throat of her own host body, driving her spirit and that of her shade into Lady Mylla. According to the last reports, Ylaire was still wearing Mylla's form when she fled into the Witchwood."

"Twenty years is a long time," Kephan said. "Are you certain you remember correctly?"

The corner of Terryn's mouth curved downward. "Yes."

Kephan compressed his mouth into a tight line. He took the ring from Terryn, holding it up to his face, and stared at it as though he could somehow, by the sheer force of his gaze, make it cease to exist. "Someone might have taken it from her. Rings can be passed around easily enough."

"True," Terryn replied. "But we would be wise to operate on the assumption that Ylaire di Jocosa has escaped the Witchwood and reentered our world. That her host body was killed, and her violently liberated soul and shade have transferred elsewhere."

"Possibly several times," Ayleth added. She hastily informed Kephan of their encounter with the bear, the terrible warping she'd observed in its body. While the Warpwitch was famous for her ability to control and warp any number of slaves, she had been known, on rare occasions, to warp her own body as well. The shade-taken bear, while possibly no more than a slave of the witch, might well have played host to the witch herself.

"Have you not been chasing a body-jumper these last several weeks?" she added. "Most shades don't practice willful transference of hosts. That's a witch's trick."

"True," Kephan agreed reluctantly. "And you're right: We have no idea how long that opening in the Great Barrier may have stood wide before someone tried to block it. I hate to imagine that one of the Crimson Devils has escaped, but . . . as you say, Terryn, we would be wise to assume as much."

"And we still don't know who killed her host body. Or Venator Nane," Ayleth said. "Whoever that was must be powerful indeed. Or very, very lucky."

"Foolish is the word I would use," Kephan said, twisting the signet ring in his fingers. "Only a fool would go up against Ylaire di Jocosa. Not even Nane would have tried it, and he was the bravest man I ever . . ." He shook his head, closing the ring tight into his fist. After a long intake of breath, his head came up, and he addressed himself to Terryn. "You know where we must go next."

Terryn nodded, his jaw clenched.

Ayleth blinked between the two men. Perfect. More information Terryn possessed that she knew nothing about.

"*I* don't know," she said irritably. "Where are we going?"

Kephan cast her a dismissive look. "You, di Ferosa, will follow *this* lead." He swiped Nane's logbook out of Terryn's grasp and pressed it into hers. "Find this Elsinoe Shrinehouse and question this Mother Vesta. Find out what you can about the inborn child. Find out if Nane ever made it that far, and pursue any leads you discover."

"And? What of you two? What will you do?"

"We will hunt the Warpwitch," Kephan answered, meeting Terryn's eye.

Ayleth's jaw hung open. Was this to be her future here in Wodechran? Shuffled off on the less important tasks while the castra-favored Terryn pursued the real hunts?

"I'm not afraid of any witch!" she said, her voice hot.

"I faced Zilla d'Utrehd and survived. I almost killed her!"

"Zilla is not Ylaire," Kephan answered darkly. "All of Dread Odile's devils were deadly, but some were worse than others. *Are* worse. The Warpwitch is the worst of the lot."

"And I punched her in the nose today!"

But Kephan shook his head firmly. "If that *was* the Warpwitch and not merely one of her slaves. Even then, you did not face her alone, and if what you tell me is true, she would have torn you apart were it not for du Balafre's intervention." Ayleth's face flamed, and she opened her mouth, but Venator Kephan put up a hand. "You *cannot* face her on your own. Believe me. If you find yourself anywhere near Ylaire di Jocosa's vicinity, do *not* engage. Fall back and find either Venator du Balafre or me. Only together can we hope to bring her down."

"Together?" Ayleth threw up her hands. "Then why are you sending me away? Take me with you." She felt Terryn's gaze on her face but refused to look his way. She hated that he should see her practically begging—begging to be treated as his equal, as a legitimate contender for this post. Damn him and his smugness and his castra connections and his stupid stoic face!

She took a step closer to Venator Kephan. "You need a tracker. I have a Feral inside me. I am much better suited to this hunt than *he* is." This with a sharp jerk of her head Terryn's way.

"I carry a Feral as well, in case you hadn't noticed," Kephan answered, his eyebrow sliding up his forehead. "We're not following a trace in any case, di Ferosa. As you ought to recall, the witch—if indeed it was she—has transferred to a new host. With no idea where her spirit is housed, we cannot trace her at all."

"Then where are you going?"

The older venator's face, already hard, turned to iron. "That is not your concern. You are not my hunt sister. You are not appointed. And if you continue in this fashion, I will be forced to make a report to the Golden Prince and see to it that you never are. Remember your place and do as you are told." He tapped the cover of the logbook with one finger. "The shrine house. Mother Vesta. Find out what you can, and report back here. Is that understood?"

Her head roaring with frustration and the ongoing

hum of the suppression songs keeping her shade at bay, Ayleth bowed her shoulders. Then she pulled herself upright and saluted smartly. "Yes, Venator," she said through clenched teeth.

CHAPTER 8

"TELL ME YOU ARE READY FOR THIS, VENATOR DU Balafre."

Terryn twitched out of the reverie into which he had sunk over the miles of a very long ride. Neither he nor Venator Kephan had bothered to speak more than a few words following a brief exchange while gathering supplies and readying their horses. There wasn't much to say, not yet. They both knew their destination. They both knew the care they must take during their approach. But for the moment, there was only miles of the open countryside of Wodechran Borough on every side.

Too much time to think.

He glanced sidelong at Kephan riding at his side. The concern in the older venator's face was grating. What did Kephan take him for? Some green apprentice?

"I am ready," he said, forcing his voice to remain level, refusing to let any hint of tension betray him. He offered no more, and Kephan didn't press him, thank the Goddess. Only an iron grip of self-control kept Terryn from urging his mare on ahead at a gallop to escape the other venator's disquieting glances. But such an act would, in and of itself, give Kephan reason to worry, so Terryn maintained firm hold on himself.

He kept seeing a certain face in his mind—a face he'd not thought of in many years. Gentle Lady Mylla. She'd always been kind to him, always cared for him. Never loved him, but then . . . neither had he loved her. As a boy he'd known he must hold her hand and call her "mother" and do as she bid him with prompt, quiet obedience.

And every afternoon, she would take him to the

princess's private chamber and leave him there for a quarter of an hour while she stood watch outside the door. For this, she had Terryn's undying gratitude.

The image of that broken skeleton, that crushed skull, flashed through his mind. He shuddered, swallowed. Lady Mylla had met her end long ago. Her poor soul had not been strong enough to withstand the power of Ylaire di Jocosa and her Anathema shade. Those possessing forces had overcome her body and ousted her spirit all in a matter of moments.

Terryn's fingers tightened around the pommel of his saddle. The Warpwitch was to blame. For Mylla and for . . . so much. The Witchwood was too good an end for her. She deserved much worse. She deserved the Haunts.

Heat writhed in the depths of his mind, responding to his anger. Terryn blenched. The suppression songs he'd played remained strong, but still he must take care. No matter how he bound it, no matter how he forced it down, his shade remained irrevocably linked to his emotions. His heart might break and long for vengeance, but he dared not give in to these feelings. He must take care, or he would end up like Mylla—a displaced spirit, watching helplessly as another being walked off wearing his body.

"There. I see it," Kephan said quietly. "Goddess! I forget every time just how . . . how bad it is."

Terryn looked over his mare's head, gazing down into the valley below. His heart lurched painfully, though he'd tried throughout the ride to brace himself for what he knew was coming.

The ruins of what was once a mighty road led down into the valley. Paved with oblidite stone, the Queen's Highway had stretched across Perrinion for a hundred miles, leading at last to Dulimurian City, the seat of Dread Odile's power. No road remained now, only a mere scar left on the landscape. Without Odile's power to sustain it, the oblidite had either sunk into the soil or disintegrated to fine dust. It wasn't a substance meant for this world.

But it wasn't the ruinous road which attracted Terryn's attention. His gaze instead turned to the fortress which had, back during the Witch Queen's reign, stood as a defense over the Queen's Highway.

Cró Ular—the Tower of Blood and Eyes.

Kephan watched him again. Terryn made certain his face remained a complete blank.

"You were there, weren't you?" Kephan said quietly. "At the battle."

A short breath. Then, "I was."

"They say Gillotin du Visgarus killed all the human slaves. That he sent their corpses into battle, while Ylaire used their spilled blood to create a blood barrier around the tower."

"Yes."

Kephan hesitated some moments. He had not served in Perrinion for the war, having been still an apprentice at the time, in Campionarre, the far north. Everything he knew about the key battles and events he had learned well after the fact.

"How . . ." He paused. Terryn sensed the older venator's rising curiosity and turned, silently daring him to ask his question. Kephan's brows drew together. "How did *you* escape that fate?"

Terryn's lip twisted. "Ylaire had other uses for me." He faced forward in the saddle again and spurred his horse into motion.

As they drew closer to the tower ruins, Terryn could no longer ignore the stench in the air. It wasn't a real stench, not something he sensed with mortal awareness. But there was no other word in his language to describe this distinct putrid funk that assaulted the soul. It made a man want to turn back, to flee.

The tower itself had fallen. Like many of those structures created by Dread Odile during her reign, it had been reinforced with oblidite. Once the Witch Queen died, her power slowly seeped away, and even an edifice as proud as Cró Ular had given in. Its walls had been broken earlier, during the battle with King Guardin.

The Crimson Devils had set up a formidable defense here at the watch tower. But even the blood barrier raised by the deaths of all those slaves had broken at last. No one could resist the coming of the Chosen King.

The remnants of the blood-barrier spell still crawled over the fallen stones of the wall. Terryn could see it, red, writhing masses of Anathema magic, like living spider webs. The curse itself had been broken, but the power that had set it in place—the sheer amount of fresh blood spilled at the moment of its creation—made such foul magic difficult to sweep away entirely. Not while the original caster, Ylaire herself, remained alive.

So, the curse, broken and sick and rotted, crawled over the walls and stank up the air. Even an untaken mortal would feel it, might even catch a glimpse of it, so powerful was the Warpwitch's working.

The horses shivered and tossed their heads, reacting to that curse which they could not see. When Terryn tried to urge his mare closer, she reared up, squealing. "Whoa, Fleeta!" he said, turning her away from the tower and stroking her neck to calm her. Her skin shivered beneath his touch. "Easy, girl, easy."

Kephan's horse tossed its head, stamping, foaming at the bit. "We'd best leave them," the older venator said, and dismounted. "And we should call up our shades. Just in case."

Terryn nodded and sprang down from his saddle. He gave his mare several more soothing pats before slipping his Vocos pipes from their sheath.

As Kephan set to work summoning the powers inside him, Terryn closed his eyes and began to play his own spell song—the Song of Searching. The world around him melted away, and he gazed upon the landscape of his own mind—the dry, hard mind which he had created for himself. A mind that would permit no weaker memories or thoughts to take root and flourish.

The only flaw on the broad, flat expanse was a huge mound which, from some angles, looked like nothing more than a pile of rock. But when approached from a certain angle, it became instead a massive, draconian being. Buried. Trapped. But still alive.

His shade.

The hum of complex suppression spells vibrated through Terryn's soul. Unlike other venators, Terryn dared not allow his possessing spirit any room for ascendancy, not even temporarily. It was much too powerful, much too dangerous. Instead, he had learned to harvest small amounts of magic at a time, which he could use at need when entering a dangerous situation.

Terryn stepped across the barren mindscape, approaching the mound with care. His spirit self reached out one hand, while his mortal body played the pipes, shifting into a new melody: the Song of Harvesting.

What is my name? Do you know my name?

Terryn halted. In the mortal world, his fingers hesitated in their playing. Only years of training enabled him to sustain his breathing, to sustain the song. He knew better than to speak, knew better than to listen to that voice. But the temptation remained: the temptation to answer. To risk everything.

With a swift plunge, Terryn slammed his fist into the side of the stone-trapped being. A shriek echoed across the heavy emptiness of sky above him, but he did not stop. He reached down, down, plunging deep to grab a great handful of power.

Then, withdrawing his arm, Terryn opened his eyes and left behind the world of his mind, reentered the mortal realm. He resolved the song spell before letting the Vocos pipes drop from his lips as summoned magic coursed through his limbs, pure white rivers of light bursting in his veins.

Terryn drew a deep breath, exhaling slowly. This feeling was . . . good. Too good, really. He had to be careful how often he indulged in such power. There was something alluring, something addictive about magic like this. If he wasn't careful, he could come to crave it.

Kephan had already completed his own summoning spell. Looking at him with shadow sight, Terryn saw the shimmering of a Feral shade coiled through him. Its shape was different from that which Venatrix di Ferosa carried, and no doubt the abilities it bestowed were likewise unique. No two shades were ever truly alike.

"Ready?" Kephan asked, sheathing his Vocos.

Terryn nodded.

They picked their way down the hillside, avoiding the remnants of the broken road. With every blink, Terryn's memory flashed back to many years ago—to a small child stumbling down that road, his new boots hurting his feet, his captors prodding him cruelly from behind. The tall captain of the princess's guard had tried to shield him from the worst of those blows.

Father . . .

Shaking his head hard, Terryn pulled himself back to the present, refusing to dwell on those images.

They did not need to find the gate. The wall was so broken down, they easily found a place to climb over. Avoiding the thicker patches of broken curse, Kephan led the way, and Terryn followed. They stood then in the ruins of the courtyard, facing the main structure of the fort itself across the piles of broken rock from the collapsed tower.

"This is our best bet," Kephan whispered. There was no real need to keep his voice down, but it was difficult to speak out loud in a place like this. Though the bodies were long gone, their souls long since either faded or dragged away to the Haunts, a heavy presence of death lingered. The deaths of the human slaves slain to create the blood barrier. The deaths of the Chosen King's brave men and women. And the deaths of the Crimson Devils who had laid down their lives to defend this citadel.

"If Ylaire has truly escaped from the Witchwood," Kephan continued, "she would most likely return to this place. Who knows what she may have left behind that she would want to reclaim."

Kephan was right. With the witch's soul loose in the borough, their best chance of finding some trace of her to follow was here. Terryn knew it.

And yet his feet stayed rooted to the ground.

The older venator turned to him, a strange expression shimmering in his eye. Or perhaps that was simply the gleam of his shade Terryn detected. "We should split up," Kephan said.

Terryn frowned. "That seems dangerous." He cleared his throat and squared his shoulders. "We're safer together."

"She's not here," Kephan answered at once, gazing out again across the ruins. "I would smell her if she were. But we should search the place over anyway, see what we can find. We're safe as long as we remain alert. Meet back here in half an hour, yes?"

Terryn didn't like it. But Venator Kephan was his superior, at least until Gerard made Terryn's appointment official. So he nodded a reluctant agreement.

As Kephan made his way right, heading for the southern part of the ruins, Terryn moved on ahead toward the main structure. The remaining patches of rotten curse obliged him to weave among the fallen stones along the way, and by the time he'd taken ten paces, he'd lost sight of Kephan.

By the time he'd gone twelve paces, he stood face to face with a ghost.

CHAPTER 9

ELSINOE SHRINEHOUSE WASN'T ON ANY OF THE MAPS stored on the outpost shelves. These maps, at least, were much more recently updated than the one she'd taken from Hollis's collection, but apparently only the very largest shrine houses merited inclusion. By the time she'd finished poring over each of the three maps she found that detailed important sites within the borough, she was ready to pull her hair out.

"Hollen," she muttered at last, her head heavy in her

hand. Her voice sounded oddly loud in the stillness of the blockhouse. Since Terryn and Kephan rode away, she had settled deep into silence, studying maps. "Hollen," she repeated with more conviction, sitting upright and rolling her tired shoulders. "The logbook said Elsinoe Shrinehouse was south of Hollen Village." How far south, she couldn't guess. But it was a start, at least.

She pulled the nearest map toward her. The labels were written in Venator Kephan's distinct, blocky handwriting, everything clear and neat. The lines of roads and major landmarks all felt blocky as well, leading her to guess that this map was of Kephan's own making. Hollen Village, if Kephan's distance measurements were accurate, was approximately twenty miles north of Milisendis and some eight miles west of the fringe forests.

Ayleth leaned back in her seat and turned to look out the window behind her. The sun was quite high in the sky already, well past its zenith. She'd already ridden Chestibor a good ten miles that day. He was a tough beast, and she knew he could handle another twenty, but not as fast as she would like. It would take her a good four hours to reach Hollen Village, if the map was even accurate. Whether or not she'd find Elsinoe Shrinehouse along her way was anyone's guess.

She heaved a sigh. Better to get started now and try to find the shrine house before dark.

Chestibor was still saddled, so it did not take her long to get back on the road. The heavy clouds had rolled by, giving way to small patches of sunlight here and there, which made for a more pleasant ride than she'd enjoyed that morning. While she hated that Venator du Tam had shuffled her off on this less interesting task rather than letting her hunt the witch, it would do her no good to sulk about it. Better to throw herself into her work with every ounce of energy she could summon.

Her spirit lightened as resolution solidified in her breast. She would find this shrine house, she would find this Mother Vesta, she would find this inborn child, and then she would . . . she would . . .

What?

If she found the child, what then?

Do you believe there is no difference?

Hollis's voice flooded her memory. Their last conversation, the night before Ayleth ran away from

Gillanluòc, her mistress's words full of anger. And warning.

Do you think you'll just as easily hunt down a child? Are you ready for all this role requires of you, all the deaths you must deal in the name of the Goddess?

Ayleth had not been able to answer then. She was devoted to honoring the Goddess and the teachings of Saint Evander. Her life was honed to a single purpose: the saving of souls from the damnation of the Haunts. A noble calling, one she had always sought to fulfill with passion and courage.

But a child.

An *inborn* child.

Flames seemed to dance before her vision.

Ayleth gritted her teeth, bent over Chestibor's neck, and drove her heels into his sides. "*Jah!*" she cried, and he broke into a gallop, churning up the track beneath his hooves, faster and faster. Ayleth clung to his back, her face to the horizon, as though she could somehow outrun her own dire purpose.

A shrine house stood at the crest of one hill, set apart from the villages surrounding. The denizens of those villages and farms walked many a long mile to meet in worship. The structure dominated the landscape, a stone building with a circular tower rising from the center, at least four stories tall. In this part of the borough, where the nearest structures were all cottages of mud and wattle and thatched roofs, it looked quite grand by contrast.

Ayleth eased Chestibor to a stop and pulled out Venator du Tam's map. Unless she'd gotten herself completely turned around, that little cluster of row cottages, sheep sheds, and ramshackle barns was Hollen Village.

She rolled up the map and eyed the shrine house ahead across a sloping field dotted with black-faced sheep. A small dormitory stood to one side of the holy structure itself, home to the priestess and a handful of nuns, no doubt. Not a particularly welcoming-looking place.

But where else could Jerlo du Bucheron's inborn child look for sanctuary when hunted by a venator?

As Ayleth rode up the green slope, scattering sheep

right and left, the bells of the shrine house rang, signaling the end of the evening service. A few of the more devout villagers appeared in its doorway soon after, their prayers and petitions complete, and prepared for the long trek back to their home villages. They spotted Ayleth from the porch steps. Her red hood stood out like a beacon, a bold declaration of her Order.

Ayleth saw the worshippers hastily make the threefold sign of the Goddess, a ward against shade-taken. Her heart sank. What exactly did they see when they looked at her? Not their protector, their defender who risked damnation for their sakes. Just another possessed monster.

Someday, perhaps, she would grow used to the fear she inspired in others. Hollis had. And Hollis never let that fear discourage her from completing her duty.

Head high, Ayleth continued up to the shrine-house door. The day lengthened fast, the setting sun casting the shadow of the tower like a long dark finger across the landscape, pointing east to the Witchwood. Someone must have warned the priestess of the venatrix's coming, for just as Ayleth approached the front steps, a tall, imposing figure in a white hood stepped into the doorway.

Ayleth dismounted, leaving Chestibor to pull up weeds around a tilting gravestone. She looked up at the priestess and made a sign of reverence, touching the first two fingers of her right hand to her heart and bowing her head. "Greetings, good Mother."

The priestess scowled. The face Ayleth glimpsed beneath that white hood was middle-aged and stern. Her brow, adorned with the silver headpiece of the Order of Saint Alicen, was constricted in what Ayleth guessed was a permanent scowl. Alicenian Sisters were devoted to the service of the GoddessHeart, and known for their charity to orphans. But an orphan would have to be desperate indeed to turn to this woman for comfort. Deep lines gouged the priestess's cheeks on either side of her severe mouth, and they deepened the longer she studied Ayleth.

"Vesta," she said abruptly. "Mother Vesta. I've served the GoddessHeart here in Wodechran nearly twenty years now, and everyone knows me and my sisters. We are pure souls. Untaken."

There was a defensive quality to the woman's voice.

Ayleth knew better than to take offense. At least now she knew she'd come to the right place.

"I'm not searching for shade-taken among Alicenians, Good Mother," she said. "I'm merely seeking information. Do you know the name Jerlo du Bucheron?"

The silver headpiece shifted as the priestess's brow tightened into an even deeper scowl. "Is this about that shade-blighted child of his?"

Ayleth blinked. Nane's logbook had said the child sought sanctuary here. But from the look in Mother Vesta's eye, no shade-taken would receive shelter under her roof. "What can you tell me about the child?" she asked carefully.

The priestess's mouth twisted as though with thought. "I sent Suvenne packing already, if that's what you're here about. When I found out what she'd been doing, she was reprimanded and returned to the temple for cleansing and re-indoctrination."

Ayleth blinked slowly. "This . . . Suvenne? She's a sister of Saint Alicen?"

"Yes."

"Did she . . ." Ayleth narrowed her eyes, trying to read

the truth in Mother Vesta's forbidding face. "Did she hide the du Bucheron child? Here?"

"I told you, she's already been punished. She's not shade-taken, so this has nothing to do with your Order."

Unsettled by the priestess's increasingly aggressive stare, Ayleth assumed a commanding stance. "Tell me," she said, "what you can about the child. Why was she said to be shade-taken?"

"Knew things she shouldn't know," the priestess answered, her voice dark beneath her hood. "*Couldn't* know, more to the point."

Ayleth waited for the priestess to elaborate. Mother Vesta folded her arms into the deep sleeves of her robe, contriving to look even more forbidding.

"We discovered her on the Eve of Uryene's Feast, when all the villages had gathered for the Twenty-First Night prayers. I learned later that she had been hidden in our granary for a fortnight beforehand. But that night, when all my congregation were gathered, she suddenly appeared in this very doorway, right during the third prayer song. She walked down the center nave, saying the same words over and over again."

"What words?" Ayleth asked.

"'Where is he?'" Mother Vesta shuddered, closing her eyes. "She kept repeating it, getting louder until everyone stopped singing, and there was only her voice, shrieking to shatter the windows. 'Where is he? Where is he?'"

"Who did she mean?"

The priestess's eyes flashed open, and her nostrils flared with a sharp intake of breath. "She stopped just beside Journeyman Gosse. She grabbed hold of his arm and began to say . . . to say . . ."

"What?"

"She told him where he had buried the body of his murdered wife."

Ayleth stared, uncertain what she had just heard. "His . . . his wife had been murdered?"

Mother Vesta leveled her gaze on Ayleth, her brows rising, moving the band of silver up her forehead. "Mistress Gosse disappeared ten years ago. Her husband claimed at the time that he did not know where she had gone. Everyone suspected him, violent man that he was, but the body was never found, and no proof could be brought to bear. Following the girl's declarations, the bailiff of Hollen went out that very night and found the woman's remains. Not much left after all these years, but enough. Her husband was taken away to the Golden Prince for judgment and duly hanged for his crimes."

Ayleth shivered at this last statement. She did not like to think of Prince Gerard in such terms—in the seat of justice, doling out sentences of life and death. Her rational mind knew this was part of his duty as master of the borough, but she preferred to imagine him above such things, pure and untainted by the dirt of this world.

"We locked the child in the cellar," Mother Vesta continued. "Sister Suvenne confessed in tears to hiding her. She knew the child was shade-taken. Stupid girl."

What the priestess described certainly sounded like shade work. Specifically, the work of a Seer: a teller of visions past, present, and sometimes even future. Not dangerous, exactly. Such abilities did not naturally translate into violence against others. But strange and unpredictable powers in their own way.

"And you are quite certain the little girl had not simply seen where Journeyman Gosse buried the body?" Ayleth asked.

Mother Vesta cast her a disgusted look. "Mistress Gosse disappeared ten years ago. The child herself was not yet born. She could not have seen any such thing. No, no. It was definitely magic afoot."

Ayleth nodded. "Did Venator du Vincent come to take the girl?"

Here the priestess looked surprised. "Don't you know? Do you people never talk amongst yourselves?"

Word of Nane's disappearance and death must not yet have traveled throughout the borough. Probably just as well. Ayleth held up a placating hand, shaking her head. "I simply want to hear your side of things."

Judging by Mother Vesta's shrewd expression, the priestess was unconvinced. But she said only, "The Red Hood arrived the next day. As did the child's father."

"Jerlo du Bucheron."

"The same. He's a woodcutter, a large man. Spends too much time in the fringe forests, I dare say. Mortal men were not meant to venture so near to cursed ground. But someone must keep our fires fueled through winter."

"And was du Bucheron present when the venator took his daughter away?"

The priestess nodded, her mouth a grim line. "He was . . . distraught, to be sure. We all of us witnessed how he struggled to take the girl back. He wanted to pluck her out of the Red Hood's arms and run off with her somewhere. As though he could somehow outrun that demon inside her!" Mother Vesta shuddered. "But the Red Hood overcame him and carried the child off. I sat with Jerlo as he lay unconscious right here in the shrine-house yard. I thought to offer him the comfort of the Goddess's truth when he awoke, but the moment he regained consciousness, he sprang up and gave chase, pursuing the Red Hood. By then it was too late for him to do anything, of course." The priestess bowed her head briefly, and Ayleth wondered if she glimpsed just the faintest hint of regret in the woman's hard face. "Du Bucheron returned a few hours later, empty-handed. The girl was gone. Dealt with."

Burned.

A shadowy hand seemed to catch hold of Ayleth's heart. She tried to shake it off, to tell herself not to be so foolish. The deed had to be done. Fire was the only way to separate a mortal soul from an inborn shade. If the child was to have any chance of heaven, her only hope was the fire.

Yet Ayleth could not deny the ache she felt, thinking of Jerlo, desperate to rescue his daughter—his poor, damned daughter. How could a man like him begin to understand?

How could anyone?

Drawing a shuddering breath, Ayleth looked up into the priestess's stony eyes once again. "Tell me where I may find Jerlo du Bucheron," she said.

CHAPTER 10

TERRYN STOPPED IN HIS TRACKS.

She stood a few yards ahead of him, surrounded by large broken stones. Her head was down and tilted so far to one side on her thin neck that it seemed to rest on her bony shoulder. Her fingers moved oddly, twirling a bright, faceted stone like a brilliant diamond round and round so that its many edges caught the light.

She spotted Terryn in the same moment he saw her. But while he drew back three paces, his breath catching painfully in his throat, she did not so much as flinch. Her face, devoid of emotion, turned slowly his way, her lips slightly parted.

She wasn't real. She couldn't be.

Dear Goddess above, let her not be real!

But Terryn knew better. His mind, no matter how fear-fogged, could not have imagined her this way. The last time he'd seen her, she wore a white wedding gown trimmed in gold. Her red hair was mounded in coils at the back of her head, a few dainty curls falling about her ears. Her throat was adorned in jewels, and her face contorted with pure terror as she screamed in a frenzy of pain.

He still saw her that way. In those few stray moments when he dared think of her at all. Whenever Gerard spoke her name, and the memories came crashing back.

Her tilted head slowly rose and tilted to the other side as she contemplated him. She still wore the remnants of her wedding gown. A flash of gold glinted beneath layers of crusted mud and grime and blood, but most of the white silk had stained to black. The once bountiful skirts hung in ragged shreds, exposing her bare legs and feet. Her hair had lost its sheen, hanging in dull hanks down to her hips. Still red, though. Even under the dirt and muck, still red.

She blinked. Only one eye. A huge fungus-like growth hid the other and extended down her cheek and neck, white and swollen and bulbous. "I know you," she said. Her voice croaked. It seemed to hurt her to speak, and she winced and swallowed, the growth on her neck lurching strangely. "I remember your name."

Terryn stood as though struck by spirit bind. But this was not the overwhelming presence of an ascendant shade lancing his soul to the quick.

"Terryn," she said at last. "You are Terryn. Am I right? Gerard always loved you. Always kept you lurking in his shadow. Even when we were children. Terryn . . . scar-faced Terryn. Venator du Balafre."

"Fayline," he breathed.

Her mouth, the half of it which could be seen, twisted in a smile. "You remember me. I thought you must have forgotten. Otherwise, why would you leave me in the dark all this time?"

It could not be her. It could *not* be. It might be her body, but it wasn't her. The being inside her, looking out through her tormented eye—it was trying to manipulate him, trying to lull him into complacency.

Terryn's hand moved to his quivers. Haunts damn! He hadn't thought to bring the paralysis used on Evanescers.

Her eye twitched as she watched him, and her horrible half smile grew. "I'd take care, if I were you. *She* knows what you're thinking. *She* wants me to kill you."

Coldness gripped Terryn's heart. "Inren—"

The girl screamed. She threw back her head, her arms flying wide to either side, every finger strained and tensed. Her throat convulsed, and the scream tore out of her in gashes of sound.

Something rose up inside her. Something invisible to mortal eyes, but which Terryn's shadow sight beheld with horror. Darkness crawled up from the pit of her soul, winding like a python of dark-light. It massed in her throat, in her head, poured out of her mouth and eyes. But through gaps in the darkness, the light of another soul gleamed, struggling to fight, struggling to suppress that choking hold, resisting with more strength than Terryn would have thought possible.

He had to do something. The heat of his own shade's

power coursed to his fingertips, but to loose that power on her risked shattering her mortal body into a million particles of dust. The intensity of such a violent death would empower her shade so profoundly, it might kill him as it shot forth from its ruined host.

No, he must try to shoot her. Without the right poison, his only option was the Gentle Death. His heart rebelled . . . but what choice did he have?

He plucked the black-fletched dart from its quiver, slammed it into his scorpiona, and took aim, his left arm crooked to brace his right.

She looked at him. Darkness poured from her mouth, from her nostrils, and wrapped around her head. "NO!" she cried, throwing up both arms.

In that same moment, Terryn heard Gerard's voice echo in his head: *No, Terryn! Don't hurt her!*

He hesitated.

The darkness exploded out of Fayline's core, enveloping her in a cloud of writhing, twining strands of anti-light. Terryn took his shot an instant too late. The dart whistled through the cloud, parting it in a narrow trail and dragging smoke behind when it bounced off a large stone and fell to the ground.

Fayline—or whatever possessed her body—was gone. *Evanesced* away to Goddess-knows-where.

Terryn panted as though he'd just run a mile at top speed. He watched the curling cloud of darkness as it shrank down and down into itself, condensing into a tight knot of nothingness, too dense to continue floating in the air. It sank to the ground, spread out like a cup of spilled water, then sank further still. It would keep on sinking, Terryn knew, until it reached the burning core of the world.

It was *oblivis*. Not the diluted form he had breathed in the Witchwood. This was pure *oblivis*, straight from the Haunts. Poured out through the slash Fayline had torn in the veils of reality as she stepped out of this world and into that chaotic realm. Somewhere far away, somewhere he could not guess, she had already torn another opening and reappeared in the mortal world, crossing through realities in an instant. As long as she had an anchor planted, she could step in and out of this world at will.

An anchor . . .

Terryn approached the still-writhing patch of dirt. It

was less than a foot square, and the *oblivis* itself was gone, but the soil now looked like the rotten, festering soil of the Witchwood. It shivered and boiled, a dead thing that felt the pain of its own decay. It would eventually stop, Terryn knew. He'd seen it happen before. But the soil itself would never recover.

He crouched over the small patch of pain, covering his nose. A bubble of black ooze popped, and something lay exposed. Dark and small, about the size of an eyeball, it rested in the center of that rotten patch of ground.

Terryn grimaced, his stomach heaving. He took out his knife and carefully, using the tip, rolled the little orb out from the patch of *oblivis* and onto the ordinary dry dust of the broken courtyard. The brilliant facets that had caught the light while Fayline toyed with it in her fingers were now dull. Something dark in the center of the stone had exploded.

"Haunts damn," Terryn hissed as he worked up the nerve to finally pick the object up between two fingers and bring it closer for a better look. It was broken. But it was an anchor. A few faint curse threads still wafted out from its center, visible to his shadow sight.

Terryn stood, slipping the orb into the small pouch on his belt. He did not fear immediate attack. If Fayline was going to return, she would have done so by now. With her anchor broken, she could not come back to this spot. She needed an active anchor in order to *evanesce* within a mile of any one location. Most likely, she had stepped away from this encounter and then broken the connection to her anchor so that it would leave no trace, no thread he could follow.

A pity Venatrix di Ferosa wasn't here. She could trace broken threads.

Terryn pushed that thought away at once. He had more important things to consider. Such as the fact that not one but two of the Crimson Devils had escaped the Witchwood. The Warpwitch—unless he was much mistaken about the identity of the dead woman in the fringe forests—and her sister. The Phantomwitch.

Inren di Karel.

"Not Fayline," Terryn whispered. "Not Fayline. Not anymore."

Were the two witches working together? If Inren was ascendant in that body, then surely she would have reunited with Ylaire, may have even escaped the Witchwood at her side. But if Inren was ascendant . . . why had she not attacked him?

Terryn frowned, slotting another Gentle Death into his scorpiona, turning slowly in place, his eyes peeled. Was it possible . . . was there even a chance . . .?

More frustrated and afraid than he liked to admit, Terryn picked his way through the rubble. He headed south, following Kephan. He needed to make certain his fellow venator had not also encountered the witch— either witch. Keeping his scorpiona up and ready, he peered into every shadow cast by the fallen tower stones. At any moment, he expected to see another patch of *oblivis* slash through the air, and to see Fayline's body step through, overflowing with the power of an ascendant spirit.

He clambered to the top of a large, ragged stone and looked down the other side. For an instant, his heart lifted with relief. Kephan stood below, alive and whole. Terryn breathed out in a sigh, opening his mouth to call out to the venator. Then his breath caught again.

Something was wrong.

In those few moments since he'd spotted him, Kephan had not moved at all. Not a muscle. He stood as though at attention, his gaze fastened on the foundation stones of the tower. The wind stirred his hair, and a big gust blew the hood back from his head, down around his shoulders.

Flaring bright with an evil, scorching light, like a brand still hot from the fire, a circle stood out on the older venator's cheek. A sigil, hot and pulsing with Anathema magic.

Terryn's heart stopped. He knew that sigil. The implanted curse of Ylaire di Jocosa. The binding mark she placed on all her slaves.

With a shout, he flung himself down from the stone, landing hard on the unforgiving ground below but springing upright again at once. Holding his scorpiona high, he called, "Venator!"

Kephan did not turn, did not move. He remained rooted in place. Only his cheek twitched with pain beneath the burning of the sigil brand.

Terryn hastened near, at every step turning this way and that, his shadow sight searching for some gleam of shade presence among the fallen stones, the crumbled walls. His gaze swiveled back to Kephan. Should he take the shot? Should he bring the man down with the Gentle Death now, before the curse could take effect, before she could *warp* him?

Terryn's finger tightened on the trigger. He took another step, bracing himself for the shot. He blinked.

Then blinked again. When did it suddenly get so dark?

Terryn groaned, wincing, and twisting his sore jaw and neck. The world seemed to have plummeted abruptly into night. He must have been so focused on what he was doing that he hadn't noticed when the sun sank beyond the horizon. Craning his neck, he looked up at the stars arching overhead, at the quarter moon gleaming like a curved blade of silver in the night.

"Oh Goddess, I'm stiff."

Terryn turned at the sound of Kephan's voice and saw the older venator standing just a few feet away, rubbing his neck and groaning. Terryn realized how tight and tense his own muscles were, as though he'd been straining his whole body to lift some heavy load for the last several hours.

Rolling his shoulders, he turned in place, taking in

their surroundings. "Where are we?" he murmured. They seemed to be standing in the middle of a hayfield recently harvested. Fragrant bales of hay loomed around them like small, bristly mountains. Not far off he saw the gleam of firelight through a set of windows, indicating some farmhouse.

"I don't . . . know exactly," Kephan answered, moonlight highlighting the creases of his frown. He drew a sharp breath, then exhaled in relief. "Ah. Our horses."

Terryn looked over his shoulder. Fleeta stood at one of the hay bales, helping herself, and Kephan's dark gelding shifted on his feet beside her.

The two venators hastened to their mounts, stumbling a little as they readjusted to using their own limbs. Terryn patted Fleeta's neck. She seemed unharmed. She must have carried him here, but he couldn't remember . . . couldn't recall . . .

"Cró Ular," he murmured.

"What's that?" Kephan asked as he heaved himself into his saddle.

Terryn frowned up at his fellow venator. "Were we not on our way to investigate the Tower of Blood and

Eyes? Searching for—"

"Yes, of course. We've just come from there." Kephan waved his hand in a brisk dismissive gesture. "We found nothing of note, remember? A pile of rocks and old broken curses. No lead to follow. If the Warpwitch was recently there, she's gone now."

"Gone. Yes. Of course." Terryn mounted, settling into his saddle with some discomfort. He cast a last glance behind. From this high, sloping field one could see the dark mass of the Witchwood in the east, impervious to moonlight. Nothing. Just a black expanse of nothing under the night sky.

"Nothing," he whispered. "We found nothing."

"Come on, lad," Kephan said, spurring his horse into motion. "Back to Milisendis for a night's sleep. If di Ferosa is there, she may have found something of interest at Elsinoe. If not, well, we'll decide tomorrow what our next step will be."

Kephan led the way across the field, and Terryn nudged his red mare to follow. They rode in silence for some while, each lost in his thoughts. Or almost-thoughts. Terryn couldn't quite pull his mind into order, and when he tried, a sharp stab of pain sliced through his temples, behind his eyes.

An hour passed, and another. At last the outpost tower loomed into sight, and Terryn's heart lifted at the prospect of sleep. That's all he needed, really. Sleep, a chance to set his mind at rest, to let this fog of bewilderment dissipate.

One hand unconsciously released Fleeta's reins and moved to the pouch on his belt. He pinched at the fabric, feeling something round and solid inside. Something no larger than an eyeball. But he couldn't remember what it was, and by the time they reached the outpost gate, he'd forgotten it entirely.

CHAPTER II

THE WOODCUTTER LIVED ALONE A FEW MILES OUTSIDE OF Hollen Village, close to the fringe forests. The sun had already set when Ayleth rode into his yard, but she saw light through the windows of his cottage. Jerlo was at home.

Ayleth's heart sank with deeper and deeper reluctance the nearer she drew to the cottage. After what she'd heard from Mother Vesta, the last thing she wanted was to face the bereaved father.

But the priestess had not been able to give her any further information as to Nane's doings following his visit to the shrine house, not even the direction he'd gone when he rode away with the child. Jerlo had pursued him. He presumably knew more.

Was it possible that he was Nane's killer? Ayleth didn't think it likely. Perhaps she could convince herself that a strong, motivated man might possibly sneak up on an experienced venator and strike him down. But in the Witchwood? Would any man, no matter how mad with rage or grief, pursue his enemy there? It didn't make sense.

Besides, she could not believe that even the strongest, most stouthearted of woodcutters would successfully kill both Venator Nane and the Warpwitch in quick succession.

Nevertheless, she needed to speak to the man, find out what he knew.

Slipping her Vocos from its sheath, she played a quick variation of the Song of Command. Laranta sprang forward in her mind, relieved at the loosening of the binding spells. *Hunt? Hunt?* she asked eagerly, her voice a growl in Ayleth's head.

"*Not now,*" Ayleth answered. "*I want you to sniff around this property. Search for some trace of . . . of Venator Nane's blood. It will be old, like the trace we found in the forest. And keep an eye out for shades.*"

Laranta slipped from her mind and manifested on the ground beside her horse. With a little bark of acknowledgement, she set off at a quick trot, making first for the woodcutter's barn. The soul tether connecting her to Ayleth tugged from here to there as the wolf shade began her exploration.

Ayleth, meanwhile, dismounted and approached the cottage's front door. Though she had tried to form some sort of theory based on the information she'd gathered, she found herself faced with more questions than before. Hopefully this man—this grieving father whose solitude she was about to invade—could give her an answer or two.

She knocked sharply and listened to the sound of footsteps inside. Heavy footsteps, a large man's tread. The door opened, and she looked up . . . and up some more. A massive figure stood before her, filling the frame of the door as he bent to peer out. His shoulders were so huge, he would have to turn sideways to exit, and a huge calloused hand gripped the doorframe.

Ayleth drew herself up as tall as she could, assuming an authoritative stance. Though she could not match this man for breadth, she could muster an impressive quantity of intimidation at need. Nevertheless, her mind reached unconsciously for the soul tether connecting her to Laranta. Goddess willing, she wouldn't need to use her wolf shade's strength, but just in case . . .

"What do you want?" the man demanded. His eyes focused on her red hood. She saw hatred glinting there. And she couldn't entirely blame him.

"I am Ayleth, Venatrix di Ferosa," she answered. "I am here by sanction of the Golden Prince. Are you Jerlo du Bucheron?"

"What if I am? What does the Golden Prince want with me?" Jerlo shifted his weight, stepping out through the cottage door onto the stone step where he could straighten to his full height. He might even make Terryn look small.

Ayleth braced herself, refusing to take even a single

step back. She chose to ignore his question and instead drove straight for the crux of the matter. "When was the last time you saw Nane du Vincent?"

The woodcutter's eyes flashed, a trace of fear mingled with the hatred. But he said only, "Nane du Vincent? I don't know this name."

"You had an altercation with him at Elsinoe Shrinehouse six weeks ago."

A vein in Jerlo's forehead bulged. Ayleth heard his teeth grinding beneath the bush of his beard. He looked as though he was ready to break something. Possibly Ayleth's head.

"You mean that man who stabbed my Fiola to the heart? That man who ripped my Nilly from my arms and carried her away to burn her alive? Is that the man you seek?"

To look into Jerlo's eyes was to behold a blazing pit of pain. Ayleth wasn't prepared. She opened her mouth, but no words would come. How could she speak in the face of such agony? She knew the law of Evander, she knew Nane had done right by the girl, but . . .

For the first time since leaving Gillanluòc, she

wondered if she should have listened to Hollis. Hunting shade-taken animals was not the same as this. Not the same at all.

Laranta approached suddenly from the side. She eyed Jerlo even as she padded closer to Ayleth. *I found no blood. No blood like the dead man's blood in the forest.*

"*Nothing?*" Ayleth asked, looking down sharply at her wolf shade.

Laranta simply repeated, *No blood.*

Ayleth's brow tightened, her gaze lifting to the woodcutter, who watched her closely, possibly guessing at her silent interactions with her shade. No blood on his property didn't necessarily clear him of guilt. He may have disposed of a weapon or of bloodstained clothes before returning home. But for the moment, she would drop this line of exploration.

"This name you mentioned," she said instead, choosing a new line of questioning. "Is Fiola your wife?"

"She was. Yes."

If the child was inborn, then one of her parents must have been shade-taken at the time of her conception. If Nane had killed Fiola, as Jerlo claimed, presumably the mother was the possessed party. But Nane should have dealt her the Gentle Death, not stabbed her through the heart. Things must have gone awry for the venator to resort to such violence.

"Tell me," Ayleth continued. "When did you know your wife had become shade-taken?"

Jerlo half turned his face away as though she'd struck him a blow. "We realized the truth, Fiola and I, nearly four years ago. Before . . . before Nilly was born."

"Nilly?" The daughter, Ayleth realized even as she spoke the name. She'd not bothered to learn it before now.

Jerlo continued as though she'd not spoken. "Fiola was expecting at the time. At first, I didn't want to believe. We knew the law, of course. We knew she ought to present herself to the Red Hood . . ." He shrugged, and his eyes shimmered in the half-light of the quarter moon. It was one thing for a man to know the law. Another thing to act on it.

"What did you do," Ayleth persisted, "when you realized the truth?"

The color drained from Jerlo's face. His huge

shoulders slumped, and his whole mighty frame seemed to shrink before her eyes. "There is a hedgewitch, lives not far from here, one Oma Githa. I took Fiola to see her, to find out if she could help us."

Ayleth sucked in both lips, chewing on them hard to keep from saying something sharp. Hedgewitches were a not-uncommon problem throughout Perrinion in these years following the Witch Wars. They were mortal practitioners of "low magic," working influence on spirits of the Haunts, though they themselves were not shade-taken. Without a possessing shade inside, these foolish individuals had little control over the results of their influences, which often led to disaster.

But hedgewitches claimed to offer alternatives to desperate shade-taken folk searching for a means to free themselves or their loved ones without undergoing the Gentle Death mandated by Saint Evander's followers.

Jerlo gave Ayleth a hooded look. "Oma Githa claimed she could drive the spirit out from Fiola. We paid her everything we could, and she performed the ceremony. We thought Fiola was safe after that. We thought the baby was safe. It wasn't until Nilly got a little older . . .

until she began to speak, that I knew . . ."

Ayleth hadn't the heart to press him, so she simply stood by, waiting, not quite looking at Jerlo while he gathered himself. At length, he continued.

"I didn't know Fiola was still shade-taken until the day the venator came to our home. She hid it all that time. Or it hid itself. I don't know which. But then that man came. He wanted to perform a test on Nilly, or take a sample or . . . or something. I thought, at first, he'd come for Fiola herself. I made them both hide, but the Red Hood found them." The woodcutter shook his head, and his next words came out strained and tight. "Fiola tried to protect Nilly. She lifted the man over her head and threw him across the yard."

Ayleth stared. She could not imagine such a thing. Strong as she was in Laranta's power, would she have the ability to lift a full-grown man over her head? Not without a fully ascendant shade.

"He fought back, of course," Jerlo said. "I thought she would kill him. But he drove his knife into her heart and . . ." He swallowed hard, and a tear escaped from his eye and fell into his beard before he could brush it roughly away. "When Fiola was dead, I thought the Red Hood would kill Nilly next. Instead, he merely inspected her with his strange implements. I don't remember what he did exactly, but when he was through, he told me to keep her with me. That he must speak to his superiors. But that he would be back soon. I think . . ." He sighed heavily. "I think he may have been giving me a chance to escape with the girl. I think he didn't want to kill her." He spoke the words resentfully, as though it pained him to give the venator any such credit.

"Why . . . why didn't you?" Ayleth asked quietly. "Escape, I mean."

Jerlo's eyes flashed, and Ayleth almost stepped back, half expecting a blow from one of those heavy hands. "Do you think I didn't want to? But by the time I'd buried my Fiola, Nilly was gone. Run off, I didn't see where. I hunted for her. I searched for weeks, everywhere I could think of. I thought that wicked spirit inside her had stolen her away from me, that it may have driven her to hide in the Witchwood even. But no. She'd gone for shelter at Elsinoe. And those Haunts-damned sisters betrayed her, and the Red Hood came back."

Ayleth watched him warily. "What about you?" she persisted. "I'm told you gave chase after Venator Nane when he left with the girl."

Jerlo shook his head, not meeting her eye. "I tried. I never saw them again. And I was afraid. To venture too far. I didn't . . . I couldn't bear to . . ."

He did not want to catch up to the venator as he killed his daughter.

Ayleth looked away, unwilling to see the expression on the big man's face. For several long moments, silence held them captive there on the doorstep of his house as each faced unthinkable thoughts.

To be honest, Ayleth didn't think she'd found her murderer. Whoever had killed Nane had not tried to face him head-on, but had taken him by surprise, from behind. Ayleth didn't see either subtlety or stealth in the large man before her. Jerlo du Bucheron couldn't move through a forest quietly enough to take an experienced venator by surprise. Much less in the Witchwood!

But was he keeping something from her? It was hard to say. Reaching out with Laranta's keen senses, she tried to detect some trace of emotion on him that would give her pause. There was guilt aplenty, but not the acrid sort of guilt one might expect to find in a murderer. And it was almost completely overwhelmed by sheer sorrow—a sorrow so mountainous, it would crush Ayleth's own soul if she dwelled on it too closely.

She pulled back her perceptions. Something told her she would need to speak to Jerlo again, but for now . . .

"I need you to tell me where I can find this Oma Githa," she said.

CHAPTER 12

ACCORDING TO JERLO, THE HEDGEWITCH MADE HER home deep in the fringe forests, not far from the Great Barrier. He told Ayleth to follow the woodcutter's track for a half mile, then to start looking for signs of the hedgewitch's presence.

"What sort of signs?"

Jerlo gave her a look. "You'll know them when you see them."

He offered nothing more. Ayleth took her leave soon

after, mounting Chestibor and riding out from the cottage yard, with Laranta trailing behind her in a stream of darkness. She breathed more easily once night closed in around her, shielding her from the woodcutter's gaze. Somehow, she knew he stood in his doorway long after she disappeared from view. Somehow, she knew he stared into the blackness, seeing the faces of his wife and his daughter, whom her Order had stolen from him.

No. Not her Order. The shades.

This was all the doing of the shades. Their evil, their parasitic malice. They damned all they touched, and only the Order of Saint Evander, only the work to which Ayleth devoted her whole heart, her whole life, offered hope of salvation. Of course, simple men like Jerlo du Bucheron could not understand it. Such men lived basic lives of dirt and sweat and labor. They did not take time to consider the needs of the soul, to consider the cost of a damned eternity. Their mortal view never stretched beyond the horizon of this world.

So Ayleth told herself, bolstering her spirit with every step Chestibor took across the dark, moonlit fields. Laranta growled now and then, sensing her mistress's distress. Ayleth ignored her.

Traveling slowly by the faint moonlight, they found the woodcutter's road Jerlo had mentioned. Halting her horse, Ayleth sat upright in her saddle, peering ahead into the dark, waiting forest. Clouds rolled in across the sky, and the darkness deepened. With shadow-light in her eyes, she could possibly navigate that gloom well enough, but Chestibor would certainly struggle. She could leave him, of course, progress on foot, but—

With a quick shake of her head, Ayleth came to a decision. She could not complete this stretch of the hunt now. And, Goddess's truth, she needed rest! She needed sleep, a proper night's sleep. And not under some hedge, with that cold wind blowing in and the taste of a storm in the air. She and Chestibor both needed shelter.

Shoulders hunched beneath her cloak, head tucked deep into her hood, Ayleth turned her horse around and gazed up at Elsinoe Shrinehouse on its hilltop. It was not exactly the most welcoming sight. But it would do.

"You again? What in the Goddess's three holy names do

you want?"

Ayleth blinked into the glaring light of the lantern held high in Mother Vesta's hand. She put up a hand to shield her eyes, half turning away.

"It is late, Good Mother," she said, "and cold. I have business in these parts tomorrow, and I ask for a place to sleep overnight. As the Order of Saint Alicen is known for its charity, would you grant a bed to a fellow sister in the Goddess's service?"

It was probably not the best tactic, all things considered. While the Order of Saint Evander was recognized under the headship of the Goddess, there were factions of the faith that still looked upon them as little better than witches. But Ayleth was in no mood to discuss theology or the validity of Saint Evander's sacred writ with one inhospitable priestess in the middle of the night. She was tired. She was cold.

So, she assumed a vaguely threatening stance. Nothing overt, merely a subtle spreading of her feet, an adjustment of her shoulders.

The priestess scowled up at her. Then, with a growl, she stepped out of the dormitory, shutting the door behind her. "You can sleep in the shrine house," she called back over her shoulder as she brushed past Ayleth. "It's late—my sisters are all in bed, and I'll not have you disturbing them with your spurs and your weaponry."

Ayleth sighed. It wasn't quite the same as a bed, but at least it would be a roof overhead. She'd already begged shelter for Chestibor in a sheep shed half a mile away in Hollen, and unless she wanted to walk all the way back to join him and the sheep, this was her only option.

The first drops of an impending thundershower fell even as Mother Vesta unlocked a side door and led Ayleth into the shrine house. They entered the north aisle, which was lined with prayer alcoves complete with privacy curtains. The priestess yanked back one of these curtains, indicating the small stone cell within. Ayleth spied a kneeling cushion under the circular window. Such luxury.

"You're out before dawn," the priestess grumbled, watching with distaste as Ayleth lowered her saddlebags from her shoulder to the floor of the tiny cell. "My sisters and I congregate at sunrise for morning prayers, and you will not be here when we begin the processional."

Ayleth shrugged and nodded.

The priestess didn't leave the lantern behind, and with her departure, tomblike darkness crept through the whole of the cold shrine house. Ayleth pulled the prayer curtain shut, wrapped her cloak around her, and nestled her head on the kneeling cushion. It smelled like sheep.

She lay for some time listening to the patter of rain on the window turn into a roaring downpour. The great darkness of the shrine house beyond her curtain echoed in her ears, an almost audible silence. Though she was bone tired, her mind kept turning and turning, and no matter how still she held her body, she could not still her thoughts.

Was this what her life was meant for? These cold nights on hard surfaces, alone in the darkness? No friend, no comrade other than a hunt brother somewhere out in the night, just as alone and cold as she.

Was this what she wanted?

She had never before stopped to ask herself that question. *Want* had nothing to do with her life. The Goddess had called her, and she must answer. She must serve the Order of Evander and save the souls of those who walked the deadly precipice of the haunts. She must be the stronger person, willing to do those terrible deeds of mercy, willing to . . .

To kill children?

How empty this stone structure around her felt. How huge, how forlorn. In olden days, the Goddess's presence was said to fill Her holy places with such spirit light that even those limited to mortal vision could almost see Her glory. But Ayleth's shadow sight detected no such trace now. Nothing that might be deemed glorious. Just darkness, hollow darkness.

Did the Goddess truly call her to this work? Or had she simply believed in her calling because Hollis had told her it was so?

Hollis, who lied to her. Hollis, who manipulated her mind.

Hollis, who taught her that mortals lived in constant threat of damnation, and it was up to the Order of Evander to save them. Could there be a greater purpose for any soul to strive after?

Seems an ineffectual Goddess who cannot save the souls of Her children.

The words seemed to whisper to her, creeping beneath the prayer curtain, across the stone floor, and into her ear. At first, she could not place where she had heard them before. Then she remembered: Gerard. The Golden Prince. The Goddess's promise to mankind made flesh. Ayleth had not realized who he was when he said those things to her, but now it struck her as strange. Could a fulfillment of ancient prophecy doubt the power and the goodness of his deity? The One who called him into being, who sent him into this world according to Her great purpose?

Ayleth realized her eyes were open. It was hard to tell the difference, but when they began to hurt, she realized she was straining her mortal vision, trying to make sense of impenetrable shadows.

Maybe because she lay on a kneeling cushion in a prayer alcove, a sudden need to pray came over her. She couldn't remember ever feeling such a need before. Hollis had trained her intensely in many aspects of her Order over the years. Prayer had not been among them. But now that the thought was in her head, Ayleth could not ignore it, not if she hoped to get any sleep that night.

Licking her dry lips, she tried to speak, tried to pull together the proper words. The right assortment of phrases that would incline a deity to listen. Surely she must know some sort of incantation, some sort of chant? Nothing came to mind.

But now that she'd worked herself up to it, she needed to say something. She swallowed. Drew a breath.

Then she whispered: "Goddess?"

The word hung in the silence and darkness before her face, tremulous and small.

She waited.

No answer.

A hot blush crept up her cheeks, as though she'd just done something incredibly foolish. With an angry growl, Ayleth rolled over, facing the wall rather than the curtain, and pulled her cloak up over her head.

"Wake up, Red Hood. It is high time you were on your way."

Ayleth jolted awake, her hands flailing out as though to catch herself from a fall, her eyes too wide and temporarily blinded by what seemed to be incredible light. The light resolved itself down into the flickering of a single candle casting dancing shadows on the prayer alcove walls.

With a groan, Ayleth got her elbows under her and pushed herself upright. Her feet didn't stretch far in the small prayer alcove, and she got herself rather painfully wedged, her cloak tangled around her legs. As she struggled to extricate herself, reason and memory flooded back. Oh, yes. She'd opted to spend the night in the shrine house, of all places.

Mother Vesta's wintry eyes stared down at her as she held a prayer candle in one hand and pushed back the prayer curtain with the other. "It's nearly time for dawn prayers," she growled.

Grimacing, Ayleth got her legs under her and managed to stand upright. Blowing on her hands and stamping her prickling feet to get the blood flowing again, she collected her saddlebags and trailed after the priestess along the prayer aisle.

"Good Mother," she said, her voice croaking and groggy, "do you know anything about a woman named

Githa? Oma Githa? A local hedgewitch, I believe."

The priestess paused on her way toward the door along the prayer aisle. She looked back, her fair eyebrows slowly rising, and made a sign of holy protection in the air, causing her candle flame to flicker wildly. "There is a woman by that name whom some folk of these parts have turned to for help, fearing her less than they fear . . . others who deal in such dark doings." She angled her head, fixing Ayleth with the full concentration of her disapproving stare. "I don't know much about her. She rarely comes for holy services, but when she does, she has the audacity to kneel at the Goddess's altar and say prayers like some pious woman." Vesta's mouth puckered with extreme distaste, and she motioned sharply with the hand holding the candle, spattering hot wax on the floor.

Responding to the gesture, Ayleth allowed herself to be hustled to the shrine-house door and out into the predawn morning. She took her leave of the old priestess, who offered a grudging blessing in return. Then, pulling her cloak tight about her, she hastened downhill. The rain from the night before had left the ground cold and shimmering with a thin sheen of ice. Her boots crunched with each footstep as she made her way to the village below. She found Chestibor warm and snug in his sheep shed, and he gave her a doleful look as she tacked him up for the day's ride.

"I'm sorry, boy," she murmured, leading him out into the damp air. "I don't like it any more than you do."

Ayleth left the shrine house behind, riding back to the fringe forest and the woodcutter's track. Occasionally she lifted her hands from the pommel of her saddle to blow feeling back into her fingers. The sun was just beginning to stain the sky pink when she plunged into the eerie half-light of the forest, but songbirds not yet flown south for the coming winter sang overhead, alleviating some of the gloom. A beam of light burst through the clouds and branches and fell upon her path.

Beloved.

Ayleth froze in her saddle, every sense alert and straining. She didn't feel the cold. She didn't feel the ache in her bones from a night on a hard shrine-house floor. She didn't feel the soreness in her legs from long days of riding, the tension in her mind from the terrible questions and worries and fears built up over the last several days.

She felt only . . . wonder.

It was there.

It was gone.

Blinking, pulling herself back into reality, Ayleth looked down at her hands, looked again at the world around her. Chestibor had come to a halt. He shuffled his feet and blew streaming vapors from his nostrils. Down in her spirit, Laranta stirred against her suppression spells, growling softly.

Had she dreamed it? That . . . not a voice. Not a sound, not a song. Hardly even a feeling. A profound sensation for which she had no name, a consciousness. An instant of pure awareness.

Her lips, chapped with cold, tried to move, tried to find the shape of a prayer. But the wind blew in her face, making her gasp, and she ducked her head, pulling her hood low.

"Walk on, Chestibor," she said, applying pressure to his ribs.

She rode on into the forest.

CHAPTER 13

TERRYN OPENED HIS EYES SLOWLY, REGRETFULLY. HE wasn't ready to be awake yet, and his entire body protested, from his heavy eyelids, to his sluggish arms, to his cold feet protruding out from under the blanket. The urge to curl up and sink back into dreamless slumber was almost too strong to resist.

The *clomp* of boots on the floorboards of the landing outside his door echoed in his ears, loud enough to jar some reason back into his lethargic mind. Terryn winced, remembering. Nane. Lady Mylla. The Warpwitch.

The ruins of Cró Ular.

That last thought hurt like an icicle shooting through his temple into his brain. "Haunts damn," he hissed, pressing the heels of his hands into his eyes and sitting upright in bed just as Venator Kephan pounded on his door.

"Are you up, du Balafre?"

"Yes," Terryn lied, but made good on the lie by swinging his legs over the edge of the bed and forcing himself to his feet. "I'm up."

"Good. We ride for Hollen in half an hour."

With those words, the pounding boots stomped away from the door, and Terryn listened to them descend the narrow staircase to the floor below. Only an exertion of willpower kept him from sinking back down onto his bed. Instead, he propelled himself into motion, staggering to the basin to splash cold water into his face. He then pulled on shirt, jerkin, boots, bracers.

"It's her," he whispered.

He paused in the middle of securing leather straps across his chest. His mouth hung open. What had he just said? He had no idea. But the compulsion to speak came again.

"It's . . . her . . ."

It's her. It's her. She's got a hold on you—

Terryn inhaled sharply, his eyes widening. With a muttered curse, he reached for the sheaths he'd slung on the footboard at the end of his bed the night before. In his exhaustion, he'd gone to sleep without taking time to reinforce the suppressions on his shade. It stirred now inside him, beneath the straining spells.

It's her. It's her. You have to remember. You must!

Terryn yanked his Vocos from its sheath, put it to his lips, and called to life the drone. The moment that low, dark reverberation touched his soul, the shade recoiled. Then it surged up again, more desperate than before.

No! No, no! It's her! It's her, it's her!

Fingers flying, Terryn deftly played a variation on the Suppression song spell. First one variation, then a second, then a third, each shifting into the next in quick succession. The threads of song wound down inside him, wrapped round and round his possessing spirit.

At last, Terryn let the fingers of his right hand still,

allowed the melody to fade away. He sustained the drone a few beats longer before letting that too fall silent. Pulling the instrument away from his lips, he blinked several times. The room came back into focus around him.

No voice anymore. Just the hum of the spell song deep inside.

He sheathed his pipes, snatched up his weapons and belts, and hurried downstairs to join Venator Kephan.

Kephan stood at the armoire, strapping bracers to his arms. He nodded as Terryn emerged from the stairwell. "Eat fast. Di Ferosa did not return during the night and has sent no message. We must assume she's pursuing a lead, and we'd better hurry if we want to catch up with her."

Terryn made a hasty meal from the store of dried meat and barley cakes in the back room. Then, holstering his scorpiona, he followed Kephan out to the stables. All the while, his mind spun. Why were they hurrying after the venatrix like this? Did Kephan not trust her to do her job capably? They would do better to fetch the body of the dead bear from yesterday, to search that surrounding area for signs of a possession. Or perhaps they'd missed some clue at Cró Ular—

His thoughts crashed to a halt as another icicle of pain lanced through his head. Terryn, in the middle of cinching the girth on his saddle, stopped and leaned against his mare's side, breathing hard until the pain passed.

Once more, his lips moved: "It's . . . her . . ."

"Snap to it, du Balafre. We have a long road before us."

Terryn shook his head and looked up to see Kephan leading his horse out to the yard. He quickly finished with his saddle and guided Fleeta out of her stall.

They spent the first hour or so of their journey in silence but for a few exchanges. The sun came out early and, while not exactly warm, at least provided a cheery break from the gloom of the day before. Terryn sank into the rhythm of Fleeta's hoofbeats on the road, letting the sound repress the clamorous thoughts in his head. Thinking . . . hurt. Better not to think at all, better to focus on the road, to focus on finding Venatrix di Ferosa.

Venatrix di Ferosa . . .

"Feral," Terryn muttered.

Kephan stirred in his saddle and looked Terryn's way. "What's that you say?"

Terryn grunted. He hadn't realized he'd spoken out loud. But now he might as well share those suspicions which had slowly been growing at the back of his brain. "The gap in the Great Barrier," he said. "When I studied it yesterday, I confirmed that the original power used to repair it was that of a Feral shade."

"Like mine." Kephan nodded. "But I wasn't there, as I've told you. I would remember something like that. I never go to the Great Barrier. That was Nane's job."

Terryn didn't answer. He let the silence speak for him.

"You're thinking of di Ferosa, aren't you?" Kephan said after several long moments. "She is likewise possessed of a Feral. And her arrival in Wodechran does seem . . . unprecedented, I will grant you. The Venator Dominus was very clear in his message that you were to take the post. No mention was made of other candidates."

Again, Terryn said nothing.

"But the prince was clear as well," Kephan continued.

"I read his message, his description of his meeting with the young venatrix. Apparently, she saved his life from a Lure. Did you know?"

"A convenient rescue," Terryn muttered.

"So, you suspect even that tale, do you?" Kephan chuckled mirthlessly. "I agree it's all a little strange. Indeed, while you two were at the fringe forest yesterday, I took time to write a message to the castra inquiring about her, a letter I intend to send as soon as opportunity presents itself. Meanwhile, I agree we would both be wise to keep an eye on your competitor. I hate to let suspicion color my view of a talented venatrix, but . . ."

But, but, but. Nane was dead. His murderer was at large. The Warpwitch may or may not be returned to this side of the Barrier.

And how did this Ayleth di Ferosa fit into the picture? She didn't. She didn't make sense at all.

Why had Zilla and Zarc d'Utrehd not killed her when they had her at their mercy?

The question hadn't occurred to Terryn during their escape from the Witchwood, when his senses were half-crazed with terror and the influence of *oblivis* in his lungs.

But it struck him now, too hard to ignore. They had her paralyzed with her own poison, lying helpless on that altar stone. She, a venatrix, an Evanderian—one of the Order which had broken their queen's power, which had slain their brethren, which had driven them into their tormented exile.

Why had they not slit her throat?

Something wasn't right here. The way she cavalierly allowed her shade so much ascendancy. The way she showed up to rescue Gerard at just the right moment. The way she'd led them straight to Nane's body, six weeks following his disappearance.

Terryn bowed his head deeper into the shadows of his hood. She'd saved his life. Several times, in fact. If she was his enemy, would she not have simply left him to die in the Witchwood?

But no. No, she needed his skill to get back out again. She couldn't leave him, because she still had use for him.

The world around him seemed suddenly shadowed despite the cold sunlight. Terryn shivered, and his hands tightened on the reins. "It's her," he whispered.

Was this why he'd woken up with those words on his

lips? Was his subconscious trying to warn him, trying to make him put together the pieces of this puzzle? The answer to all these mysteries seemed tantalizingly close, if he could only see what connected them. If he could just—

"Help! Help, please! *Please!*"

Terryn, startled, turned in his saddle and looked out to the right. He and Kephan rode a venator's circuit through a stretch of recently harvested fields. A man in rough farmer's garb ran toward them, waving his hat with one hand like a signal flag.

This couldn't be good. As a rule, citizens of the borough avoided all contact with venators. The last thing anyone wanted was to be the object of a shade hunter's interest. But this man's desperation drove him straight to them. Which could mean only one thing.

Kephan glanced Terryn's way. Without a word, both men reined in their horses and waited for the stranger to catch up.

The farmer, a middle-aged man with an impressive growth of reddish beard, came to a puffing halt, hands resting on his bony knees. "Thank the Goddess you're here!" he gasped, trying not to meet their eyes as he spoke. Even now, frantic as he was, he feared them. "You've got to help me. My wife!"

"What about your wife?" Kephan demanded. Terryn switched to shadow sight and peered into the man's soul. He saw no indication of shade presence, nothing readily visible.

"She's gone mad," the farmer said, standing upright and twisting his hat in both hands. His eyes bugged out from his face, huge with terror. "She's lost her mind, raving like a monster. I shut her into the woodshed, but she's pounding at the door, and . . . and . . ."

Kephan caught Terryn's eye again. "We should go with him," he said, a sigh in his voice. "We need to make certain."

Terryn shrugged. He wanted to protest. If the farmer had claimed possession regarding his horse or his dog, that would be different. But in a situation like this . . . it was sadly not uncommon for a difficult spouse to be falsely accused of shade possession, especially in cases of insanity.

Still, they could not know if the farmer's claim was

true without seeing for themselves. Terryn nodded his agreement, and Kephan turned back to the farmer. "Your name, my man?"

"Foulke, Namon Foulke," came the quick response, along with an awkward bow.

Kephan waved his hand, the fastenings on his bracer glinting. "Lead on then, Farmer Foulke."

The farmer's homestead lay two fields over. Scanning the house and yard with shadow sight, Terryn detected no sign of shade presence, but his shadow sight was limited while his spirit lay under deep suppressions. He did see signs of a struggle in the yard—an ax lying in the grass as though flung there, a pile of wood knocked over, a spilled basket of eggs.

Grooves in the dirt. Torn by clawing hands.

Farmer Foulke hesitated to reenter his own yard. His hand trembled when he pointed to the woodshed behind his house. "There. I locked her in, but you see . . ." He choked on his own words, unable to finish.

The doorframe of the shed was broken, splintered. The door itself lay in pieces on the ground. Whatever had been imprisoned inside had broken free. Blasted free, rather.

This didn't look good.

Terryn dismounted and strode into the yard. Kephan held back until he had summoned up his shade, then joined Terryn, walking around the shed. "I smell shade," Kephan said, his Feral shade senses keen and searching.

So, the farmer wasn't lying. That was something at least. Terryn drew his scorpiona from its holster and snapped it onto the bracer. "Can you sense the variety?" he asked.

Kephan shook his head. Nevertheless, Terryn's hand moved to his quivers, and he withdrew an Anathema poison. If the Warpwitch was near, he wanted to be ready.

Moving in synchronization, the two venators stalked the periphery of the farmyard before returning to Farmer Foulke where he stood trembling, staring at the wreckage of his shed door. "What happened exactly?" Venator Kephan demanded. "Did the fit come on her suddenly?"

The farmer nodded. "I was just having my midday meal inside, and she was fetching eggs. She opened the door and . . . and screamed." He covered his face with his hands, his body quaking with terror. "One minute it's her, the next, she was something else. Something terrible. I thought she'd kill me, I thought sure she'd kill me! I got her into the shed, and I ran as fast as I could."

Terryn's eyes narrowed. A sudden taking was not unheard of, but it was unusual. Most shades newly possessing their hosts lay dormant for some time, weeks, even months, slowly gaining control and ascendancy without any overt displays of power. A sudden overwhelming like this indicated violence—a shade violently ousted from its previous host and, propelled by that violence, possessing a new host while still suffering from the pain of its previous host's death.

Terryn met Kephan's eye. "There has to be a dead host around here somewhere," he said.

Kephan nodded and sniffed the air, no doubt reaching again with his shade senses. "Inside," he said after a moment. The two of them stepped through the open farmhouse door into the low-ceilinged front room. Something smoldered on the fire. Kephan made for it at once, snatching up a poker and digging into the coals.

He dragged a tiny, scorched body out onto the hearth

stone. Terryn crouched for a closer look. A bird? A sparrow, perhaps.

"Is this it?"

"Maybe," Kephan said. "I'm getting . . . something off of it."

Sliding his bone knife from its sheath, Terryn cut into the tiny, charred corpse. With a hiss, boiling black blood poured out, burning into the stone. This small creature had certainly been shade-taken. Perhaps a long while, given the state of its blood. Or perhaps the shade inside had simply overwhelmed and destroyed its frail host body too quickly, thus driving the bird to commit this act of self-destruction in a bid to propel the shade into a better host. It may have intended to possess Farmer Foulke himself, who—judging by the wooden dishes scattered around the floor—had been eating his meal by the hearth.

But it wasn't Foulke who'd proved habitable. Instead, the shade had taken his wife.

Terryn sat back on his heels and looked up at Kephan. "The Warpwitch," he said. "It has to be."

Kephan's face was drawn and dark. "We can't assume that," he said. "Other shades can and do shift hosts upon occasion."

"We know the Warpwitch is loose in Wodechran," Terryn persisted. "When I killed that bear yesterday, she could have taken the bird's body and gone hunting for a better host. She could have—"

"She could have done many things," Kephan said. "We don't know. We don't even know for certain whether the dead woman you found in the forest was Ylaire di Jocosa's host. To assume anything at this juncture is dangerous. Even one mistake could cost everything."

Terryn breathed hard, his nostrils flaring. He saw again in his mind's eye Lady Mylla's ring. That dainty gold ring with its carving of the rose. No, he couldn't know for certain, but . . . but somehow, he *did* know. That was Mylla's body he'd seen, and that had been the Warpwitch twisting the body of that bear. She was near.

He stood up, raising his scorpiona. "We need to hunt down this woman," he said. "We need to find her trail."

Kephan eyed him closely. "I agree this shade-taken must be dealt with," he said, his voice too calm, too careful. "She cannot have gone far, and I should be able to pick up her scent. So, I will track her down now and deal with her. I want you to ride on to Hollen and find di Ferosa. If she hasn't discovered anything of interest in her investigation, the two of you may come back here and join me—if I haven't finished the job already."

Terryn stared, hardly believing what he was hearing. "You can't . . . I'm going with you!"

Kephan shook his head. "I don't need some hair-trigger young ass on my heels, firing off the wrong poisons at the wrong time. Look at you, boy!" He caught Terryn's scorpiona arm, pulled it down, and yanked out the dart, holding it up to Terryn's eye level. "You've already loaded. You have no idea what you're hunting, but you've already decided, based on nothing but guesses and assumption."

Terryn opened his mouth to protest, but Kephan pushed him away firmly. "You go on to Hollen and cool your hot head. Find di Ferosa. Do you hear me, Venator du Balafre?"

Heart pounding in his throat, Terryn swallowed back his frustration. He pulled himself together and offered a brisk salute. "Yes, sir."

Kephan gave him a close look. Then he clapped him on the upper arm and shook his head. "Be off with you. Go!"

Feeling like a disciplined child, Terryn stepped from the farmhouse, passed the quivering Farmer Foulke, and strode swiftly across the yard to his horse. Everything inside him told him this was the wrong choice, the wrong move. Every instinct of training urged him to turn around now, to find the shade-taken farmwife's trail.

His lips tried to shape the words again. "It's . . . her . . ."

Terryn clenched his teeth hard, mounted his horse, and turned her back toward the circuit road.

CHAPTER 14

THE BROAD, RUTTED WOODCUTTER'S TRACK WOUND slowly through the fringe forest, seemingly without aim. Ayleth followed it deeper and deeper, her bones tense with expectation of that strange, buzzing sensation she knew heralded proximity to the Great Barrier. But whoever had made this trail—Jerlo, presumably, and other woodcutters before him—must have been eager to avoid the Witchwood, so the road never led close enough for her to sense the spell.

"Who would choose to live way out here?" Ayleth muttered out loud after she and Chestibor had journeyed into the forest for over an hour. Hedgewitches had suffered no little persecution throughout the years, both during and after the reign of the Witch Queen. But still, to hide this deep in the forest seemed strange. What was the point of practicing her weird craft if this Oma Githa wasn't accessible to the people she allegedly helped?

But Jerlo had said signs of her presence would be visible enough, so Ayleth kept her eyes peeled and continued following the road.

Suddenly, Laranta reared up in her awareness, shadow senses prickling curiously. Ayleth had not bothered to reinforce the suppression spells this morning, and she felt their laxness now as her shade tugged against them.

Look, Laranta growled. Though she remained inside Ayleth's head, Ayleth got a sensation of fur rising along a spine. *Look, look, look.*

Almost against her will, Ayleth's gaze turned to the left. A little tree stood not far off the track. It would have been hidden entirely had the bounty of its red berries not seemed to glow in the solemn green shadows. A rowan tree—sacred to the Goddess and almost never seen growing wild. The sight caught Ayleth's attention, even as it had Laranta's. She drew Chestibor to a halt.

Could this be the sign Jerlo had meant?

Almost unconsciously, Ayleth slipped her red hood from her head and tucked it away out of sight. If she was now on the trail of the hedgewitch, she didn't want to give away her identity too easily. Clucking to her horse, she guided Chestibor off the track and into the foliage. At first it seemed too dense for much progress, but as they drew nearer to the rowan tree, a narrow path appeared to her view, almost as though by magic. It led into the denser forest. If she had not approached the tree, she would have missed it entirely.

"Well, it's a place to start," she murmured, and nudged Chestibor on.

Rowan. Laranta shuddered inside her. *I smell rowan. Ugh!*

"*I know, Laranta,*" Ayleth answered soothingly. "*We'll be past it soon.*"

Though sacred to the Goddess, rowan trees were repellent to shades. Often peasants would pin sprigs of rowan leaves and berries over their doors or around babies' cradles as protection against evil influences. Whether it worked or not, Ayleth couldn't say. She knew only that the practice was unsanctioned by Saint Evander and considered low magic. Judging by Laranta's reaction, however, it might prove useful.

They passed more rowan trees as they followed the winding path, and, strung in the branches of yew, oak, and birch, Ayleth spotted strange little hoops of willow stems woven in unique and often beautiful patterns. She recognized these at once as "spirit catchers," another form of low magic. They were intended to snare any loose shades escaped from the Haunts, preventing them from finding host bodies.

Ayleth rode Chestibor close to a birch tree strung with three of these dainty snares. Switching to her shadow sight, she plucked one from its branches and studied the weave. To her surprise, the woven stems hummed with what could almost be described as a song spell. Not a complex spell and not an effective one either, so far as she could discern. None of these traps had actually caught any spirits. But something about the spell seemed *almost* right. If the maker possessed the ability to see into the spirit realm, she might be able to make them work properly.

Ayleth frowned and hung the spirit-catcher back on its branch. It didn't behoove one of Evander's followers to indulge in curiosity over low magic.

The path led at last to a little clearing in the forest. The ground was ragged with tall ferns and clumps of gorse, but the morning sunshine pouring down made it feel oddly bright and welcoming. A cottage stood in the center of the clearing, small and squat, boasting a musty thatch and a listing front door. Spirit-catchers were strung all around the periphery, their sheer number generating a hum audible to Ayleth's shade senses.

But what struck her as most peculiar were the cages. Dozens and dozens of willow-woven cages containing various animals—rabbits, mice, a fox, a pair of raccoons, hedgehogs. All these watched Ayleth's approach, their bodies so still she would have thought they were dead and stuffed if not for the intensity of their gazes fixed upon her.

What was it Jerlo du Bucheron had said? That he and his wife had come to the hedgewitch, looking for her to oust the shade within Fiola's body. How the woman had attempted this feat, Ayleth couldn't guess, but something about those animals . . . She shivered and studied each of them carefully, searching for some sign of indwelling shades. She found nothing. Were these more protections, like the spirit-catchers? Options for any loose shades to possess before reaching the cottage's owner? Or did the hedgewitch keep them for other, grimmer purposes?

Ayleth turned her attention from the cages to the cottage door. All was quiet inside. The hedgewitch might not be at home. Or perhaps, aware of a venatrix's approach, she simply crouched on the other side of the door, unwilling to emerge.

"*Laranta,*" Ayleth said, "*check inside.*"

Laranta flowed out from her head and floated through the ferns up to the ramshackle door. As she drew near, her form solidified to Ayleth's vision, becoming more wolfish and less formless darkness. By the time she sniffed at the door, she looked almost real.

A low growl vibrated their connecting soul tether.

Shade, Laranta said.

Ayleth, who had dismounted and begun slowly

approaching the cottage, stopped abruptly. *"Shade-taken? In the cottage?"* This was unexpected.

Laranta growled again and backed away from the door, every black hair on her manifested body rising. An icy chill ran down Ayleth's neck. Her hand moved to the poisons across her breast, but she didn't know what sort of shade waited inside. If she used the wrong dart, she would only make things worse.

"Does it know we're here?" she asked, whispering even in her own mind.

Another growl, long and low, as Laranta reached out with her senses again. Then: *Yes.*

Ayleth drew her bone knife. Whatever hid within that cottage, it had to be wearing a host body. And a host body could bleed. She took another step toward the cottage, then another. "Oma Githa?" she called out loud. "Oma Githa, I have come to consult with you. Are you there?"

No answer.

Shade, Laranta said. *Shade, shade . . .*

"I just have a few questions for you," Ayleth said, taking another careful step, raising the knife slightly, its blade angled for defense. "I want to ask you about Fiola du Bucheron. You tried to help her a few years back. Do you remember that name?"

Something stirred inside the cottage. Ayleth saw it with her shadow sight, a flick of a soul. Two souls?

Then a small, plaintive voice called out, *"Mama?"*

The door burst open. Laranta started back, the soul tether sparking with her surprise. Something flared in Ayleth's vision, a brilliance of soul so bright, her shadow sight was dazzled. She struggled to blink back into mortal vision, to see what stood in the doorway. She glimpsed something run through the door, around the side of the cottage, making for the forest.

A child?

Shade! Laranta roared.

Ayleth sprang into motion, moving on instinct rather than reason, her mind still half blinded by that flare of souls. "Stop!" she cried. "Stop right there!"

The little figure fell headlong, nearly vanishing in the tall ferns. A head popped back into view, craning to look back at Ayleth. Ayleth skidded to a halt despite Laranta's frantic warnings of *Shade! Shade, shade!*

Shadow-light gleamed in the child's wide, jade-colored eyes. Looking down inside her, Ayleth saw the powerful pulse of a spirit wound tight around the mortal soul so that the two were almost indistinguishable from one another.

"Nilly?" Ayleth's voice cracked on the name. "Nilly du Bucheron? Is that you?"

The girl sprang up, magic flowing through every limb. She turned from Ayleth and fled for the trees as fast as her short legs could carry her.

"Wait!" Ayleth cried, extending a hand. "Please, wait! I won't hurt you!"

SHADE! Laranta roared.

Ayleth turned to her wolf, saw her coil together and then spring, losing all shape of wolfishness and becoming a column of pure black spirit, bolting through the air straight for Ayleth's head. No, not for her head—over it. Aiming at something just above, just behind.

Ayleth realized. With a gasp, she flung herself to one side.

Not in time.

A terrible blow struck the back of her head. Her mind

exploded with brutal red pain. Then . . . darkness.

CHAPTER 15

THE BELLS OF ELSINOE SHRINEHOUSE RANG OUT across the surrounding countryside, signaling the end of afternoon prayer hour. A small collection of worshippers, wrapped in scarves against the cold, hustled out through the front door. Many of them spied Terryn in his red hood as they descended the porch steps and froze in their tracks, eyes rounding. Then, hastily making the sign of the Goddess, they hurried on their way, ducking their faces to avoid his gaze.

Terryn waited until the last of them had gone, then dismounted and approached the door. A priestess appeared in the doorway before he was halfway up the porch. She folded her arms, assuming a forbidding posture and expression, like an austere angel in her white robes, barring the way to heaven.

"Good morrow, Mother," Terryn said respectfully, making the holy sign.

She returned the gesture grudgingly. "You're another one of *them,* aren't you? Saints preserve us, haven't we had enough of your kind in these parts already?"

Terryn's eyebrow twitched. "You have spoken with another of my Order recently?"

"Yes. A girl." The priestess's lip curled. "A venatrix. She was here asking about the shade-taken du Bucheron child. Nasty business that."

"And what can you tell me of that nasty business?"

"Ask your order sister." Folding her arms deep into the sleeves of her robe, the older woman contrived to make herself as large as possible. Even so, she was scarcely tall enough to look Terryn straight in the eye, though he was several steps down from her. "I'm not recounting all that misery again. We've had enough of shade doings around here. I gave the venatrix a place to sleep for the night and sent her on her way this morning."

"Sent her on where?"

"To the hedgewitch's cottage."

Terryn blinked. This was a new development. "What did she want with a hedgewitch?"

"Blessed if I know!" the priestess snarled. The lines framing her thin lips deepened with sour condemnation. "Yesterday she was here asking for directions to Jerlo du Bucheron's home, this morning she's pestering me with questions about the hedgewitch. I don't want anything to do with you or your kind. I let her sleep here last night, and I'm done."

With those words, spoken with finality, she stepped back into the shrine house and made as though to close the door. Terryn took the last three steps up the porch in a single stride and stretched out his long arm to block her. "Your pardon, Good Mother," he said as she glared ferociously up at him. "But if I might trouble you to point my way to the du Bucheron household?"

With a hoarse growl in her throat, the priestess pushed

the door wide enough that she could stick an arm and shoulder through. She pointed north, down the hill on which the shrine house stood toward the little village nestled in a valley below. "That's Hollen," she said. "His house is east of the village, near to the fringe forest. He's a woodcutter."

Terryn backed away from the door, offering a quick salute, which the priestess did not see, for she slammed the door the moment she could. Terryn rolled his eyes and stomped back down the steps to his horse.

Village folk watched him ride by, their faces masks of pure dread. It could be discouraging, the ingratitude so often directed his way. How would any of these people like it if the venators packed up and left Perrinion? How quickly would shade-taken and witches overwhelm all those mortals who had no means to fight back? Goddess above, did they *want* to return to the enslavement they'd known when Dread Odile ruled these parts?

Terryn shrugged off these thoughts as he left the village behind, making his way into the lonelier stretch of country between Hollen and the fringe forest. He had enough concerns filling his head as it was.

A hedgewitch. Why would Venatrix di Ferosa be asking about a local hedgewitch? Had she learned of some doings between the hedgewitch and Nane? Or was this related to some other purpose she pursued?

His teeth clenched so hard, his jaw hurt. He ought not to be here, following in di Ferosa's footsteps like some lost hound trying to sniff its way back to its master. He ought to be on the hunt with Kephan. Yes, perhaps he'd been a little too hot-headed, but he was a true hunter, and his skills would be put to better use on the trail of a shade-taken than wandering around these country villages.

Then again, if his suspicions concerning Venatrix di Ferosa proved true . . . suspicions he hardly dared name, suspicions not yet fully formed . . .

Spying a humble homestead, a cottage and barn, ahead, Terryn urged Fleeta into a brisk trot, hastening on his way. Was this the du Bucheron home? He saw a dray out in the yard such as a woodcutter might use to haul logs out from the forest. And he saw—

Terryn's heart stopped.

A large animal body lay on its side several yards from

the dray. An ox, perhaps. Its side was torn wide open, entrails spilling.

Fleeta tossed her head as the stench of blood carried on the breeze. She pranced and whinnied until Terryn sprang from her saddle, leaving her behind as he approached the cottage for a better view. His senses sparked, and down beneath the suppressing song spells, his shade stirred warningly.

The venatrix. Her shade was powerful, vicious. Vicious enough to tear an animal wide open?

Terryn dropped to the ground, making himself a smaller target. Shadow-light blazed in his eyes as he scanned the yard, searching for souls. A miasma of death hovered around the slaughtered ox. Death and . . . a trace of magic? No ordinary animal had done this brutal killing. This was shade-taken work.

The killer could still be near. Terryn strained his gaze, but with his shade suppressed, his shadow sight could discern only so much. The killer could still be somewhere down there. In the house. In the barn.

His hand moved to his Vocos pipes, and after an instant of hesitation, he slipped them free and played a quick spell, grabbing a handful of magic from the soul of his shade. Power flowed through his limbs, channeled into his hands, glowed at his fingertips. He clenched his fists, holding it back, saving it for the right moment.

The stench of blood and death assaulted his mortal senses as he approached the yard. Flies had already gathered on the ox corpse. How long had it been dead? Since yesterday? Since the venatrix's visit? And where . . . where was the other ox? Looking at the dray, Terryn noted that the halter was meant for a pair. The huge head-join bar was broken in two.

Impossible.

His hand up, power burning in his fingertips, Terryn approached the dead beast. Its side had been ripped wide open, the bones of its ribcage broken like matchsticks. This didn't look like damage teeth might inflict. Unless he was much mistaken, this was a goring.

A door slammed.

Terryn jumped, spinning toward the barn, his hands upraised and ready to blast. Nothing there. The barn door was open, blown against the wall by the wind, perhaps. But what was that lying on the floor just through the open doorway?

Terryn's eyes widened. Leaving the body of the ox, he strode to the barn, his eyes fixed on the shadows inside. He channeled a small amount of power into the palm of his hand, creating a sphere of illumination.

The glow lit upon the face of a huge bearded man. Broken. Bloody. His body almost unrecognizable as human, but his face strangely untouched.

Terryn stopped. For an instant, he stood rooted to the floor as though caught in spirit bind. He simply could not make himself take another step. He'd seen many things in the years of his training, the years of his service, but this . . . this was . . .

A deep, guttural moan filled the air.

Galvanized into action, Terryn sprang to the doorway, sprang over the body of the broken man, his hand upraised. The small sphere of light roiled into a brighter beam, ready to be shot like a bolt of lightning. By that fierce glow, he saw the monster.

It lay in a pile of ruin in the center of the barn. A huge ax protruded from its neck, and it sprawled out, its sides heaving as it gasped and gurgled for last breaths. Once it might have been an ox. But this . . . this thing looked like nothing of this world. Not anymore. The horns were huge, curved, and stained with blood. The bones of its spine broke through its skin in great spikes. The head was warped, the jaw disjointed to hold enormous, fang-like teeth.

He'd seen this work before. He knew it.

The Warpwitch.

It's her. It's her. It's her . . .

Terryn pulled his bone knife free and moved across the barn toward that dying creature. This was no shade-taken, so no Gentle Death would be required here. The one blow the woodcutter managed to strike before he was killed had almost done the trick; the ax was embedded deep in the monster's neck. Only the terrible magic of the Warpwitch's curse had kept the beast alive this long.

While it lived, the curse thread connecting it to its mistress remained intact. If di Ferosa were here, she might manage it with ease, her shade frighteningly ascendant inside her. But she was not.

One rolling eye, still strangely ox-like, watched Terryn as he approached, watched as he pulled out his Vocos and put it to his lips. With extreme care, Terryn began to weave a variation of the Song of Unbinding. He needed more access to his shade's senses if he was to have any hope of following a curse thread. Carefully, cautiously, he reached down into his soul with the spell song and loosened the suppressions holding his shade at bay. Only a little, only the slightest amount.

His shade lurched in reaction.

It's her! it cried. *It's her! Remember! Remember, remember!*

"*Silence,*" Terryn said, speaking in his mind. With his mortal body, he shifted the spell into a powerful variation of the Song of Command. He whipped the harsh melody at his shade, and the spirit bound inside him shuddered in response, retreating. Sweat beaded Terryn's brow. But Fendrel had trained him well over the years.

Modulating between the spell songs, he took hold of the power he needed, an increase of the shadow sight which allowed him to look beyond the mortal world into the world of spirit.

Resolving the song spells with a flourish, he sheathed his Vocos once more and trained his eyes upon the dying ox monster. His eyes shimmered with their augmented power, and he saw the curse latched deep down inside it, implanted with a sigil of blood. Anathema magic—Terryn recognized it at once.

He drew his scorpiona and loaded it with an Anathema dart. He was ready. Now, if the Goddess was with him, the warped ox would live in this agonized suffering long enough for him to trace the curse back to its source.

"I'm coming for you, Ylaire," he whispered. He strode from the barn, stepping over the remains of the woodcutter, and ran across the yard, following the strained, shimmering curse.

CHAPTER 16

HER EYELIDS FELT LIKE LEAD WEIGHTS. AYLETH struggled to open them, but the effort required was too great, so she gave up for the moment. Instead, she reached out with her other senses, trying to make heads or tails of her slowly reawakening awareness.

She felt prickling. A hundred and more itchy prickles up and down her arms, in her neck, at the back of her head. It felt like . . . straw? A straw mattress, perhaps. Inhaling deeply, she was quite certain she smelled straw as well, along with many other earthy, musky scents. Smoke. And another scent she almost recognized but couldn't quite name. The air was close and still, and she heard the crackle of a fire and what might be the scrape of a wooden spoon around the lip of a pot.

"*Laranta?*" she whispered, searching down inside herself. The pine forest of her mind was dark and still save for a dull, pulsing throb. Her own pain, she realized. Pushing through the sensation, she found her shade deep down in the forest, crouched and trembling. "*Laranta, come here,*" Ayleth said, without any real force in the command.

Laranta's rumbling voice answered from the depths of the dark pines. *No. Iron. No.*

That was the scent she could not name. Ayleth's face wrinkled, and with her next inhalation, her stomach clenched. Screwing up her strength, she made another effort to open her eyes and just managed to force the lids up. Her blurred vision slowly slid back into focus.

Directly overhead hung an assortment of discarded horseshoes, strung on stout woolen thread and arranged in a strangely complex cluster. It spun slightly, pulled by its own counterbalancing weights, and the air around it hummed with a faint but effective suppression spell.

"Ah. You're awake."

The voice had a humming quality to it, much like the sound of the spell. But unlike the spell, it didn't make Ayleth's innards churn. A stumping of feet, and a face creased with a most incredible assortment of delicate wrinkles loomed into Ayleth's view.

"Don't move too quickly. You took a nasty blow to the back of the head. The iron ward is keeping your shade quiet, but I'll give you something stronger if you resist."

Ayleth winced. Her last few moments of consciousness slowly reformed in her brain. The child. The little girl running, falling. Staring up at her with such terror in her jade eyes. The shade spirit shining bright, twined with her young soul.

The blow from behind.

Her fingers trembling, Ayleth lifted a hand and gently touched the throbbing place just behind her right ear. Her fingertips found a bandage damp with either medicine or blood, she wasn't certain which.

"Don't worry," the old woman said. "You took a

glancing hit but no permanent damage. A direct blow like that would have killed you."

Swallowing to wet her parched throat, Ayleth blinked up into the wrinkle-hooded eyes. "Oma Githa?" she croaked.

The old woman acknowledged this with a smile and a nod. She lifted a rough wooden cup full of some brew. "Try to drink this down." At the look Ayleth gave her, she added, "It's neither poison nor low magic. Merely a concoction to reduce swelling and help ease the pain. You'll feel better for it."

Though she probably ought not to trust a hedgewitch, Ayleth's head pounded too hard for her to think of a protest. With painful slowness, she propped up onto her elbows and let the old woman lift the cup to her mouth, taking careful sips. The brew was sweet, which surprised her, and she drank it all rather more hastily than she'd planned.

Clucking with satisfaction, Oma Githa set the cup to one side and settled back in a spindly chair. She crossed a pair of absolutely enormous, calloused bare feet, displaying great gnarled toes. Her hands, by contrast, were quite dainty, and she folded these over her stomach and leaned back, eyeing Ayleth from beneath bristling black brows. "Tell me, what is a young venatrix doing at my door?"

Ayleth, who had just rested her head back on the scratchy mattress, lifted it again too quickly. The room spun, and she closed her eyes. Then, peering at the hedgewitch, she said, "You know what I am?"

The old woman nodded. "I've had encounters with the Order of Saint Evander before." She chuckled, a cheerful gleam brightening her eyes. "I've been a thorn in Nane du Vincent's side for many years now! Has he grown so weary of dealing with me that he must send young blood such as yourself in his place?"

Ayleth opened her mouth, but stopped herself and chose her words carefully before speaking. "Do you . . . not know what happened to Venator du Vincent?"

Those bristling brows shot up the old woman's forehead, bunching its wrinkles into mounds. "Is he dead?"

Though she did not speak, Ayleth knew her face gave away the answer.

Oma Githa shook her head, chuckling again, this time without any mirth. "When you spend your life hunting the defenseless, you're bound to make a bad end."

"The defenseless?" Ayleth pushed herself back up onto her elbows, then, with an effort, all the way to a seated position. She glared at the hedgewitch. "Venator du Vincent devoted his life to purging the world of evil. Spirits possessed of extraordinary and dangerous powers are hardly defenseless!"

Oma Githa considered her with some interest. "Such devotion to the teachings of your saint. So, you agree with the burning of children?"

"I—" Ayleth stopped. Her head swam, and she closed her eyes again, wishing she'd not sat up so quickly. Bowing her head, she waited for the dizziness to pass. Once more she saw the little girl in her memory, her face white with terror, staring up at Ayleth from among broad fern leaves. A child not yet four years of age. Eyes so wide, so innocent, so frightened.

Eyes so full of shadow-light.

"That was Jerlo's daughter I saw fleeing this house, wasn't it." Ayleth lifted her chin and looked at the hedgewitch. "Nilly du Bucheron."

Oma Githa nodded.

"So . . . it was Jerlo who killed Venator du Vincent and hid his daughter here."

The hedgewitch frowned at this. "I wouldn't be knowing about that." She sucked reflectively at one of three teeth remaining to her. "All I know is that Fiola showed up at my door four weeks ago, leading her daughter and begging me to hide her. She told me the girl was shade-taken, that a man had come to kill her. To burn her. I took from this that Nilly was an inborn . . . which surprised me, I won't deny."

Ayleth frowned, struggling to make sense of what she'd just heard. "Wait. Wait a moment. Fiola, you say? Fiola du Bucheron?"

The hedgewitch tilted her head to the other side.

"But . . . she was dead." Ayleth persisted. "Jerlo witnessed her death. Nane killed her six weeks ago."

"Killed her body, yes," the old woman said.

Realization struck. Ayleth put both hands to her face, rubbing hard as though she could somehow push own thoughts into order. If Fiola du Bucheron was violently killed, her indwelling shade had certainly been propelled on to find and possess another body. But her mortal spirit should have been left to wander revenant and fade unless . . . unless . . .

"She's a witch," Ayleth whispered. "She turned to witchcraft."

Only the souls of inborn or witches remained bound to their shades after death. Inborn were naturally entwined with their possessing spirits, while witches fostered the binding through unnatural means. With such a binding, they gained control over the powers indwelling them. If Fiola du Bucheron had turned to witchcraft, she could have taken control of her shade and successfully hidden its powers even from her husband for years.

Witchcraft of all kinds was forbidden on pain of death in Perrinion. Only death by fire could separate a bound soul from its shade—but the Order of Evander never offered such a death to witches. They deserved their ultimate torment.

Pyres were saved for innocent souls.

Ayleth pressed her hands into her eyes. The pieces of the puzzle seemed to scatter before her vision. Did she have all of them now? If she could only ask the right question, perhaps she could see how to put it all together.

"What . . . what form did Fiola wear when she visited you?"

Oma Githa scratched her stomach, then reached out one scrawny arm and plucked a pipe from a nearby table. She set about stuffing and lighting it, taking decidedly more time than necessary. Ayleth inwardly writhed with impatience but knew better than to push. She waited, her question hanging unanswered until the hedgewitch had puffed several large clouds into the air, filling the close cottage room with the powerful stink of tobacco.

At long last, Oma Githa tapped the stem of her pipe against one tooth and said, "I've always been willing to help the Order insofar as my conscience allows. It seems to me that you are investigating the death of your fellow venator, and to that end, I see no harm in telling you what I know."

Following this declaration, she took three more long draws on her pipe, gathering her thoughts. At last she began:

"Fiola and Jerlo du Bucheron came to me nigh unto

four years ago, desperate and frightened. Fiola had become shade-taken, and she was also with child. The law of Perrinion dictates, of course, that they should go at once to the Red Hoods and submit to the necessary end. But they came to me to see if there was aught else to be done.

"My first task was to determine whether or not the taking was true. As I am not possessed myself, I cannot see spirits as you do." She raised a bushy eyebrow and nodded at Ayleth. "But in this instance, it was simple enough to verify the truth. I asked Fiola to demonstrate her powers, and she answered by picking her husband up and lifting him over her head."

Ayleth nodded. It was impressive to consider any woman lifting a man of Jerlo du Bucheron's height and breadth. If the story was true, there could be no doubt that a powerful Feral shade possessed Fiola's body.

Oma Githa, taking another draw on her pipe, chuckled at the expression on Ayleth's face. "Following this little demonstration, I set about the difficult task of transferring the shade she carried into a different host body."

242

"That's impossible," Ayleth blurted. Immediately, she wished she could take the words back, for the old woman gave her such a look, Ayleth half feared she would be turned out of the cottage on the spot. But the hedgewitch simply drew another several puffs on her pipe, waiting.

Ayleth ducked her head. "I apologize, Oma Githa. Please continue."

"Hmmm." Oma Githa drew the pipe from her mouth and pointed the stem at Ayleth. "Just because your saint forbade the practice of low magic doesn't make the low magic itself ineffective. You'd do well to remember as much, child."

Ayleth nodded silently. With another grunt, the hedgewitch went on:

"I took blood from Fiola and blood from the animal I'd chosen as the shade's new host, a raven I'd caught the previous week. The bird was eye-torn but as yet untaken. A healthy creature and a worthy enough host for a spirit such as Fiola carried. So, I took blood from each, mingling them together, saying the *run gwedhíath*"—Oma Githa gave Ayleth a narrow look—"a secret and ancient prayer to the Goddess, of which your Saint Evander disapproved. When the prayers were complete, I used this."

She withdrew a curious object from the depths of her ragged robes. It was a little crystal triangle hung on a bit of gut. It dangled in the air, silent except . . . Ayleth's ears pricked, her shade senses quickening. She detected a faint hum, beyond the range of human hearing, audible only to spirits. The hedgewitch herself probably could not hear it, untaken as she was, though she was apparently aware of the quality of sound it made.

"When struck with a silver spoon," Oma Githa said, "this little instrument opens a connection between two souls. Like a soul bridge. Once that connection is established, it is only a matter of gently—Oh! So gently!—coaxing the shade out of its current host and into the other. The hum of the triangle helps. As do the prayers. And the blood."

The old woman grinned around her pipe. "I can see the disapproval in your face, young venatrix. But tell me, has your saint offered you and your Order any such solutions? Have you means by which to save mortal souls without destroying mortal bodies?" When Ayleth gave no answer, she shook her head. "I thought not."

"What happened to Fiola?" Ayleth pressed. "Did your ceremony . . . Did it work?"

"In a way, it did," the hedgewitch said, though her lips twisted in a funny expression. "A connection between souls was certainly made, and I thought . . . I believed the transference took place." She tapped her pipe on the side of the table, spilling dead ashes onto the floor and scuffing them with one bare foot. "Fiola woke up many hours later. She was disoriented, but she claimed that the ceremony had done the trick. Wishful thinking, perhaps. I saw no sign of shade power in the raven, but that gave me no undue concern. Often shades will hide down deep within a new host body, not manifesting in power for weeks or even years. I sent Fiola and her husband home in good faith that my work was accomplished."

"What of the raven?" Ayleth asked.

"I took the raven to the Barriers and sent it through." Oma Githa toyed with her pipe, twiddling it around in her dainty fingers. "This has long been my practice with shade-taken creatures. They are too unpredictable to live free in this world, but I see no reason to turn them over to the likes of Nane or his hunt brother."

Knowing what lay beyond the Great Barrier as she did, Ayleth didn't consider the choice particularly merciful on the hedgewitch's part. Many would prefer death over life in the Witchwood.

With a shiver, she pressed on. "What of the du Bucherons? Did you see anything of them following the . . . the ceremony?"

The hedgewitch shook her head. "I rarely see my customers a second time. But I glimpsed them now and then, when I made my few lonely journeys to Elsinoe Shrinehouse for the Feast Day prayers. I saw Fiola with a babe in her arms. and later, a little child toddling at her heels. She never acknowledged me. I never expected it. But I was glad to think I had helped them through a difficult time." She shrugged. "Or so I believed."

Ayleth drew her legs up into a crisscross position and studied her hands resting in her lap. Whatever brew Oma Githa had given her seemed to have done its work, for her head no longer throbbed with so much pain. "You told me," she said, "that Fiola came to you four weeks ago. With her daughter."

Oma Githa nodded. "She did."

"In what body?"

"Fiola wore the body of a raven."

Ayleth stared. Her mind seemed to have hit a solid wall and stopped, unable to accept what she had just heard. "She . . . what?"

"It would seem the connection I had formed between the souls worked," the hedgewitch said. "Only not as I had intended. When Fiola's body was killed by Nane, she and her possessing spirit followed that connection. Across the Great Barrier, into the body of the bird."

Ayleth drew a long, long breath. Her mouth tried to form questions, but she couldn't figure out the words to speak.

"I've had to piece the bits of the story together as I could over the last few weeks," the hedgewitch continued. "Little Nilly is much too frightened to tell me, but Fiola communicated what she could. She has no ability to speak mortal language anymore, not with a raven's tongue. But I have, over the years, become sensitive to . . . *impressions* of spirit. From what I understand, Fiola found herself in the raven's body, trapped on the far side of the Barrier. She could do nothing for her daughter, and she despaired. But then, a few weeks following her entrapment, the unbelievable happened—she felt her daughter's spirit near. In the Witchwood.

"A few weeks after his first visit to the du Bucheron household, Nane returned to take little Nilly away. I'm hazy on the details, but somehow the child escaped him and fled deep into the forest, across the Barrier. Venator Nane pursued her even there, but Fiola kept her daughter hidden from him. Then, using the opening the venator himself made in the barrier spell, they crossed back into our world, and Fiola brought the child to me."

Ayleth's hands curled into fists. She felt as though she heard all the words which Oma Githa either chose not to tell, or which Fiola herself had chosen not to relate. The pieces . . . the pieces of the puzzle slowly came together.

Jerlo had pursued Nane. Though he'd told Ayleth he'd not caught up with them, they must have had another confrontation after all. And during that fight, Nilly had slipped free of her captor and run away into the Witchwood.

Nane would not want a child to suffer the horrors of the cursed forest. The poisonous air, the monsters, the despairing evil that ate away at the soul. While most shade-taken he would leave to their fate, for Nilly's sake, he went in after her. To find her, to save her. To burn her.

But when he failed to find the girl, Nane returned to the Barrier, opening a gate for his own escape. And Fiola, hiding nearby with her daughter, had seen her chance. She'd swooped in and delivered a killing blow to the back of Nane's head. Killed him with a blade-like beak driven with the power of a Feral shade. Then she and her daughter slipped free of the Witchwood, back into their own world.

"But . . . but that can't be all," Ayleth whispered, her face twisting with something like pain as she tried to make the rest of the story work. What about the logbook taken from Nane's body? What about the attempt to patch the break in the Great Barrier? What about the dead woman—the woman Terryn claimed was the Warpwitch? How did she fit into this bizarre picture?

Ayleth shifted on the straw mattress so that she could

lean her back against the cottage wall. No matter how she tried to twist the information into shape, she couldn't get it all to fit where it should. She eyed the hedgewitch, who eyed her back.

"Why are you telling me all this?" she asked at last. "You've been hiding Nilly for weeks. Why give it all up now?"

"Well, for one thing, I'm about to die," Oma Githa answered. "I figure it is better to pass on what I know now rather than take it all with me. For another, Nilly told me to."

"What?" Ayleth shook her head. "What do you mean Nilly told you—? What do you mean you're about to—? *What?*"

The hedgewitch tossed her head back and laughed loud and long, snorting and snuffling with each breath. When at last the fit of mirth passed, she wiped the soft skin around her eyes with the back of one finger. "Oh, the look on your face, girl! As if you didn't know that we all of us die eventually. It's not as though it's such shocking news as all that. But yes." She folded her hands across her stomach again. "Nilly is . . . a seer of visions.

Her shade enables her to perceive things past, present, and future. When a vision takes her, she cannot stop herself from speaking it to the one for whom it's intended. To try to hold it back causes her terrible pain, and she's too young to learn how to suppress it. She told me I would die the day the young venatrix came to visit me. Which means my end must be coming soon now, I should think."

Ayleth continued shaking her head, harder and harder. "I'm not going to kill you," she said.

"That doesn't mean I won't die."

"Why did you help me then?" Ayleth flung up both hands. "When you saw me, why didn't you turn around and run the other way?"

"Doing so might well have speeded my death. I thought you'd like a little soothing tea first. And possibly a chance to hear what I had to say." The old woman's face settled into stern frown lines, every wrinkle deepening. "So much for gratitude."

"And what am I supposed to do now?" Ayleth demanded. "What am I supposed to do with what you've told me?"

"Your job, I imagine." Oma Githa sucked on her teeth again before adding, "Unless, of course, you have no taste for murdering children. In which case, you'll have to think of something cleverer." She shrugged. "All the same, it's not my business anymore. I'm about to die, and I can no longer protect little Nilly from the likes of you. She still has her mother at least, so she's not entirely alone in the world. But you might want to—"

The old woman broke off as a sudden clamor started up outside. Ayleth flinched, staring across the room to the listing cottage door. Those were animal voices, different kinds of animal voices, shrieking, screaming. All the little creatures in their cages outside.

"What—?" she began.

Oma Githa's eyes snapped to Ayleth's face, glinting bright. "Ah. So *she's* the one who'll do it."

The door flung open with a bang.

A woman loomed in the doorway, so tall she had to stoop to enter. Long snarls of lank, colorless hair framed a hard-featured face, and bright, red-rimmed eyes stared into the dark gloom of the cottage, flashing with unsuppressed shadow-light.

"Where is the child?" she roared.

CHAPTER 17

THE SHADE-TAKEN WOMAN DUCKED HER HEAD TO pass under the lintel, then straightened to her full height, her head nearly touching the low ceiling rafters. Her lips curled back in a hideous grimace, revealing teeth dark and streaked with red stains. More stains surrounded her mouth and coated her chin, and the stench of blood filled the room. Her flashing eyes burned into Oma Githa, and she lifted one trembling, blood-stained hand, pointing.

"Where is the child?"

For an instant, the question hung in the air.

The next instant, Ayleth's instincts surged to life. Her eyes darted to one side, spying her weapons in a pile on a table across the small room. She lunged in the same moment the shade-taken moved to intercept her. Catching the hilt of her bone knife, she yanked it from its sheath, turning just in time to slash at the woman. The blade bit a savage cut across her upraised arm.

The shade-taken woman's snarl turned to a smile. Moving with incredible speed, she caught Ayleth by the wrist and slammed her arm against the wall. The whole cottage shook, and debris fell from the ceiling. Ayleth dropped her knife but swung her left fist at the woman's face. Her blow was blocked, and the next thing she knew, she was hurtled bodily to one side, striking the edge of the table and falling to the floor.

"*Laranta!*" Ayleth screamed inside. Her wolf shade lunged, struggling against the still-potent restrictions of the iron-ward spell. For the moment, she could offer no strength.

A clatter in her ears. Ayleth, her vision spinning, felt rather than saw her scorpiona land on the floor, jostled from the impact of her collision with the table. Though she wanted nothing more than to rest her throbbing head, to take a breath, she rolled—just in time. A knife blade sang a vicious note as it stabbed into the floor where her head had been an instant before.

Scrambling under the table, Ayleth snatched up her scorpiona. No time to fix it to her arm, no time to use it as she had always trained. She must shoot it free-handed.

Ayleth pushed out from underneath the table, standing on the far side, across from the shade-taken. Her quivers lay before her, darts scattered across the tabletop. A single instant spread like an eternity before her. A single instant to grab the first poison she could lay hands on.

Ayleth's hand caught a dart and slammed it into the scorpiona. The shade-taken, roaring like a demon, flung herself at the table, her blade lashing out—but stopped short, choking, gagging from the bite of a dart quivering in the hollow of her throat.

For a sweet, beautiful moment, the shadow-light in her eyes faded.

Then she screamed, flung out both arms, and threw back her head. A burst of raw magic erupted straight from the core of her being. She pulled her chin back down, her eyes lancing into Ayleth.

Before Ayleth could react, the shade-taken's knife flashed, tearing into the flesh of her own hand. Blood flowed, bursting with magic. In a swift, slashing motion, she sent droplets of blood out from her in an arc, and with them flew an eruption of power so great, it hurtled Ayleth off her feet. She crashed into the wall, the air crushed from her lungs.

Pinned, paralyzed, Ayleth could neither turn her face away nor close her eyes as the shade-taken approached. The woman threw the table across the room with one arm. Her teeth gnashing with a need for death, she drew her knife back to strike.

The blow didn't fall.

The woman's mouth dropped open, the snarl of bloodlust vanishing behind an expression of utter shock followed by awe. Her magic-maddened eyes widened.

"Y-you?" she breathed.

Ayleth felt her heartbeat slow. She felt the pulse of blood in her ears, a pounding drumbeat, a rhythm of doom. Not death, but worse. Something shuddered inside her brain, some wall of protection she'd never realized was there, and beyond it . . . beyond it . . .

A bright, clear, vicious note of deadly music sliced through the air, burning down into Ayleth's soul. It struck her and the shade-taken woman simultaneously, and their voices mingled in a scream. The blast of power which had held Ayleth to the wall broke, and she fell to her knees. The very marrow of her soul quaked with pain, but she realized this was not a pain that attacked her directly. It was aimed at Laranta. Her wolf shade writhed inside her in helpless agony.

On the very edges of her awareness, Ayleth realized that the shade-taken woman had fallen as well, and was similarly thrashing on the floor.

The piercing sound faded, and Ayleth, panting hard, looked up. She saw Oma Githa, a little crystal triangle in her dainty hands quivering from the note she'd struck—a note the hedgewitch could not hear, a note heard and felt only by shade souls and those possessed by them.

Ayleth tried to pull herself back upright. But she could not master her own limbs. Oma Githa's attack had struck her much harder than it had her foe. She could only watch in horror as the shade-taken woman rose, turning on the hedgewitch.

Oma Githa lifted her silver spoon, striking at the quivering triangle again. But before the note could sound, the shade-taken flung out her bleeding hand, sending another arc of droplets flying at the old woman.

The droplets became black spears. Curse bolts. They tore through Oma Githa's flesh, pierced her gut, her torso.

The hedgewitch uttered a single horrible scream and fell, bleeding. Protrusions of curse magic quivered where they'd pierced her. She lay gasping, unable to pull herself upright as the shade-taken approached her.

The strange woman knelt, catching the hedgewitch by her throat, pulling her up to snarl into her face. "Where is the child? Where is the little Seer? I've been tracking her for weeks, and all signs have pointed me here. I need her. Now!"

Oma Githa's mouth worked as though trying to form words. But instead, she spat a great gob of blood directly into the witch's face.

The witch reeled back. Then she struck the old woman

across the face, roaring, "Tell me! Tell me where she is!"

She was too late. Oma Githa's head lolled as the last of her strength faded. Ayleth, lying broken on the floor, watched a thread of mortal spirit slip out of the broken, bleeding body which had been its host.

The shade-taken saw it as well. "*No!*" she shrieked, snatching with her bloody hand as though to catch the soul, which slipped through her fingers and away, up through the ceiling and gone. She slammed the hedgewitch's body to the floor, tore at its flesh with her nails.

Then, still crouched over her kill, she whirled suddenly, her gaze fixed on Ayleth. With a hiss through bared teeth, she turned and crawled across the floor, dragging her knife as she came. Ayleth, her body still seized with the pain of Oma Githa's attack, couldn't even cringe as the shade-taken reached out to her, caught her by the base of her braid, and yanked her head up, exposing her neck. She peered intently down at Ayleth.

"I know your face," she said, blood dripping from her lips. "I know your face, but I don't know you. Who are you?"

The muscles of Ayleth's throat worked, but no words came. The shade-taken leaned in closer, her foul breath hot against Ayleth's skin.

"Just a little blood," she murmured, raising her knife and pressing the edge delicately beneath Ayleth's ear. "Just a little drop. I don't need more than that. Just enough . . ."

Burning pain ripped across Ayleth's skin. She screamed. Her blood flowed warm down her neck, flowed onto the shade-taken's knife, caught in the grooves etched in the blade.

"Get away from her!"

The deep voice burst through Ayleth's brain like a bolt of lightning. The shade-taken turned, brandishing her knife. Ayleth, her vision swimming, saw a tall figure filling the doorway, saw light gleaming on the fastenings of a scorpiona.

"Terryn!" she tried to scream. But her mouth would not obey her.

Hissing like a snake, the shade-taken dropped her hold on Ayleth's hair and sprang to her feet. With a snap, Terryn fired.

Not fast enough. The shade-taken ducked to one side, and the dart struck the wall over Ayleth's head. But the shade-taken fell to her knees, carried down by her own momentum, and before she could pick herself up, Terryn had reloaded and shot again. She was quick, but the dart scraped her cheek.

Ayleth stared, her shadow vision straining. She saw the flash of the Anathema spirit inside the woman's body. She saw the burst and the shudder of poison, burning down.

Terryn had chosen the right dart.

With a shriek that would shatter souls, the shade-taken sprang to her feet. She leapt straight at her attacker, her knife flashing. He could not reload fast enough, but he brought his left arm up, deflecting her knife with the iron spike. The witch swiped at his face with her hands. Her nails dug into his skin, drawing scratches of blood across the puckered skin of his scar.

The next instant she whirled away, leaping for the small door at the back of the cottage. Terryn made a grab for her, his fingers closing on a fistful of hair, but she pulled free, leaving a hank of scraggly locks twined through his fingers. Bursting through the door, she fled out into the yard even as poison pulsed through her veins.

A pounding of footsteps. Ayleth's blurring vision saw boots cross her line of sight as Terryn raced out in pursuit of his quarry. She let her forehead sink to the floor and passed into unconsciousness.

CHAPTER 18

SOMEONE GRABBED HER FOREARMS, ROLLED HER over. An arm slid under her shoulders and heaved her up. In a half-aware haze, Ayleth tried to respond, tried to react. Her muscles twitched, her hands flailed, desperate to catch hold of something, anything.

A brief instant of weightlessness, then she landed hard. Her fingers tightened on reflex around a handful of fabric, and though she felt weak as a kitten, she pulled hard. Something moved in response, and her slowly returning senses felt the warmth of a solid body over hers and breath on her face.

With an effort of extreme will, she forced her eyelids open and found herself staring into a pair of ice-cold eyes mere inches from her own. Both her hands gripped the front of Venator Terryn's jerkin, pulling him down over her where she lay.

"Let go of me, Venatrix." His voice rumbled low in her ear, edged with danger.

For an instant she tried to refuse, to resist. Her fingers tightened their hold, but the effort required was too great. A painful humming in her ear seemed to pierce down inside her, weakening not only her body but also her spirit.

With a sigh, she released him and fell back. Terryn straightened and stepped away, then reached up to adjust something over her head. The humming increased, and Ayleth, wincing, lifted her heavy gaze and saw Oma Githa's iron ward still hung from the ceiling above her. Her heart lifted with the hope that Terryn was taking it down, dismantling it, so that the low-magic spell would break.

Instead, he backed away. His gaze moved from the ward to her and back again as he realized what it was.

"P-p-please," Ayleth gasped. His face was a mask without a trace of compassion. Was he or was he not here to help her? She closed her eyes. The effort required to stay awake was too much. Pain crawled through her senses: pain in her throat where the knife had cut into her skin, and, worse still, the pain of a curse trying to penetrate down into her soul.

Her teeth clenched in a vicious, growling snarl. She tried to sit up but couldn't. With a start, she lurched back into full wakefulness only to find that Terryn had bound her hands and feet to the bed. She lifted her head as far as it would go and looked down to where he crouched at the foot of the bed, securing the last rope.

"What are you doing?" The words tore through her grinding teeth.

Terryn met her gaze even as he tugged his final knot tight. "Making certain you lie still."

"Let me go." Fear pulsed in her throat. Ayleth strained against the bindings, which should have been nothing for Laranta's strength. But Laranta, though frantically active down in her soul, couldn't find a way past the iron-ward spell. "Let me up! The . . . the shade-taken woman . . . we've got to— Haunts damn!" Severe stabs of pain shot through every inch of her body.

"The more you struggle, the more you'll hurt yourself." Terryn stood, looming tall over her, his head and shoulders bent to avoid hitting the ceiling rafters. "The Warpwitch caught you with a curse, and it's still wearing off. It looks like a basic attack to me, but I'm not certain. It might be a compulsion. She could still call it into play, take control of you, warp your body."

Ayleth drew several long breaths through her nostrils. The Warpwitch. The Warpwitch! That was the Warpwitch she'd just faced? That was the Warpwitch who had . . . who had . . .

Turning her head to one side, Ayleth stared into the room, searching for . . . she wasn't sure what. Not until her eyes landed on the table did she realize. Her weapons were gone, scattered across the floor. In their place, the table supported a blanket-wrapped corpse. Two huge gnarled feet protruded from the end. Countless bloodstains soaked through the rough woven fibers.

She told me I would die the day the young venatrix came to visit me. The hedgewitch's voice floated back through Ayleth's memory.

"She was going to die today," Ayleth whispered. "The day she met me . . ."

Terryn grabbed a chair, pulled it between the bed and the table, and sat, blocking her view of the dead woman. Three red lines from where the Warpwitch had scratched him marred his already-maimed right cheek. He rested his elbows on his knees, tilting his head to look at her, his eyes cold and hooded. He said nothing for a long while, merely studied her, his expression unreadable.

At last he said, "What did the hedgewitch tell you?"

Her brain was so numb. Ayleth's lips cracked as she opened her mouth. Rather than tell her tale, she could only croak, "Water?"

He hesitated a long moment, watching her closely. Then, as though reaching the end of some silent internal debate, he nodded, got up, and drifted out of her line of sight. He returned a moment later and, putting out one large hand, caught Ayleth by the back of the head. With surprising gentleness, he lifted her up high enough that she could sip from the cup he held to her lips. Her arms were still bound, but she contrived to balance on her elbows and drank gratefully.

By the time she'd drained the cup, all her energy seemed to have fled her. She lay back down again, wincing as she looked at Terryn. How long had she been unconscious? How long had he been playing nursemaid to her? Judging from the faint light coming through the long cracks in the door, the day was well advanced toward evening. She might have lain here for hours.

"All right, Venatrix," Terryn said, setting aside the cup. "Tell me why you're here. Tell me what you learned from the hedgewitch."

Haltingly, Ayleth related her recent adventures. Her conversation with Mother Vesta, with Jerlo. The story of the vision-seeing child and her mother, and their connection to Oma Githa. She suspected she didn't tell all, didn't clearly draw the connections necessary within her own tale. Her head was too numb, her body too distracted by pain.

Terryn said nothing the whole time she spoke, save for a question here or there when her words were too garbled to make sense. When at last she finished, he rested his elbow on his knee, cupping his chin in his hand, looking off into some empty space over her bed, his brow drawn into a tight frown.

It was Ayleth's turn to watch him now. The scar on his cheek seemed to stand out starkly, the puckered skin red against his dark skin. In this lighting, it struck her as uglier than before.

"Why . . . Why are you here?" she demanded. "Why aren't you after the witch? Or did you get her already?"

A strange expression flashed across Terryn's face. Then he shook his head quickly. "You were hurt. And cursed. I stopped to . . . to make certain . . ." Another expression Ayleth couldn't quite name flared in his eyes. Was it pain? He looked away, tilting his head oddly.

Ayleth opened her mouth to chastise him. How could he let that shade-taken murderess get away? She ground her teeth, wanting to scream in frustration, and yet . . . would she rather he'd left her lying cursed on the cottage floor?

"How did you get here?" she asked instead, realizing suddenly how odd it was. The last she'd seen of Terryn, he was riding south with Venator Kephan, the two of them making for some secret destination. "What happened to your investigation?"

Terryn shrugged dismissively. "That proved a dead end. Venator du Tam and I were riding to join you, but he was called to another trail. I continued on to Hollen, and the Warpwitch led me here. I found a still-active curse thread near Jerlo du Bucheron's body, and—"

Ayleth's eyes flashed to meet his. "His body? Jerlo is dead? He was alive just last . . . Tell me what you found."

"I will tell you if you stop pulling at your bindings. Lie still."

A jolt of rage nearly started her yanking at the ropes even harder. But in truth, the room was slowly spinning around her, and she felt darkness creeping in at the edges. She scowled at the venator but acquiesced enough to rest her head back on the straw mattress.

Terryn waited to be certain she truly was settled. Then he told her of finding Jerlo's body and the hideous monster his ox had been transformed into. As he described the horror of the scene, Ayleth's stomach twisted. It seemed impossible, somehow, that the man she'd spoken to just the night before could have met such a fate.

"But why?" she whispered at last. "Why would the Warpwitch target Jerlo? How does she connect with all this?"

"You tell me," Terryn replied. "Did she say anything? During your encounter, before I got here."

Ayleth struggled to remember. The awful hum of the iron ward lanced down into her head, and she winced. "I can't think," she said, glaring up at the weird low-magic spell caster. "Take that thing down. It hurts, and it's blocking my shade."

"I know," Terryn said. "It seems this hedgewitch had some talent. She's created a spell refined specifically to affect your Feral. I can hear it, but it does not touch me. Neither did it affect the Warpwitch, apparently."

"Well, it affects me. So, take the Haunts-damned thing down, will you?"

Terryn shook his head. "I think not." He leaned back in the chair. "Not until you tell me how exactly you're connected to the Crimson Devils."

Ayleth stared at him. The humming of the iron ward

seemed to intensify, painful in her ear. "What . . . what are you . . .?"

"Twice now," he said, his eyes boring into hers. "Twice you have been at the mercy of Odile's Devils. Twice you should have been killed. But here you are."

Ayleth shook her head. "You're mad, du Balafre. This one *did* try to kill me. You saw her. She had a festering knife to my throat!"

Terryn surged up out of his seat, bending over Ayleth, his teeth flashing white in his dark face. "If Ylaire di Jocosa wanted to kill you, you would be dead," he growled. "So, I ask again, *Venatrix*—what is your connection to Dread Odile and her Devils? Who are you really?"

Memory came back to her of the terrible moment when she'd been crumpled at the witch's feet, her head caught and viciously pulled back. The knife was at her throat, blood trickling down its edge.

Why had the witch stopped? Why had she not sliced her prey's neck wide open?

I know your face, but I don't know you . . .

Ayleth squeezed her eyes shut, plunging herself down

into the darkness of her mind. But there the hum of the iron-ward spell was too piercing, and beyond that hum, something else . . . something powerful . . . some magic she recognized . . .

Hollis's magic . . .

Ayleth's eyes flew open. She looked up into Terryn's face and met his gaze, saw the writhing gleam of his shade in the depths of his pupils. She clenched her fists, every muscle in her body longing for the rush of shade power, power enough to tear apart these bindings, to fling the venator across the room.

"I am Ayleth, Venatrix di Ferosa," she said through her teeth. "I was trained by my mistress, Hollis di Theldry, at Gillanluòc Outpost in Drauval Borough. I am a loyal daughter of Saint Evander's Order, devoted to the hunt, devoted to the will of our Goddess. This is who I am, this is who I have been. This is who I will always be. So, untie these ropes and let me do my job!"

Terryn backed away from the bed, his face falling into shadows. "You're not going anywhere," he said, drawing his scorpiona from its holster.

Was he going to shoot her? Ayleth roared and hauled

at her bindings, only for a stab of pain to shoot from her head down her spine to the very soles of her feet. The iron ward over her head hummed, and the horseshoes twisted gently on their many suspending threads. Sweat beaded Ayleth's brow, and she panted, her fingers curling and relaxing and curling again.

Terryn plucked a dart from its quiver and loaded it into the scorpiona, never taking his eyes from Ayleth. "You're staying here," he said, his voice so low, she wondered if he spoke to himself rather than to her, not caring whether or not she heard him, "where you can't cause any trouble. I'll come back for you when this hunt is over. Then we'll get to the bottom of this."

"No. No, du Balafre, no!" Ayleth shook her head wildly, and her hair, pulled loose from her long braid, clung to her damp face. "Let me up. Let me come with you. You can't hunt her alone! You need me. And the girl, Nilly. And Fiola du Bucheron. They're still out there! Fiola killed Nane. She'll kill you too!"

But Terryn was already at the door. She might as well be shouting at a deaf man. He glanced back at her once, shadow-light transforming his eyes to two eerie pinpoint embers.

"We'll get to the bottom of this," he said again.

The next moment, he was out the door, slamming it shut behind him.

CHAPTER 19

"TERRYN! *TERRYN!*" AYLETH SCREAMED. HER FINGERS shredded the mattress ticking within their reach. Musty straw fell to the floor, but the bindings on her wrists held firm.

"Haunts damn you, du Balafre!" she roared. "Haunts take and damn you to oblivion!"

She collapsed back on the mattress, staring at the rafters overhead, staring at the weird turnings of that iron ward. Daylight had almost completely faded outside, and the cottage fell into darkness. Remnant glow from a small fire on the hearth illuminated one corner, not enough to offer much visual aid. Ayleth tried to switch to shadow sight, but with Laranta trapped behind the ward, her vision was hazy and uncomfortable, and she soon shifted back to her mortal sight.

What could she do? Her choices were limited enough. She could just lie here and wait for Terryn to return. Goddess above, but she was tired! It wouldn't be all that horrible to close her eyes and simply let herself fall asleep.

But that wasn't an option. The Warpwitch was out there, and Nane's murderer. And the child. Nilly. The little inborn girl.

If Terryn found her, what would he do?

His duty, of course. He was Terryn du Balafre, protégé of the Venator Dominus. The perfect Evanderian, the ideal venator, devout in his service to the Goddess and her saint.

If he found Nilly du Bucheron, he would kill her. To save her soul.

Ayleth's breath shuddered in her throat. She could stay here, out of the fight, out of the hunt. She didn't have to throw herself into this mess. It wasn't her fault if her fellow venator tied her to a bed and left her trapped under a hedgewitch's spell. She could let whatever was going to happen take place out of her sight. Let others accomplish these holy deeds.

She closed her eyes. And she saw that little face peering at her from among the broad fern leaves.

"I won't let him," she whispered.

Maybe she wasn't as devoted as she had always believed.

Maybe she wasn't cut out to be a venatrix in the Order of Saint Evander.

Maybe she was a Haunts-damned heretic.

But, by the Goddess's three holy names, she would not let anyone burn that little girl alive!

Her right hand relaxed, going as limp and lifeless as possible. Then slowly, very slowly, she began to twist. The rope fibers bit into her flesh, but she clenched her teeth and kept turning, rotating back and forth very gently. The bones of her hand crushed together, the skin tore, began to bleed. Still she rotated and pulled.

Her hand came free. With a triumphant cry, Ayleth

reached over and tore at the knot securing her left hand. It was tough and well tied, and she couldn't loosen it one-handed. In her frantic urgency, her numb and bleeding fingers refused to work for her.

"Calm down. Calm down," she told herself, lying back and closing her eyes, forcing herself to take several breaths. "Calm down. You can do this." She opened her eyes and rolled slightly to get a better angle on the knot.

The cottage door opened. Ayleth looked up. Her heart lurched to her throat so hard she almost choked on it.

Nilly du Bucheron stood in the darkness of swiftly falling evening, her hand still on the door latch, her wide eyes blinking slowly as she looked around the room. Her gaze landed on Ayleth, and a whimper escaped her quivering lips.

"*Blood to blood,*" she said in a lisping voice. "*Bone to bone.*"

Ayleth scrabbled again at her bindings, her fingers ineffective against Terryn's knots. Fear jumped in her veins as the child took a step into the room. Fear of *what* exactly, she couldn't say, but fear as palpable as she'd ever experienced it.

"*Blood to blood,*" Nilly said again. "*Bone to bone.*"

The iron ward. As the girl took another step, Ayleth twisted on the bed, her legs and hand still bound, but her right arm free. She looked up at the ward suspended over her head. Could she reach it?

"*Blood to blood. Bone to bone.*" The girl took a third step into the cottage. Her feet were bare, her clothes ragged. Fair hair straggled over her round face. "*The Queen will rise to claim her own.*"

Ayleth stretched out her arm. The tips of her fingers just brushed the lowest-hanging horseshoe. The bite of iron made her flinch back, hissing sharply. Down inside her, Laranta howled. But she could reach it . . . if she stretched just a little higher . . .

"*Blood to blood.*" Nilly approached the foot of the bed. The shadow-light in her eyes bathed her in a jade-colored halo. "*Bone to bone.*" She reached out one small hand.

Ayleth lunged as high as she could and caught the bottom horseshoe. Pain shot through her hand, down her arm, straight to her soul, but she closed her fingers tight and, with a snarl, yanked the horseshoe down from the rafters, breaking the threads. The whole assortment spun and clanged, its balance thrown off. Three horseshoes fell, one of them just missing her head as it landed on the straw mattress and bounced to the floor. The hedgewitch's humming spell turned to a knife-like shriek, and Ayleth screamed in response.

"*Laranta, give me your strength!*" she cried.

Her shade sprang forward in her mind with a roar. Ayleth crashed into the shattered remnants of the iron ward, and it scattered to nothing, vanishing in a last burst of spirit-splitting sound. Raw power coursed through Ayleth's limbs. She tore her left arm loose from its bindings and sat upright in the bed. One leg kicked free, and she reached down to tear off the last of her bonds.

"*Blood to blood,*" Nilly said and caught Ayleth by the hand. "*Bone to bone.*"

Ayleth screamed—

She climbs a narrow staircase. Innumerable steps leading round and round, higher and higher, as the walls close in around her. There are no windows, there are no doors. She squeezes on, desperate to reach the top, desperate to escape the crushing walls.

At last, up ahead, a doorway! Her heart leaps with relief.

Setting her jaw, she scrambles up the last turn of stairs, her shoulders scraping stone until she bursts through the opening and stands in a wide-open space.

The air feels thin up here. Five stone pillars surround her, shaped like four curling fingers and a curving thumb, all tipped in talon-like nails. Beyond those pillars she sees open sky and, far below, the endless expanse of a dark, dead forest. Cold wind whips through the stones, stinging her face, catching and snarling her long, loose hair.

A figure stands between two of the pillars. At the sight of him, a stone drops in her stomach. She knows him, or she believes she does, but when her mouth opens to cry out his name, she can't remember, and only silence emerges from her lips.

The figure starts as though he hears her. He turns. Shadows shroud his face from view, but her heart lurches, nonetheless. She knows him. She trusts him. She wants to go to him.

Starlight glints on the edge of the sword in his right hand.

"I'm so sorry," he says, taking three long strides toward her.

She tries again to speak, but cannot. And suddenly, terribly, her head burns as though wrapped in a band of fired iron. The pain sears through her skull, and she sees her blowing hair catch fire, blazing away in coiling strands of ember, ash, and smoke.

The man draws nearer. The light streaming from her own burning head falls upon his face, and she sees him clearly.

Prince Gerard gazes at her, his face stricken with sorrow.

"I'm so sorry, Ayleth," he says.

Then he swings his sword and, with a single blow, severs her head from her shoulders.

—and her chin hit the floor first, the rest of her body collapsing hard around her.

For a few breaths, she simply lay there, stunned.

Then her hands clutched at her throat. Her heart pounded wildly, and she felt the flow of blood gushing over her fingers. But no. No, there was no blood. Only the bandages over the witch's knife wound. Her trembling hands touched her jaw, her cheeks, ran slowly down her neck and wrappings. With a painful gasp, she drew in a breath of sweet air.

Then she growled and pushed herself up onto her elbows.

Shade! Shade, shade! Laranta barked inside her head, and Ayleth turned, teeth bared, to see Nilly slowly back away toward the door. The jade light—light of a Seer shade—

whirled in the centers of her pupils, bright and brilliant with ascendant power.

"*Blood to blood. Bone to bone,*" she said in that multitudinous voice that didn't belong to Nilly at all. "*The Queen will rise to claim her own. Blood to blood. Bone to bone. The Queen will rise to claim her own. Blood to bl—*"

"Stop!" Ayleth cried. With great effort, she pulled her knees beneath her and, drawing on Laranta's power, hauled herself to her feet. "Stop, please! You've got to tell me! Tell me the rest! What was that place? Why was I there? Why would the prince . . .?"

She didn't understand. Nothing about that vision made sense to her. But it had felt so real, so agonizingly real!

Nilly shook her head. Her little body stood framed in the doorway, and still her lips moved, never pausing as the words spilled out, "*Blood to blood. Bone to bone. The Queen will rise to claim her own. Blood to blood. Bone to bone.*"

"Wait!" Ayleth took a lunging step. The child screamed in her own voice and sprang out of the cottage into the dark yard. She would be off into the night in another moment, into the forest where Terryn prowled. If

Ayleth didn't catch her, didn't hide her, she would end up . . .

"Don't go!" Ayleth leapt to the door out into the yard.

Something swooped down from the darkness above.

Laranta roared to the forefront of Ayleth's mind, bursting with power and perception. Ayleth, giving over to her shade's impulses, threw herself flat to the ground, rolling. A large, feathered body hurtled into the place where she had been. A blade-like beak drove into the floor just inside the cottage doorway.

Ayleth pushed herself up and saw the raven. More than that, her shadow sight beheld the whirling vortex of spirits in the center of that small host. Two souls: shade and human.

The raven yanked its beak from the ground, uttering a hoarse and utterly unnatural shriek that tore at her ears. Behind Ayleth in the darkness, Nilly screamed.

The raven fixed a single eye upon Ayleth's face. With a powerful pulse of wings, it rose into the air and plunged straight for her eyes. Ayleth got her left arm up just in time, and the talons tore against the iron spike. Claws scrabbled to get around it, and the beak clacked a mere inch from her nose, lunging as though to impale her through the eye, straight to her brain. Though the body was small, the strength was far greater than anything Ayleth had prepared to meet. Laranta's magic burned inside her, but she struggled to hold back such primal force.

A human spirit looked out through the raven's eye, wild with merciless hatred.

CHAPTER 20

TERRYN GROUND HIS TEETH AS HE HASTENED THROUGH the forest, his mind flagellating his heart with self-reproach. Why had he stopped? Why hadn't he stayed on the Warpwitch's trail? He'd grazed her with poison, and while it wouldn't be enough to bring her down, it would certainly slow her, inhibiting her ability to control her shade. He should have armed his scorpiona with the Gentle Death and left di Ferosa where she lay on the cottage floor.

So why had he made it not even fifty paces from the cottage before he turned and ran back to kneel beside the fallen venatrix, his fingers trembling as he felt for a pulse?

He growled, frustrated, furious. Servants of Evander ought to work alone. He'd always thought so. The practice of hunt brothers and hunt sisters was overrated. Out in the field, to be concerned about a fellow hunter's welfare was to be distracted from the task at hand. If he'd only continued, he might have caught the witch, might have already ended her existence in this world.

Now her trail was old, and the day was fading fast. Terryn snapped his fingers, cupping a fistful of gleaming light to illuminate the shadows before him. Signs of the witch's flight were clear enough—she'd staggered and fallen again and again as the paralysis poison coursed through her limbs. But it wouldn't be enough to overwhelm her completely.

Her trail led him toward the Great Barrier. Did she intend to cross back over? Somehow Terryn doubted it. Once having escaped the Witchwood, no sane soul would willingly return.

It's her. It's her.

The thought pulsed in the back of his brain, inexplicable and yet undeniable.

It's her. And she has you. She has a hold on you—

"No!" Terryn growled. He staggered to a halt and leaned suddenly against a tree. He closed his eyes, his head twisting to one side. The scarred skin on his cheek seemed to tighten, to burn. "No . . . she doesn't have me. Not anymore."

Memories seared across his brain. A battle. Blood pouring down stone walls. Corpses marching out to face the living. Men and women taken, warped, turned into inhuman monsters.

A king in golden armor.

When the bloodshed was over, when all the curses were cast, when all the spirits of the dead had faded from this world, Terryn had crouched hidden beneath dead bodies, trembling lest anyone should find him. But someone had. Fendrel.

Fendrel had dug him out from among the corpses. Fendrel had taken his knife and . . .

Terryn caught hold of the tree but could not stop his knees from buckling. They hit the ground so hard that his bones jarred, and he only just kept from falling on his face. Pain lanced through his cheek. But it was just a memory, nothing but a memory.

Fendrel had saved him. Fendrel had purged his blood, carved Ylaire's sigil from his cheek. He was scarred, yes, but he was no longer cursed. The witch could no longer compel him, could no longer warp his body and his will. He was—

A scream tore through the forest.

Terryn jerked upright, turning to look over his shoulder, back in the direction he had just come. His eyes widened, staring into the shadows. When had it gotten so dark? How long had he knelt here beneath this tree? Where . . . where was . . .?

Another scream. Followed by a shrieking roar, wholly unnatural. A shade's voice.

"Damn!" Terryn snarled, pulling himself to his feet. "Damn, damn!" He took two running steps before nearly falling over with a wave of dizziness. His face spasmed, and he rubbed at the scar. His hand came away streaked with blood. *That's right,* he remembered. The Warpwitch had scratched him during their encounter in the cottage.

She'd scratched him and—

His ears split as another hideous shriek tore through the forest.

Terryn set off at a run, making for the cottage. With every step, the pain in his face decreased until he almost forgot it entirely.

Laranta roared. The sound burst from Ayleth's mouth, and she lashed out to catch the raven by its throat. It sliced at her hand, ripping it open, then made another lunge for her face. The tip of the beak snapped a mere breath from her eyeball, cutting her eyelashes.

Pure, unsuppressed power pulsed from the raven's core, surrounding Ayleth in a haze of Feral magic. The raven's body strained to bursting with the magnitude of force inside it.

It wrapped its talons around Ayleth's arm. With a rapid beating of wings, it took off, lifting Ayleth from the ground. She screamed, not in terror but in surprise, her legs kicking the air uselessly behind her. The bird rose up and up, over the trees. If it carried her too high and dropped her, she might not survive the fall. Laranta wasn't ascendant enough to offer complete protection.

With a wrench and a tearing of cruel talons through her sleeve and down her arm, Ayleth pulled herself free just as the raven broke through the uppermost foliage of the fringe forest. She fell hard, plunging back through branches and leaves, adding more scrapes and cuts to her collection. One flailing arm managed to catch hold of a branch, and she dangled thirty feet in the air. At any second, she expected that iron-hard beak to break her head open from behind.

"Laranta, give me your sight!" she cried, shifting fully to shadow vision. Drawing on her shade's strength, she caught hold of the branch with her other arm and heaved herself up. Her feet still dangled, but her hold was secure. She twisted in the air, her eyes peeled for any flash of shade spirit.

A blaze of Feral magic lit up the sky, through the interlacing branches above her head. Ayleth's eyes widened as the bird plunged straight toward her. With a terrified gasp, she did the only thing she could think of in the fraction of an instant she had to decide: She let go.

Her fall carried her faster than the raven's approach. She slammed through branches, calling on Laranta's strength to shield her bones. The ground seemed to rise up and slam her body, knocking the air out of her lungs.

The raven landed in the ground just beside her face, only a fraction off from her eye. Its beak embedded into the earth so deep, it fluttered as it tried to pull free.

Ayleth gasped for a breath that would not come. She couldn't wait. Her lungs bursting with the need for air, she forced her body into motion. One arm slammed down, catching the raven by a beating wing. It yanked its beak free and slashed at her, cutting into her upper arm, then lunged at her face. Ayleth struggled to maintain her hold, struggled to catch a breath of air. She flung up one arm to defend herself as unsuppressed shade power blasted her with fury.

Suddenly, a burst of sound—not a raven's croaking cry, but human. A woman's despairing voice crying out in short, sharp agony.

A shudder passed through the raven's body, reverberating through Ayleth's arm.

The raven fell away, landing in a heap of feathers and

talons, its eyes round with shock and horror. The hilt of a quivering bone knife protruded from between its wings.

Dragging a breath into her lungs, Ayleth pushed herself up onto her elbows. Her shadow sight flaring in her eyes, she looked across the cottage clearing and saw Terryn standing just within the ringing trees. His arm was still extended from his well-aimed throw.

"What have you done?" Ayleth breathed. Then she bolted upright, crying, "What have you done?"

A violent death—he'd dealt a violent death! Again! Scrambling to her knees, Ayleth gazed down in horror at the shade-taken. The pain of its death radiated out from it in a spirit aura that was nearly blinding. She thrust out a hand to protect her gaze from that glare, knowing that she had moments, mere moments before the shade inside that dying host launched free, empowered to search out a new body.

And there were all those eye-torn animals in their cages surrounding the cottage, just waiting to be possessed.

Ayleth yanked her Detrudos pipe from its sheath. "*Laranta! Help me!*" she cried, and blew the drone into life.

Her wolf shade leaped forward in her mind, and brute strength flowed through her, supporting every note she played. The Song of Binding filled the air, reaching out to wrap around the dying bird.

Just as Ayleth played the first notes of the melody, the shade leapt free from its host body. It flung itself against the ensnaring song in a burst of magic so strong it made Ayleth gasp and stagger. She almost dropped the pipes, almost lost the song. But Laranta supported her from inside, and she braced herself and continued playing, moving into the first variation.

She felt the yawning opening of the Haunts. Eager to devour, eager to reclaim that which it had lost. She felt dark, churning chaos overhead.

The shade shrieked and flung itself with redoubled force against the spell. Ayleth played a second variation on the melody, binding the shade fast. She needed to switch to the Song of Expulsion. But first . . .

First, she must search. First, she must find Fiola.

"*Help me, Laranta,*" she said. "*Is there another spirit?*"

Laranta's shade senses reached out, sinking into the lashing tangle of terror that was the Feral spirit caught in the song spell. It had no shape, no substance, only roaring rage and fear, pulsing so hot, it threatened to burn away the Detrudos song. Ayleth played a third variation, this one more complex than the last. She feared her fingers would stumble, would miss notes or play a sour trill. But she maintained the song.

Laranta's vision revealed what she sought: a human spirit tangled up with the shade. A small, gleaming orb of silver amid the snarl of wrath.

"*Fiola,*" Ayleth called in spirit even as her physical body continued to play. "*Fiola, I see you. Can you hear me?*"

The silver orb struggled, trying to escape the snare of the Feral shade that held it so fast. But the poor mortal soul was utterly caught in the parasitic force which had overtaken her.

If she was a witch, there would be no saving her. Ayleth could never undo the bindings that soldered a witch's soul to its possessing shade. But . . . but there was a chance. Oma Githa's low magic had formed the connection between the shade and the raven. It could be that Fiola's soul had been drawn into this host against her will.

If so, she might yet be saved.

But how? Ayleth would have to weave yet another level of complexity into this song, mingling the Binding and the Expulsion spells simultaneously. Her skills were stretched to the limit already, simply holding this wrathful shade in place. The draw of the Haunts was intense. If she loosened the Binding for a moment, she knew the shade would be immediately drawn into the realm of its origin, dragging Fiola with it.

Ayleth moved her hands along the recorder, trying a complex variation that would blend the Binding and the Expulsion into one. She could feel the shape of it in her head, could almost, *almost* hear what it was meant to be. But her fingers faltered. She couldn't play like this! She hadn't the skill, hadn't the training.

The shade, sensing her lack of control, threw itself against the Binding. It almost broke through—and it screamed as it realized that to succeed would mean to be lost to the Haunts. The gaping void loomed closer, reaching down from its own strange dimension, eager for its prey. Only Ayleth's song kept the shade from its ultimate doom.

Her strength faltered. Even Laranta shuddered inside her. Ayleth despaired, realizing she would lose. She could not hold onto the mortal spirit, not a moment more . . .

Music flared. Bright and brilliant, winding through her own Detrudos song, a second song appeared. A new melody, deep and throbbing, a melody Ayleth had never before heard. It brushed against her song, softly at first. Then it wound itself tight, like a lover's embrace, and the two became one.

Ayleth did not open her physical eyes. To do so would be to become distracted, and she could not afford that now. All of her being concentrated on maintaining the Binding, on keeping the two spirits in this world. As she played, the new song slowly severed the ties between that writhing shade and the silver orb that was Fiola. The new song caught Fiola's soul, drawing it away.

A deep voice murmured, speaking spirit to spirit: *"It's all right. I've got her now."*

Immediately, Ayleth modulated the Binding into the Expulsion. The Feral shade gave a last shriek, desperately grasping at this world. But it could catch nothing. The Haunts pulled, and the shade whirled up and away, still screaming until the gates to that other realm snapped shut.

Ayleth let her Detrudos drop. The Expulsion spell broke into a million frayed ends, sparkling as they withered away in an instant. Drawing a shuddering breath, Ayleth opened her eyes.

Terryn stood only an arm's length away from her, his legs braced, his forehead gleaming with sweat. He played his Detrudos pipe, the song touching the spirit but silent to mortal ears. Ayleth, looking with shadow sight, could see how gently he held Fiola's sundered spirit in the lines of his strange melody.

She'd never encountered anyone who played their pipes as Venator du Balafre did.

Before the song ended, before the soul vanished, a little figure stepped from the shadows of the cottage doorway. Nilly du Bucheron, shadow-light gleaming in her eyes, rushed forward, standing between Terryn and Ayleth. She lifted one hand, reaching up into that silver soul. It hovered between her fingers, and with the eyes of her spirit, Ayleth saw the child's face lit with a soft glow like moonlight.

"*Mama!*" Nilly said, her voice a strange mingling of spirit and mortality. "*Mama, don't leave me!*"

The spirit answered. Its voice was so faint, Ayleth could not discern the words, but the girl did. Two tears escaped through her lashes and fell from her chin. The silver orb in her hand reached out threads of soul and caught those droplets before they landed on the ground. Clutching them close so that they seemed like two brilliant diamonds in Ayleth's vision, the orb suddenly shot away, up through the trees and away into the night sky.

Ayleth tipped her head back, watching Fiola's soul streak higher and higher, like a shooting star streaking backwards. Then it was gone.

Terryn's song faded. He lowered his Detrudos pipes. With a shuddering gasp, he fell to his knees.

And Ayleth watched as the shade-taken child knelt beside the broken body of the raven, weeping and stroking its feathers.

CHAPTER 21

AYLETH TURNED ON TERRYN, HER SOUL JUMPING with anger and gratitude and confusion all mingled into a single painful and nameless emotion. He had left her trapped under the iron ward. He had accused her of collusion with witches. He had treated her like the enemy.

And he had saved her life yet again.

"Why did you do that?" she demanded, spitting the words in a sharp whisper so as not to draw Nilly's attention. "Why did you . . . help me?"

It wasn't the question she'd intended to ask. It forced its way from her lips and now hung in the air between them. He could have let the raven kill her, after all. He could have stood back and let the monster solve the problem of her presence right then and there. No one would have been the wiser.

A dangerous expression flashed across his face as he met her eyes. "I am a servant of Saint Evander," he answered in a deep growl of a voice. "We take care of our own." Then he pointed at the body of the raven. "This is the host? Of Fiola du Bucheron?"

Ayleth nodded, looking from him to the monstrous bird and the little girl crouched in tears over its body.

"Why did you insist on saving her soul?" Terryn demanded. "She killed Nane."

"She was . . . she was not a witch." Ayleth shrugged. "It's up to the Goddess to judge the dead. Not us."

She didn't speak aloud the answer that rested forefront in her mind: *She was only trying to protect her daughter. From Nane. From us.*

She didn't have to say it. Her shade-augmented senses detected the tension in Terryn's spirit as he too looked at the child and the raven. As he realized who this girl was. What she was. What she carried inside her.

Realized what the law of Evander required of his servants.

Ayleth stepped to Nilly's side and crouched. The girl rocked back and forth over the fallen bird, stroking its feathers with her small fingers and murmuring, "Mama! Mama! Mama!" The profound presence of her ascendant shade surrounded her in an aura of magic.

Putting out a hesitant hand, Ayleth rested her fingers lightly on Nilly's bowed shoulder. "We must . . . I must . . ." She licked her dry lips. She ought to bag the bird up and carry it back to Milisendis for dissection and inspection.

Instead, she said, "I must bury the body. Shall I dig a grave, Nilly?"

The girl wiped her nose and nodded, tears still falling down her soft round face. She sat down crosslegged in the dirt, and Ayleth lifted the bird and rested it in her lap. The girl cradled the broken remains to her heart, stroking the head softly.

Ayleth had nothing but her knife with which to dig in

the soil, but that, combined with the strength of Laranta in her hands, should be sufficient. She looked around the cottage clearing and discovered a bit of what might pass for a garden nearby. The soil there would be softer. Her bleeding arm protested, but she ignored it as best she could and soon managed to dig a hole deep enough for a raven.

All the while she worked, she expected Terryn to protest, to point out all the ways in which she broke protocol, to scold her for wasting his time. But he held his peace. When Ayleth dared look his way, his gaze was fixed upon Nilly, studying her closely, his expression cold and calculating.

She shuddered from the inside out.

When the grave was ready, Ayleth approached Nilly, her hands out. She didn't have to say a word. Nilly handed her the raven but remained weeping where she sat. Though Ayleth motioned for her to come, she would not join her at the graveside. So Ayleth returned to the kitchen garden, gently lowered the bird into its final resting place, and slid dirt over its wings. She sniffed and dashed at her face before a tear could escape, then smoothed out the grave mound and patted it down, determined no foxes or other scavengers of the forest would find it. As she worked, her lips murmured a prayer she had heard not too long ago:

"May the Mother receive you, who hath called you, and may the heavenly spirits conduct you to the Gates of Life. GoddessHeart have mercy. GoddessSoul have mercy. GoddessHead have mercy."

When she finished, she stood a few moments in silence, simply looking down at the grave. Then, with a last sniff and a short shake of her head, she turned around.

Her heart jumped in surprise.

Venator Terryn knelt on the ground with Nilly du Bucheron in his lap, his arms wrapped around her. By the gleam of the pale moon rising over the trees, Ayleth saw little Nilly's face resting on the venator's shoulder. Tears stained the child's cheeks but no longer flowed. Her eyes were wide, round, and peaceful, and one little hand patted his shoulder, as though it were she who offered him comfort.

It was the strangest, most horrible sight.

Ayleth rose slowly, her feet braced in the dirt over the

bird's grave. Her shadow vision watched the roiling tension in Terryn's soul as he leaned his head against Nilly's, his scarred cheek pressed into her tangle of hair. With a flick of shadow-light, his gaze moved to meet Ayleth's.

"You go on," he said, his voice low and husky. "Go on back to Hollen. Find Venator Kephan. I'll . . . I'll meet you there soon."

Ayleth stared at him. She heard his words, but for a moment she could not answer, could not even breathe.

"You . . . can't," she gasped.

His arms tightened fractionally around the little girl. "There is nothing else to be done."

Ayleth's mind whirled into a storm of half thoughts, none of which could fully form. The child was doomed to the Haunts. Bound to her shade, destined to follow it to its final damnation when her body inevitably gave out. Today, tomorrow, next year . . . or sixty years from now. Whenever it happened, she would face that inescapable destiny. Her only chance was the pain of death, a violent enough death to allow for separation from that damning inborn spirit.

They could wait, though. Why did it have to be now? They could wait a while, a few years at least. Give her time. But . . . would it be any easier to kill an older child? An adult? One who knew what was happening, who fought back? Seer shades were not naturally violent, but who knew what one could do if driven to desperation? It would be hard enough to control it now, while its host was so small, so vulnerable.

But . . . but . . .

"Are you ready for all this role requires of you, all the deaths you must deal in the name of the Goddess?"

This was Evander's law. This was the sacred teaching, the transcribed will of the Divine.

"Goddess," Ayleth whispered, a prayer, a plea, a fountain of desperation rising from the depths of her soul. But she could not find words in her language to express her need. She could say only, "Goddess. Goddess . . ."

Terryn watched her. He stood, hoisting the girl up with him, her little arms wrapped around his neck. Had she fallen asleep on his shoulder? His breathing came rough and ragged, and his eyes flashed again, like cold lightning.

"Do you want to do this yourself?" he demanded. "Are you venatrix enough to see this through?"

She had glimpsed the Haunts. Every time the gates opened, she'd caught visions of that horror, that chaos, that crushing abyss. She'd heard the echo of the tormented souls screaming within.

The pain of fire was temporary. The Haunts were eternity.

She looked at the girl, telling herself that she knew what was right. Telling herself that she had the will to accomplish the Goddess's purpose on this earth. Telling herself that true compassion meant inflicting pain where need dictated.

"Goddess," Ayleth breathed.

A resolve like steel came over her spirit, so firm, so sharp, even Laranta trembled. She faced the venator and spoke clearly, without dropping her voice: "No."

Terryn's eyes narrowed to slits. "What do you think you will do with her? You can't hide her. You can't send her away. There is nowhere you can take her where she will be safe. She carries her own worst enemy inside her.

Death is her only hope for salvation."

"Maybe you're right," Ayleth said. She flexed her fingers, and shade magic surged up inside her, more and more power, pushing the boundaries of ascendancy. The wolf in her head howled, and Ayleth bared her teeth. "But I won't let you take her."

Terryn took a step back, then another. His shadow sight saw the mounting magic in her soul. "Do you realize what you're doing, Venatrix di Ferosa?"

Ayleth lowered her head, her hands clenching into fists. "Yes."

She took a step.

Sudden movement to her left drew her eye. Ayleth looked, almost against her will, just as a figure emerged through the trees. He wore a red hood over his head, and his right arm was upraised, scorpiona trained on Terryn.

"Stop right there, du Balafre," said Venator Kephan. "Put the girl down and back away. No one needs to get hurt."

CHAPTER 22

IT WAS THE GENTLE DEATH. FROM HER ANGLE, Ayleth could just see the black fletching on the dart Kephan aimed at Terryn's face.

Terryn stared at Kephan, his eyes rounding. He opened his mouth but could not speak, surprise stealing his words. He, too, must have seen the black feathers on the dart, for his arms tightened around the girl. She lifted her head from his shoulder and peered round at the group of them standing in the yard.

"What . . . what are you doing?" Ayleth demanded. Though only an instant before she had been prepared to charge Terryn with all the force Laranta had to offer, her heart jolted at the sight of that dart aimed between his eyes. One small prick, and Terryn would die.

Kephan only repeated, "Put the girl down. Carefully. And back away."

Confusion clamored in Ayleth's head, making her dizzy. Would Kephan truly kill Terryn to save the girl? But why? Had he turned heretic? Or was he . . .?

Terryn turned sideways, angling himself so that his shoulder and arm shielded Nilly from the Gentle Death. But he didn't put her down.

"So, what, Kephan?" he said, his voice a rough growl. "Are you on *her* side then? Are you both turning against the teachings of our saint?"

At Terryn's accusation, Kephan's gaze flicked to Ayleth. He saw her brace herself, rising on the balls of her feet in preparation for a lunge. Swinging his scorpiona, he trained the Gentle Death on her next. "Back away, di Ferosa," he said, indicating with a jerk of his head that she should move to stand beside Terryn. "I don't want anyone to get hurt. All I want is the child."

Her fingernails digging into her palms, Ayleth moved with care, shifted closer to Terryn, though still not within arm's reach. Terryn adjusted his own angle, trying to keep Nilly away from Ayleth while simultaneously protecting her from Kephan's aim. His teeth flashed in a grimace.

"It was you, wasn't it, Kephan," he snarled. "It was you who closed the Great Barrier after Nane died. And did you kill him too? Because of . . . of what he intended toward this child?"

"I would never hurt Nane," Kephan answered, each word tight and tense from his lips. "And I never went to the . . . I never saw the . . ." He choked, the cords of his throat straining. His face contorted in a flash of pain, and for an instant, his scorpiona arm drooped. At a quick step from Terryn, he yanked it back up. "I never saw the Great Barrier!"

Laranta snarled suddenly in Ayleth's head. *Wrong,* she said. *Wrong, wrong, wrong.*

Her shade's awareness sharpened her own perceptions. Ayleth looked more closely at Kephan, looked beyond her mortal vision and into the world of spirit. She saw Kephan's soul, twisted, writhing in flashes of pain. His shade was ascendant, called up for the hunt, but there were no song spells binding it. Instead, a weird, wrong thread of dark magic wound tight around both shade and mortal souls, twisting them into unnatural contortions.

Ayleth, using her shade senses, latched her gaze on that thread of wrong magic, following it back to where it implanted in Kephan's body. Her shadow sight saw what her mortal vision could not—a blazing sigil carved into his cheek. An implantation of blood and curse, burning bright in the spirit world with ugly, scorching Anathema magic.

Kephan was not under his own control.

"The Warpwitch," she gasped. Then she spread her hands, trying to draw Kephan's eye away from Terryn and Nilly. "Venator du Tam!" she called out. "You don't want to do this. This isn't you!"

The venator's face twisted in a pained facsimile of a smile. A half smile, for the cheek in which the sigil blazed didn't move. "I don't," he said, shaking his head. "You're right. But I . . . I have to!" He swung the scorpiona back at Terryn, his jaw set, his finger snug against the trigger, ready to squeeze. "Put her down and walk away. Slowly."

"No." Terryn's voice was rough as stone. "You're cursed, Kephan." So, he'd seen and recognized the implanted sigil too. "Ylaire's got a hold on you."

Kephan's neck twisted, first one way, then the other, and his jaw worked, strained. Then he snapped his face back, his eyes focused and blazing with too-bright light. A strange rippling moved under his skin, like some living thing pressing against his cheek from the inside, then crawling down his throat into his torso. His scorpiona arm shook harder, and he had to raise his left arm to brace it. "Put her down," he said again. "Put her down, put her down, put her down, put her *dooooarrrrrrgh!*" He broke off in an inhuman screech, his mouth wide, his head shaking wildly.

Ayleth lunged—not for Kephan, but at Terryn. She caught his arm and, using her shade strength, yanked him and Nilly to the ground. She felt rather than saw the dart pass through the air over their heads, missing Terryn by a breath.

Nilly screamed, but Terryn had caught himself to keep

from landing with his full weight on top of her, and rolled to one side, one arm still holding her close. The girl continued screaming as Terryn pushed upright. His gaze met Ayleth's for an instant as she sprang into a crouch.

Ayleth turned, her long braid whipping back over her shoulder. Venator Kephan bent double, his hands tearing at his own head. She watched the same change work through him as she'd witnessed in the bear yesterday morning. Anathema magic flared out from his core, poured from his nostrils, his eyes, the ends of his fingers, tearing through his flesh. His skeleton shifted, twisted, grew. From his curved spine, terrible protrusions of bone tore through skin, their ragged ends dripping with his own blood. His arms lengthened, the bones of his fingers stretching out into long, razor-sharp claws. His jaw disjointed, sagging to his chest to make room for a cage of sharp fangs.

Suddenly, he stood up straight, his arms outflung, his head thrown back as he bellowed his pain to the sky. Then he snapped his face forward with a predatory intensity, fastening his gaze on Terryn and Nilly.

Ayleth's hand went for her darts. But she was

unarmed. The hedgewitch had taken all her weapons and piled them on the table, and now they were strewn across the floor. She had no poisons.

But she had Laranta.

Kephan crouched, his bone talons tearing into the soil. With a roar he sprang, the power of his Feral shade propelling him across the space. His elongated arms extended, reaching for Terryn, who pulled Nilly to him and turned to shield her. Claws gouging for his face passed through Terryn's hair as he twisted his head away.

Then Ayleth crashed into Kephan, knocking him off course. Laranta's power pulsed through her arms, which she wrapped around the older venator's torso. They landed hard, and Ayleth only just had the nimbleness to spring free before getting caught in a tangle of limbs and claws and spines. She found her balance, her feet skidding beneath her, then threw herself at Kephan's head, her arm drawn back for a punch. She had no clear plan, but somewhere in the back of her brain she knew that if she could knock Kephan unconscious, subduing the mortal host, she could then find her poisons and subdue the power inside.

That warped face snarled up at her in a flash of fangs. One arm swiped in an arc, blocked her blow, and caught her in the side. Claws tore great gashes in her cloak even as she flew through the air. She landed hard, the wind knocked from her lungs. Laranta's magic spiked in her head, preventing her bones from being broken, but in that space of time, as she struggled to draw a breath, she could not force her body into action.

The monster Kephan shook his head, spattering foaming spittle from his peeled-back lips. Huge arms reached out, and claws tore into the soil as he pulled himself toward her. He reared up, fingers splayed, and Ayleth flung herself into a roll just before those claws could tear straight through her chest and rip out her heart. Instead, they dug into the dirt, gouging out a great clump of earth.

Ayleth rotated swiftly, trying to get her limbs under her. The monster moved fast, snatching at her head. She was just fast enough to avoid being skewered through the ear, but one long claw caught in her braid, pinning her to the ground. She caught hold of that hand, applying Laranta's strength in an attempt to break it at the wrist.

But Kephan's Feral was highly ascendant, and Laranta was still partially bound by suppressing spell songs, preventing her from accessing her full range of force. Ayleth screamed.

A flare of white light burned across the darkness like a bolt of lightning. It struck the monster straight in the chest, ripped it off its feet, and carried it several yards through the air to smack against a tree trunk. Ayleth's head jerked to one side as the claw tangled in her braid tore free, and her hair came undone, falling over the ground and her face. Her eyes, dazzled with the glare of light and magic, stared blindly in the direction the monster had flown.

She felt rather than saw Terryn's approach, the pound of his boots on the ground as he hastened to her side. He crouched and grabbed her arm, his deep voice demanding, "Are you alive? Venatrix, are you alive?"

"Yes, I'm alive!" she growled, allowing him to haul her to her feet. His fingers on her arm were hot enough to burn through her sleeve if he held on too long. Magic pulsed from his center out through his shoulders, down into the palms of his hands. "Warn me next time you're going to let loose like that!"

He didn't answer. The moment she was upright, he let her go, and she almost went sprawling again. Catching herself and giving her head a quick shake, she hurried after Terryn as he approached the fallen form of Kephan. The older venator lay in a heap of misshapen limbs, curls of smoke rising from his body.

"Is he . . . did you kill him?"

Terryn held his glowing hands up, curling his fingers tight. "It shouldn't have—"

Before he could finish, a savage yell ripped the air behind them. Ayleth and Terryn both whirled to see a second horrible shape rush out from the trees. As with Kephan, its arms were elongated and terrible spines burst from its bleeding back. The bearded chin gaped to make room for the too-large teeth. A snarl of Anathema magic surrounded it, bright and discordant, a powerful curse which, like Kephan's, was anchored to a sigil planted in the man's cheek.

The monster tore up the ground as it ran, making straight for Nilly du Bucheron.

The child stood in the middle of the yard, screaming,

her shade spirit whirling about her but unable to offer defense against the oncoming creature. Terryn lifted his hand and took a shot, pure light beaming from his palm in a powerful bolt of energy. He cried out in pain, his arms spasming with the burn of magic, and lost control of the blast. It went over the monster's head, striking a tree so hard, the trunk broke in two, and the upper limbs crashed down hard.

The monster lunged, eluding the falling branches, and snatched Nilly up in a close embrace, pressing her to its misshapen chest. The girl shrieked in terror.

Ayleth, not yet steady on her feet, took a single step after the monster as it turned to flee back into the woods. Before she could take the next step, she hit the ground hard, one leg pulled out from under her. Twisting her torso to look behind her, she found her ankle caught by long, claw-tipped fingers. Kephan's warped face snarled at her even as he struggled to pull himself upright, his skin still smoking from the magic blast.

A scream of shocked surprise tore from Ayleth's throat. Terryn, already in pursuit of the second monster and Nilly, turned to look back, his eyes blazing with shadow-light, his hands throbbing with magic. He staggered, hesitated.

"Go!" Ayleth shouted. They couldn't let that fiend take Nilly.

His face hardening, Terryn whirled and ran on.

Ayleth twisted in Kephan's grasp. He dragged her toward his leering jaws, but she raised her other foot and kicked with all the strength Laranta could give her. Kephan, still reeling from the blast he'd taken, shrieked and let go, giving Ayleth enough time to scramble back and get to her feet.

Then the monster was up and barreling for her. Ayleth turned and ran. She did not have access to enough of Laranta's power to end this fight. Her shade senses sparking, she felt the pursuing creature close behind her. She didn't need to look back to sense how quickly he closed the gap between them.

Moving on pure survival instinct, she jinked in mid-stride, altering her course to the cottage rather than the forest. Kephan, unprepared for her maneuver, lumbered forward several strides, giving her a chance to gain a few steps.

She ran for the cottage and leapt for the roof. Her fingers caught in the thatch and tore out two great handfuls before finding a solid hold. Hoisting her legs up, she climbed to the pinnacle of the roof. For the moment at least, she had higher ground.

Kephan, less nimble in his cursed form, rammed into the cottage wall. The whole structure shook.

Her weapons. Ayleth's mind fixed on a single thought. Her weapons, her darts. They were down below, scattered across the cottage floor. If she could find a Feral paralysis, it should work on Kephan, curse or no curse. But she had to get inside.

A hideous howl, and twisted hands latched hold of the roof edge. Kephan pulled himself up, claws tearing through the thatch as he climbed.

Ayleth sucked in a breath and skidded down the far slope of the roof, falling to the ground, her bones jarred. Seeing the side door standing wide, she scrambled on her hands and skidding feet, propelling herself through the opening into the dark cottage interior.

Thatching fell inside like rain. Overhead, Kephan's claws tore an opening, letting shafts of moonlight spear to the floor. By the gleam of that pale light, Ayleth spied one of her small quivers.

"Goddess!" she gasped in desperate prayer and leaped to snatch it up.

Then she was falling out through the front door just as part of the roof caved in and Kephan dropped from above. Ayleth almost lost her footing but managed to keep on her feet as she hurtled across the cottage yard, making for the forest.

Only as she plunged into the deeper shadows of the trees did she remember: She didn't have her scorpiona. To deliver this poison, she'd have to get up close.

"*Laranta, get ready,*" she said.

Laranta growled with cruel delight. *Hunt! Hunt, hunt!*

She pushed her way into the trees, deeper and deeper. She could hear Kephan behind her and knew his shade-heightened senses would lead him directly to her. As she ran, she grabbed two darts from the quiver, holding them up to glimpse which poison she'd grabbed. Feral! Somehow, against all odds, she'd grabbed Feral darts. The Goddess must have heard her prayer.

She had to slow down to uncork the tips. Otherwise,

she risked pricking herself and falling paralyzed and powerless. But those few slowed steps were enough to let the warped Kephan close the distance between them. She could hear his breath pulse savagely through his gaping mouth.

Pressing her back to a thick tree, she held up both darts in her fists, poisoned ends out and ready. "Goddess," she breathed one last time. Let divine grace shine on her just once more tonight.

Here! Laranta cried.

Ayleth whirled out from behind her tree, face to face with the curse-warped monster. He recoiled for just an instant—time enough to let her spring straight at his face. Laranta's power hurled her forward, and before Kephan could dodge or knock her away, she plunged both darts into his neck, one on either side.

A huge hand caught her by the fabric on her shoulder, one claw tearing into her skin. The monster flung her into the dirt, straight down, so hard that her spine would have shattered if not for Laranta's protections. With darts protruding from his neck, the warped Kephan loomed over her. Even with two doses of poison in his system, the curse drove him on, and his ascendant shade empowered him. He planted one palm in the center of her chest, pinning her in place. His huge teeth clattered together as he bit for her face.

Ayleth managed to get both hands up, to catch hold of the monster by its upper and lower jaws. His razor teeth cut into her fingers, and blood flowed, but she applied Laranta's strength, preventing him from closing his mouth and cutting her fingers off at the knuckles. He leaned in closer, closer, his breath hot on her face, intending to rip her head from her body.

"*Laranta!*" Ayleth screamed.

Her wolf shade burst forward in her brain, straining against the suppressing spells. She struggled frantically, and Ayleth screamed and screamed as blood poured down her hands, her arms, into her face. Those slavering jaws pressed nearer, nearer.

Then, with a suddenness like lightning, the monster slumped, fell. The poison took effect, paralyzing body and soul alike. Kephan's misshapen form collapsed on top of Ayleth, heavy and horrible. She could do nothing but lie there beneath it for some moments.

Tears fell from the corners of her eyes, and her hands shuddered as she pulled them free of those sharp teeth.

The curse binding Kephan loosened, faded. Ayleth felt the change in his body as the warping mutations shifted back into the ordinary shape of a man. A bloody, battered man.

CHAPTER 23

TERRYN SNATCHED A DART FROM THE QUIVERS across his chest and armed his scorpiona as he ran. He couldn't tell what kind of shade this second monster carried, if any, but he knew from the warping effect on its body that it must be under the Warpwitch's control. Which meant she was somewhere near. The poison he'd grazed her with earlier would have slowed down her physical body, motivating her to send these servants in her place. But if he could find her, if he could kill her, her curses on these unfortunate men would break.

Poor Kephan, implanted with the sigil of Ylaire di Jocosa! How long had Kephan not been his own master? Since they parted ways that afternoon? Or since before Terryn came to Milisendis?

Terryn shook his head and redoubled his pace. He had no time to dwell on these questions now. He could hear the monster ahead of him, crashing through the foliage. It was making for the Great Barrier, carrying the little girl in its arms. The monster must have taken her at the bidding of its mistress, but what the Warpwitch wanted with Nilly du Bucheron was anyone's guess.

It didn't matter. He had to catch them. He had to save the child. He had to save her soul . . .

His shadow vision straining, he saw the pulse of three spirits ahead of him. Two mortals, one shade. And the glaring, searing snare of the curse.

The monster stopped. It had reached the strip of clearing between the fringe forest and the Great Barrier. Turning, it snarled at Terryn as he burst through the trees and into the moonlit stretch of open ground. Little Nilly, clutched under the monster's arm and tucked close to its body, saw Terryn and screamed, stretching out one small hand to him.

"Let her go!" Terryn cried.

The monster opened wide its gaping mouth, flashing its knife-like teeth. With a bolt of horror straight to his heart, Terryn recognized him—Farmer Foulke! The man whose wife was possessed earlier that day, the man who had come running to Kephan and Terryn for help. The Warpwitch must have implanted him with her sigil. She may even have done it before he came to Kephan and Terryn, may have used him to lure them off their path, to separate them.

His poisons would be useless against an untaken foe. Though he didn't want to hurt the cursed man, Terryn drew his knife.

"Let her go," he called again. "I know you're in there, Foulke. I know you can hear me. I don't want to hurt you, but you have to fight this curse."

The monster shook its head, a long sinuous tongue protruding from between its teeth.

"Fight it, man! Fight her hold on you!" Terryn urged. "Let the girl go."

With a high-pitched shriek, the monster went down onto its clawed right hand, still clutching Nilly in its left arm, and lumbered toward Terryn with alarming speed. Terryn braced himself, waiting until the last moment before he darted to one side. Unable to stop its momentum, the monster careened past him, and Terryn crouched, twisted, slashing at its leg with his knife as it went by. His blow connected; Terryn felt the blade cut through sinew and muscle.

The ground shuddered as the monster crashed to its knees. Nilly cried out in a thin voice. Gnashing its teeth, the warped man swung out its free arm in a wide arc, connecting with Terryn and sending him tumbling to earth.

Propelling itself with its uninjured leg, the monster hurtled at him. Terryn barely had time to get his left arm up. Those long bone claws clashed against the iron spike with a grating ring. Terryn found himself face to face with Nilly. She stared down at him from the warped man's grasp, her face tear-streaked, her eyes round.

Terryn saw how those monstrous claws pressed her close, saw how easily they could kill her. One small flick of its wrist, and her head would roll.

He had to act. Now, while he had the opening.

With a curse that was almost a prayer, Terryn twisted his left arm, knocking aside the monster's scrabbling claws. His right arm shot out, and he drove the blade of his knife up under the warped man's sternum, straight to his heart. A deathblow.

For an instant, the blazing sigil implanted in Foulke's cheek flared bright as a sun, dazzling Terryn's eyes. The next instant, it snuffed out completely, leaving the world black as pitch.

The warped man fell, dropping Nilly from his lifeless arms as he collapsed in ruin.

With a strangled gasp, Terryn swept the girl up in his arms. Her skinny arms trembling, she clung to his neck, weeping as she pressed her face into his shoulder. Terryn stood, staggered to catch his balance, and backed away from the monster. He couldn't tear his eyes from that horrible wreckage of humanity. As he watched, the mortal soul inside worked itself free from the fraying snare of the Anathema curse and flew off into the night sky, leaving the monster-man's husk behind.

Terryn's chest heaved with labored breaths. His arms tightened around Nilly's small body even as she clung to him. He'd never killed an untaken man before. He'd never realized he was capable of such a thing.

"I had no choice," he whispered. But the words tasted false on his tongue.

Nilly sobbed, her voice finally breaking through the pounding of blood in his ears. Terryn shifted her in his arms, cradling her close to his heart, and turned her to be certain she could not see the dead man. "It's all right," he murmured in her ear. "It's all right now. You're safe. Hush, hush."

His stomach twisted with sickening dread at every word he spoke. For now, he realized, he had to deal with her. With the inborn child doomed to the Haunts unless he took action.

"Hush," he whispered, staring off into the darkness of the forest, staring hard as though he could somehow discern in those shadows some path, some alternate way. Something, anything he might do other than the duty weighing down upon his soul. "Hush."

The little girl tucked her face close to his chest. Her

body shuddered, but her sobs quieted.

"She trusts you, you know. She believes you are her friend."

Terryn's limbs froze. Not with fear, not with surprise. They simply . . . froze. As though he'd turned to stone.

The scars on his cheek blazed with sudden pain.

A figure moved through the trees, swaying heavily with each step. She left the shadows behind, and moonlight shone on her face. A hard, square face, one half of it slack and numb where paralysis poison had touched it. Drool poured from her sagging lips, but one side curled in a vicious smile.

"It's such a shame, sweet boy," she said, slurring each word. "Those Evanderians have turned you into their weapon. A murderer of children! I had far better plans for you and that strong frame of yours."

Terryn tried to speak. He tried to turn away, to put his body between Nilly and the witch. He tried to raise his scorpiona, still armed with the Anathema dart. But he could only stand where he was, holding Nilly, as the Warpwitch slowly made her way to him.

"I see they tried to carve out my sigil," she said,

waving a hand to indicate his cheek. "A good attempt! But they underestimated how deep my curses penetrate and how well I can hide them when I wish. They've only managed to mar your pretty face. Such a shame! Such a shame."

Terryn's heart shuddered. He remembered now, suddenly and horribly. He remembered yesterday afternoon, approaching Venator Kephan in the ruins of Cró Ular. Kephan had stepped into a ward trap the Warpwitch had set in place, and when Terryn drew near, he'd walked into the same trap. Their sigils activated, they had obeyed the compulsion of the ward: Walk away from Cró Ular and forget what they had seen.

Only now did he remember. Now, as his curse once more awakened.

His heart pounded thunderously in his throat. He was her slave. Just like Kephan. Just like poor Foulke.

"I don't let go of my toys so easily," the Warpwitch said, standing before him, wearing the stolen body of Foulke's wife. Her mad gaze studied his face with interest. She raised one hand to caress his cheek where her sigil burned beneath his scars. "I have use for you still, pretty boy. I always knew you would serve me, somehow."

She took Nilly from his arms. The child cried out a thin little "No!" and tried to hold onto Terryn's jerkin. But the Warpwitch ground her teeth and yanked her back.

"Come to me, little one," she said, spitting the words through her poison-numbed lips. "He would only burn you and drive out that beautiful spirit you carry. I have better plans in mind for you. You're going to help me, child. Together we will restore this land. We will restore our kind to their rightful place of rule, and no Evanderian will ever dare raise a hand against you again!"

He could not let her get away. Summoning all the will he still possessed, Terryn jerked his head to one side. But even that single motion increased the burn in his cheek. The curse flared so hot, he felt as though the skin on his face would melt away and the skull beneath would blacken and crumble to dust. With a cry he fell to his knees, clutching at his face, clutching at the burn.

The witch crouched over him, Nilly still in her arms. "Don't forget. You are mine. No shade, no song spells, no prayers to your Goddess will ever change that fact."

Terryn swore. Then he screamed and fell onto his side, writhing and flailing as pain overtook his body. His bones . . . his bones were breaking, warping, changing! He felt his spine crack, felt something try to stab out through his skin. He couldn't bear it. He screamed again, and this time it wasn't his own voice emerging from his throat—it was a monstrous roar.

"We can't have this, now can we?" the Warpwitch said, setting Nilly to one side before she lunged at him and caught his face in her hands, her fingers digging into his skull. "Quiet," she said, spittle falling on his cheeks. "Quiet!"

The pain eased almost at once. Terryn, his body contorting as though he sought to escape himself, almost blessed the witch for the relief she gave. With agonizing slowness, his bones reduced, returning to their proper shape. He lay panting, darkness closing in around the edges of his vision.

"You were easier to control as an un-taken," the Warpwitch said, stroking his forehead as he lay prostrate before her. "But no matter. You'll be useful to me in time, I'm sure. My sweetest pet."

She bent and pressed that horrible, sagging mouth on his cheek. When she drew back slowly, a trail of saliva dangled from her lip, gleaming in the moonlight until it broke. "I'm so glad our paths have crossed again. But for now, don't tell a soul of our happy reunion. Wouldn't want anyone trying to break this curse, now would we? You tell your companions that you saw me and this girl cross the Barrier and vanish into the Witchwood. You tell them we are gone and never coming back. Then forget our conversation. Forget your curse."

She stood, still unsteady on her feet from the paralysis poison. Terryn's vision blurred, and he could see nothing more than a vague, shadowy outline as she swept Nilly up onto her hip and staggered away several paces. But she turned back and looked at him once more, saying, "Until we meet again, sweet boy."

With that, she vanished into the forest, carrying the girl with her.

Terryn bowed his head and let the darkness of compulsion overcome him.

CHAPTER 24

BITING OUT A STRING OF CURSES, AYLETH ROLLED
Kephan's body off her. Her bleeding hands shook, and
her head spun wildly, adrenaline and shade magic
exploding in her brain. She lay on the forest floor beside
the cursed venator, staring up at the starry sky through
the interlacing branches and concentrating everything she
had on simply taking one ragged breath after another.

Laranta careened around inside her. *Mistress? Mistress?
Mistress?*

"Hush," Ayleth soothed her, speaking in her mind. *"I'm . . . I'm all right. Hush, Laranta."*

Her wolf shade crouched, still simmering with excitement and power, still straining at her remaining suppressions. But she held her peace.

Ayleth, drawing one more long breath through her nostrils, rolled onto her side and pushed herself up in order to study Kephan beside her. Shadow sight told her that his soul remained within his body, and when she pressed her shivering, bleeding fingers to his neck, feeling for his pulse, she found it steady and calm. Thank the Goddess! Her double dose of poison wouldn't kill him outright.

She turned her attention to the sigil on his cheek, her eyes narrowing as her shadow sight focused. It was completely invisible to mortal vision, and now it faded so quickly that even her shade senses could hardly discern it. Only when activated by the Warpwitch would it blaze so bright, like fire irons heated in the furnace.

Eyes widening, Ayleth gasped just as the last of the sigil faded completely from her sight. She continued staring at Kephan's cheek for several startled heartbeats, hardly daring to acknowledge the realization that had come to her. Was she mistaken? Had she imagined it amid the haze of pain from her various wounds?

Was it the same pattern as the scars carved into Terryn's cheek?

Terryn.

She jumped to her feet. Each cut and graze and gash in her skin protested violently, and her hands trembled so hard, she pressed them against her chest to try to still them. She couldn't stay here. Terryn had gone after the second monster. Terryn had gone after Nilly. She had to . . . she had to . . .

"*Laranta!*" she called, and her wolf shade immediately sprang upright in her head. "*Laranta, find the venator! Find Terryn!*"

Laranta manifested in her huge wolf shape and set off at once through the trees, her nose to the ground as she sought to catch a scent. Ayleth cast a glance down at Kephan where he lay. She hated to leave him. He looked so frail, so helpless, his clothing torn where his own bones had protruded through skin and fabric, his face contorted in pain even in sleep. But the double dose of paralysis should keep him quiet for many hours. She would return and—

Here! Here, here!

At Laranta's barked warning, Ayleth's head whipped around. She peered through the trees using her shadow vision and saw the glow of a spirit approaching. A spirit she recognized.

"Venator du Balafre?" she called, bracing herself to meet him. The connection between his scar and the sigil in Kephan's face was too clear in her head. She didn't know who he would be when he drew near, but she knew better than to meet him unprepared. "*Laranta, to me,*" she commanded.

Her wolf shade flowed along the soul tether connecting her to Ayleth's body and entered Ayleth's head, snarling, brimming with power. Ayleth leaned into that power, allowing awareness of her body's hurts and needs to be swallowed by the pulse of magic. Her bloody hands clenched into fists.

"Venator du Balafre!" she called a second time.

"Venatrix di Ferosa," Terryn's deep voice rumbled in answer. He didn't *sound* cursed. If that meant anything at all. "Are you hurt? Where is Kephan?"

Ayleth adjusted her footing, rising to the balls of her feet, ready to spring. She watched the gleam of Terryn's spirit approaching through the trees. Then Terryn himself appeared, pushing through foliage to stand before her. Moonlight illuminated his face in a ghostly glow, revealing a tense jaw, fear-widened eyes, and strain lines surrounding his mouth. But neither her mortal vision nor her shadow sight caught any sign of a sigil beneath the ugly scars on his cheek.

His gaze shot from her to the fallen body at her feet. He swooped down beside Kephan, hands outstretched but hesitant to touch their comrade's body.

"He's alive," Ayleth said quickly, kneeling on the venator's other side. "He's subdued for now."

Terryn nodded. His eyes lifted to her face and slowly scanned down the rest of her, noting in particular her bleeding hands. Ayleth tucked her hands under her arms, little caring about the stains she would leave on her jerkin. "It was . . . rough," she said. "Not as bad as it could have been. You?"

A stricken look shot across his face, but he hid it

quickly, so quickly, Ayleth almost doubted she'd seen it. "I killed him," he said darkly.

"Killed whom?" Ayleth's throat thickened before she asked the question to which she feared to hear an answer: "Where's Nilly?"

"The Warpwitch took her." Terryn didn't meet her eye when he answered. He seemed suddenly very focused on Kephan. Perhaps feeling the intensity of her stare on the side of his face, he glanced up quickly, then away again. Clearing his throat, he said, "Kephan and I encountered a farmer on our ride to Elsinoe. His wife was possessed by the Warpwitch. Apparently, Ylaire cursed the husband as well."

"And you didn't notice?" Ayleth asked. Which was unfair of her, she knew. Kephan had almost certainly been cursed since long before she met him, and she'd not detected a thing. The Warpwitch hid her curses deep.

"Sorry," she muttered. Then, "Was that the farmer who took Nilly?"

Terryn nodded, then told her of his fight with the cursed man. Foulke had dropped Nilly during the battle, and after Terryn subdued his enemy he'd gone after the girl at once. But he wasn't fast enough. Her trail had led him straight for the Barrier, and by the time he got there, the girl had already crossed over.

"She wasn't alone," Terryn finished, the hand resting on his bent knee clenching tight. "She was with the Warpwitch. I'm sure it was her. I took a shot, but I wasn't quick enough." He bowed his head, running his fingers through his thick dark curls and cursing softly. "At least they're gone. The Barrier is solid, and they'll not escape again."

Ayleth wanted to reach out and slap him across his scarred face, to leave her own bloody handprint on his cheek. Instead, she said in a low voice, "I'll take Kephan back to the hedgewitch's cottage. He'll rest better there, and we can decide what to do next."

Terryn glanced her way, his eyes meeting hers for another flashing instant. Then he nodded and stood up, sliding his hands under Kephan's arms. "Don't bother," Ayleth said, and nudged him aside. Summoning Laranta's strength, she hefted the venator up and over her shoulder, holding him tight with her lacerated fingers.

She grimaced against the pain and nodded to Terryn.

"Lead on, du Balafre."

Oma Githa's cottage could hardly count as shelter now, with a great hole broken through the roof. But the bed was still intact, and Ayleth laid Kephan down as gently as she could, while Terryn set about lighting a fire on the small hearth and clearing away debris. The corpse of the poor hedgewitch had been knocked to the ground during Ayleth's fight with Kephan. Ayleth carefully gathered up the poor woman, wrapping her once more in a blanket, and arranged her in a corner of the cottage.

Then, Laranta's senses keen in her mind, she went hunting for their horses, leaving Terryn to stand watch over Kephan.

Chestibor proved simple enough to find. Her faithful steed had wandered no more than a mile away since she first dismounted and left him in the cottage yard. Terryn's red mare proved more difficult to locate, and the night was well advanced by the time Ayleth, footsore, exhausted, and sustained only by her shade's ongoing magical strength, led both mounts back to the cottage.

Her wounds, all surface scrapes and not serious, had mostly stopped bleeding, but her hands were stiff and sore.

Terryn's tall frame, silhouetted by firelight, stooped to exit the cottage doorway as Ayleth approached across the yard. "He's stirring," he said.

After tying the horses up in the yard, Ayleth stepped into the cottage after Terryn. Although painfully aware of the hedgewitch's poor little broken body wrapped in its blanket in the corner, she focused her attention on the venator lying on the narrow bed. His eyes slowly blinked as he gazed up at the broken ceiling above.

Ayleth took a seat beside him. "Venator du Tam?"

He blinked again and turned his gaze to her.

Ayleth tried to smile but suspected it appeared less than soothing. "You're . . . you're all right, Venator," she said. "I had to dose you with paralysis. A large dose. You'll be immobile for a while, but you will recover."

The muscles around his eyes twitched. No doubt he wanted to speak, wanted to demand what she was thinking, drugging him, her superior! How much did he remember of his time under the curse? Nothing at all, she suspected.

"I'm sorry about the poison," she said. "You were trying to . . . to kill me."

Terryn stepped in behind Ayleth, towering over her and drawing the venator's gaze. "You're cursed, Kephan," he said. "The Warpwitch got to you. You won't remember it, but you might feel pain in your right cheek. That's where the sigil is."

As Kephan's eyes slowly widened, they explained to him what had happened. Terryn offered his suspicion that the cursing had taken place earlier that day, after he and Kephan parted ways. But Ayleth shook her head. She'd been thinking about it during her search for the horses. Kephan had repaired the opening in the Great Barrier. He must have. But the Warpwitch had caught him and made him forget all about the encounter. Made him forget so thoroughly that he continued to believe he'd not been near the Barrier at all in recent history.

She didn't try to argue the point, however. There was no use in it, not when complete answers were beyond their ability to grasp.

"I was cursed by Ylaire as a child," Terryn continued,

stepping to one side and leaning his shoulder against the cottage wall. He looked ready to drop but refused to take a seat. "Unless she's called the curse to life, it will remain dormant. Not even shadow vision will discern the sigil unless the influence is active. And the individual under her power won't remember anything if she doesn't want them to." He rubbed a hand down the side of his face, pulling at the scars on his cheek. "I didn't remember anything. Not until Fendrel purged my blood."

Bowing his head, he stood for several heartbeats in silence, grappling with painful memories, no doubt. But he pulled himself together and addressed Kephan once more. "You'll need to go to Castra Breçar and receive treatment as soon as you're recovered. When the curse is gone, you'll be able to remember the details of your cursing, and perhaps we can sort through this mystery and lay it to rest once and for all."

Kephan blinked helplessly several times, looking from Terryn to Ayleth, and then up to the hole in the ceiling overhead. His nostrils flared and thinned as he drew long breaths, and the corner of his mouth twitched. Ayleth pitied him, pitied the revelations he faced. To realize he'd not been his own master for who knows how long . . . and to hear that, at another's bidding, he had tried to kill his comrades . . . it would be a lot for any man to take in.

On an impulse quite unlike herself, Ayleth caught Kephan's hand. She knew he couldn't feel it, but she gave his fingers a gentle squeeze even so. "Rest, sir," she said, trying another smile, which felt no more natural than the last one. "Sleep. We'll wait here with you, and we'll set out for Milisendis as soon as you are able."

Kephan blinked again in acknowledgement. Then, obediently, he closed his eyes, still breathing hard. A tear escaped through pale lashes and raced swiftly down the side of his face, over the space where the witch's sigil had burned, invisible but potent.

Could Ylaire still control her slaves from across the Barrier? Ayleth shuddered at the question and got up, backing away from the bed.

With only the briefest of glances Terryn's way, she moved to the corner of the cottage and gathered Oma Githa in her arms. Though she wanted more than anything to curl up on the hearth beside the fire and sleep like a worn-out hound after the hunt, she couldn't bear to leave the poor old hedgewitch's remains bundled off to the side like that.

So, she carried the corpse outside and set about digging another grave, this one much bigger than the grave she'd dug for the raven, and she was that much more exhausted now. But she called Laranta forward in her brain and, using her shade's strength, tore with her knife into the soil of the cottage garden, using her bare hands as scoops.

A few minutes into her work, Terryn joined her. He carried a spade with him. "Found this inside," he said. "Back up."

She nodded, using one arm to sweep loose hair from her face and wiping her hands on her trousers. Terryn dug silently and rhythmically, and though Ayleth several times thought she ought to offer to relieve him, she couldn't quite bring herself to speak.

The night was at its heaviest, at that dark brink before plunging toward dawn, and the air was bitter cold when at last Terryn stood back, panting a little. He nodded to Ayleth, and she heaved the hedgewitch's remains into the grave. As Terryn covered the blanket-wrapped corpse with the soil he had just turned, Ayleth whispered the same prayer she had said over the raven: *"May the Mother receive you who hath called you . . ."*

When the job was done, they stood for some moments on either side of the grave. Not speaking. Not looking at one another.

Finally, Terryn said, "I don't understand."

"What?" Ayleth asked.

He shook his head, gripping the spade handle hard. "How did she end up dead? Ylaire's host, I mean. Lady Mylla's body."

Ayleth thought of the shattered skull she'd found in the forest. "Fiola killed her," she said. "For trying to take Nilly."

"But what would Ylaire want with the child?"

"Nilly carries a Seer." Ayleth shrugged. "Perhaps . . . perhaps the Warpwitch is looking for something. For a vision."

"If that's the case, why would she cross the Barrier again?" Terryn shook his head, glaring at the mound of earth before him. "Even if she managed to harness the completely unpredictable powers of a Seer, she's now trapped back in the Witchwood. What good can a vision do her there?"

Ayleth's stomach knotted, and she decided not to venture a guess. Not now. Not yet. There were too many other issues requiring immediate attention.

She turned and made her way back to the cottage. Rather than enter, however, she moved to the stacks of wooden cages containing the eye-torn animals. Some of the cages had been overturned and crushed during her fight with Kephan, but most remained shut fast, the animals inside crouched and silent.

With quick flicks of her wrist, Ayleth began breaking locks and opening cages wide. Animals darted free: squirrels, birds, hedgehogs, a badger.

"Tell me, Venator du Balafre," she said over her shoulder as she worked, "do you still think I'm somehow in league with the Crimson Devils?"

He didn't answer. Not for some while. His silence lasted so long, Ayleth began to wonder if he'd simply walked away. She stopped with her hand resting on the last cage door and looked around.

Terryn still stood over the grave, regarding her, his

arms folded. "I don't know what I think of you," he said at last. His voice was rough, his face hidden in the depths of his hood. Only his cold eyes glinting with shadow-light were visible.

She held his gaze across the darkness of the yard. In the silence between them, she saw again that moment . . . that moment when they faced each other, he with his arms around Nilly, she with her hands fisted, her shade's power rising in force. What would have happened had Kephan not attacked? What would she have done? Would she have thrown away everything—her life of training, her vows of devotion, her future—for the sake of one inborn shade-taken?

Ayleth turned away. She felt sick even thinking of that little girl in the Witchwood. But at least Nilly was alive. At least she hadn't fallen back into Evanderian hands. For now.

Hollis's voice whispered in the back of her memory: "*Are you ready for all this role requires of you?*"

With a snarl, Ayleth broke the last cage lock, flinging the door wide. She watched as a young fox darted free and fled for the forest, plunging into the deeper shadows, never to be seen again. For a moment, she wished with all her heart that she could run with it. Run and run and run and never look back.

CHAPTER 25

"YOUR HIGHNESS!"

Gerard didn't look up from the papers spread before him on his desk. Instead, as the door to his office opened and Chancellor Yves stepped into the room, he pinched his nose between two fingers, supporting the weight of his head on one elbow. "Yes, what is it?" he asked rather more sharply than necessary.

"A courier arrived just now." Yves crossed the room in brisk strides and slid a scroll across the desk under

Gerard's nose. "It's the third message this month," he continued. "From the duke."

Gerard didn't need to ask which duke Yves meant. He stared down at the seal pressed into the blob of red wax, the unmistakable hart-and-hind of Duke d'Aldreda. He sat upright, taking his elbows off the desktop, and leaned back in his chair. His heart beat a little too fast, but he took care not to let any emotion show in his face. Yves watched him closely.

Knowing his chancellor wouldn't leave until he was certain the missive had been read, Gerard grabbed the scroll, broke the seal, and unrolled the parchment. He scanned the lines quickly.

"Well, Your Highness?" Yves said after a perfunctory silence.

"Well, Yves." Gerard let the scroll roll back up again and fall to the desk atop his other work. Work which he would not be continuing that day. He looked up and met his chancellor's eager gaze. "You must congratulate me. I'm to be married."

An almost-smile pulled at the corner of Yves's mustache. "Goddess's blessings be upon you. We all hoped this day would come agai— would come. When, may I ask, is the happy event to take place?"

"Hallow's Well Night," Gerard replied.

"Saints have mercy!" All color drained from his chancellor's face. "That's a mere month from now! And . . . and will *all* of them be coming? The king? The duke? Their households? The whole court of Telianor?"

"As far as I know." Gerard shrugged. "It's only my wedding. I'm not privy to the details."

"Oh, Saints," Yves whispered again, looking as though he'd just heard rumor of invading armies marching to besiege Dunloch. He made the holy sign, then turned to the door, muttering, "I will begin preparations at once, Your Highness. Word must be sent to the Sisters Siveline. Surely Grand Mother Didienne may be prevailed upon to perform the ceremony. And we'll have to hire extra hands to account for the . . ." His voice trailed off as he reached the door. He paused with his hand on the latch and looked back. "I nearly forgot. The Evanderians are here."

Startled, Gerard looked up sharply. "The Evanderians? Which ones?"

"All of them." Yves curled his lip in distaste. "Venator

du Tam, Venator du Balafre, and that new venatrix."

"Di Ferosa," Gerard said. "Venatrix di Ferosa. Learn her name. Where are they?"

"I made them wait in the kitchen yard," Yves said. "They are a sight to behold, their uniforms befouled with I know not what. I couldn't bear to let them through the door."

"How long have they been waiting, Yves?"

"The last half hour or so."

Gerard cursed and stood up at the desk, his chair's legs scraping on the floor. "Send them up to me at once. And never, *never* make any Evanderian wait to be announced again. Do I make myself clear?"

One fair brow slid up Yves's forehead. "Very clear, Your Highness," he said, and shut the door on his way out.

Gerard waited until he heard his chancellor's footsteps retreat down the hall. Then he pounded a fist on the desktop and turned to the window behind him to gaze at a view of the lake shining bright under cold afternoon sun. But his vision glazed over, blind to the beauty of the scene. Instead, he saw the lines written on that scroll in the duke's firm hand.

Cerine has agreed to the marriage and signed the papers at last. After all these years, I look forward to clasping your hand as I would clasp the hand of my own son.

And that was it. Signed in d'Aldreda's firm hand.

"Cerine has agreed," Gerard whispered, his face close enough to the window to fog the glass. He didn't know if he should believe it. Not after all that had transpired between them. What threats, what leverage had the duke used to strong-arm his youngest daughter into this marriage?

Or was there a chance, even the smallest chance, that she came of her own free will?

Gerard cursed again and started to turn away from the window. Just as he did, a flash of red caught his eye. He turned back. His heart leaped to his throat. The glare of sunlight on the water dazzled his eyes, but he put up a hand to shade them and stared across the lake to the tree-lined far shore.

Who was that standing behind the gold curtain of

autumnal willow boughs? A slim, almost skeletal figure in a tattered, stained white gown. A phantom, an illusion.

Gone.

Gerard opened his window. Ignoring the blast of cold air that bit into his skin, he leaned out over the sill, trying to force his eyes to see farther, to study those empty shadows beneath the willows. Was he mad? Was he dreaming? This was twice now in the space of five days that he'd thought he'd seen her. The first time had proved nothing more than an illusion cast by a predatory Lure shade. But this . . .?

"Fayline," he whispered.

A knock at the door startled him. He pulled his head back into the room and swiftly drew the window shut. "Come!" he called.

The door opened, and Chancellor Yves stepped through, sweeping a long velvet sleeve. "The Evanderians of Milisendis, Your Highness," he said and withdrew swiftly.

The three shade hunters entered—first Kephan, looking much the worse for wear in a battered uniform riddled with strange tears and holes. His face was haggard, as though he'd just survived some terrible ordeal, his eyes hollow in their sockets. Terryn followed him, looking grim and stern as only Terryn could.

Ayleth entered last of all, her uniform a wreck of dirt and mud and blood, but her hair tightly braided out of her face. She had the look of a caged wolf about her, head down and eyes alert. Those eyes fixed hard upon Gerard as she entered, but the moment she saw him, she visibly relaxed.

Kephan approached the prince's desk, and Terryn and Ayleth flanked him. The three of them bowed, Ayleth a little later than the other two. Gerard again took a seat behind his desk and motioned for all three of them to be at ease. Their attitude of attention scarcely altered, their shoulders square and hands fisted behind their backs. Gerard surveyed them wordlessly, noting any number of small cuts, scrapes, and bruises.

"What in the Goddess's three holy names have you been up to?"

Kephan took a step forward, drawing the prince's gaze. "Your Highness," he said, "I am sorry to report that I have apparently fallen prey to a curse."

"A curse?" Gerard's eyebrows went up. Although he'd been instructed in basic understanding of Saint Evander's Order and its workings, he was a little vague on the specifics. "How?"

"Ylaire di Jocosa," Terryn said. "The Warpwitch."

Gerard felt as though a lance had pierced him to the quick. He turned his gaze from Terryn to Kephan to Ayleth and back again, hoping to see some doubt in one of their faces. He read only certainty. And fear.

"Report," he said, his voice firm.

Terryn and Kephan hastened to fill him in on all that had taken place in the last three days. Ayleth stood by, mostly silent, offering only a word or two here and there as to her own part in events.

Gerard listened with mounting horror. A breach in the Great Barrier was unheard of! It had not happened, so far as he knew, in the nearly twenty years since Fendrel du Glaive had played the song spell into being. For one of the Crimson Devils to escape was surely a disaster.

But then . . . if Ylaire di Jocosa had somehow slipped free of the Witchwood, did it not follow that one of her brethren might have escaped as well? Which meant that phantom glimpse Gerard had caught among the willows . . .

It might have been real.

"I must apologize," Kephan said as they reached the end of their tale, "that I do not remember more details. But as you know, du Balafre suffered under the same curse in his childhood. Which means a cure is possible. I fear I must temporarily step down from my service here in Wodechran and go seek that cure at Castra Breçar."

Gerard nodded. "Of course, Venator du Tam. You must take care of yourself. We don't want to lose another good man."

Kephan's face tightened at this indirect mention of Nane, but he said no more, offering only a short nod.

Gerard's gaze slid to Ayleth, standing silently to one side, her chin high. She looked more wolfish than ever in her intensity, but something about her stance told Gerard she was the one to ask his next question.

"What about the inborn child?" he said. "What did you do with her?"

"She was taken by the Warpwitch back across the Barrier, into the Witchwood," Terryn answered, but

Gerard never took his gaze off Ayleth's face. She stared hard at the edge of his desk rather than at him. He watched how her jaw tightened, how her nostrils flared as she drew in a silent breath.

Pinching the bridge of his nose, Gerard once again leaned his head on his hand, elbow propped on the desk. He considered all they had told him. Were they truly going to . . . to burn a child alive? The very idea made him sick. Sick, and angry enough to turn on his childhood friend. What sort of justice was this?

His father maintained a rigid policy of leaving the Evanderian Order to go about its business unquestioned. The king trusted Fendrel to oversee the Order's role in the kingdom, and Gerard had likewise been brought up never to interfere in castra affairs. But . . .

"If you find her," he said, directing his words to Ayleth specifically, "bring her to me. Before you do *anything* else. Bring her to me. The same goes for all inborn you discover in Wodechran Borough."

The tension in the venatrix's face relaxed. Her hard eyes flicked to meet Gerard's, speaking volumes of hopeful gratitude.

Gerard addressed himself to Kephan once more. "I will look forward to your swift return, Venator," he said. "Meanwhile, I trust you will offer both Venator du Balafre and Venatrix di Ferosa counsel to aid them while they manage Milisendis Outpost in your absence. I commend you all for the work you have done. Though the Warpwitch was not killed, at least we have the assurance that she is back behind the Barrier where she belongs. And Nane's murderer . . . she is no longer a threat either. Well done, all of you."

The Evanderians saluted and turned to leave. Kephan led the way, Ayleth hastening behind him. Terryn stood a moment longer, his eyes intent upon Gerard's face. Just as he turned to join the others, Gerard said, "Wait, Terryn."

Kephan and Ayleth paused at the door, looking back over their shoulders. At a wave from the prince, they continued out, closing the door behind them. Gerard rose and moved around to the other side of his desk, facing Terryn.

"I saw Fayline," he said without preamble.

Terryn's anger vanished in a flash of surprise. He

wasn't expecting that. He recovered himself quickly, however. "Are you certain?"

"No," Gerard answered heavily. "I'm not. I'm not certain of anything."

His friend shook his head. He looked away from Gerard out the window, an odd expression on his face. Strained and somewhat confused, as though he tried to remember something but couldn't quite catch it.

"What's wrong?" Gerard asked.

"I . . ." Terryn swallowed hard, his eyes narrowing. "I thought, perhaps . . . No. Never mind. It's nothing." He pulled himself together and faced Gerard once more. "I will hunt down what information I can," he said. "You have my word. If there is even a chance that *she* got out, I will find her."

"And you will save her soul?" The words came out small, hopeless. But he had to ask.

Terryn did not answer at once, and a long, terrible silence hung between them. At last, he whispered, "If her soul is still there to be saved."

Gerard nodded. He knew he could ask for nothing more.

CHAPTER 26

LEAVING THE PRESENCE OF THE GOLDEN PRINCE WAS, Ayleth thought, like stepping out of sunlight into shadow. But she couldn't deny that it was also something of a relief to escape that office. Sight of Gerard's beautiful face only called to mind the brief glimpse she'd had of him in the vision Nilly's shade had pressed into her head. That vision of a star-filled night sky, of a sword's edge, of burning heat around her brow . . .

"*I'm so sorry, Ayleth,*" he'd said just before raising his

sword.

Ayleth shook the memory away quickly. The powers of Seers were unpredictable, strange, and ultimately untrustworthy. No good could come from dwelling on images so incomprehensible, so confused.

Terryn joined her and Kephan on the porch steps as they waited for their horses to be brought around. Ayleth stood behind the two men, a few steps higher, and crossed her arms. None of them spoke.

Throughout their interview with the prince, Ayleth had half expected Terryn to spout his crazed accusations, linking her with the Crimson Devils. And how would Gerard, for all his magnanimity, react to his longtime friend's claims? Would he still look on Ayleth as a worthy candidate? Or would he suddenly see her as a threat?

But the words had never crossed Terryn's lips.

Their three horses were brought eventually. Terryn moved fast to claim and mount his red mare. Ayleth and Kephan moved more leisurely, taking time to check their stirrups and bridles before mounting and crossing the bridge. Terryn was already well into the outer gardens by the time they passed through the gate.

"Well, di Ferosa," Kephan said after they'd left Dunloch behind them, "it seems we must part."

Ayleth cast the older venator a quick, uneasy glance. Riding next to a man who had, only the night before, tried to eat her face off felt strangely . . . vulnerable.

"I can't say our acquaintance has been entirely pleasurable." He spoke in a light tone which contrasted oddly with the hardness in his face. "This being said . . ." Kephan paused a moment, then continued in the same vein: "While at our first meeting I thought it odd that our prince would even consider you as competition for Venator du Balafre, now . . . Well, now I think I see the wisdom in his thinking. You are a formidable hunter, and you might actually have what it takes to steal Terryn's future right out from under him."

The way he said it didn't sound entirely complimentary. Uncertain how else to respond, Ayleth murmured, "Thank . . . you?"

When Kephan chuckled and briefly met her gaze, Ayleth recognized a sad sort of resignation in his eyes. Despite the uncertainty of his future, he mustered a smile that was surprisingly sincere and tossed it casually

Ayleth's way. "All I ask is that you and that boy up ahead don't prove too effective a team. I want to be certain I still have a position here when I return from the castra."

She snorted. "I don't think there's any danger."

"Don't you?" The smile went wryly lopsided, and Kephan shook his head. The road ahead of them split, and the venator reined in his horse even as Ayleth started to turn Chestibor east. "I'll be on my way at once," he said, and nodded in the direction of Terryn, riding ahead down the east road. "Say goodbye to du Balafre for me. And don't be fooled, di Ferosa. He's not all frost. There's fire in his core, and it'll burn true when need arises."

Pausing, Ayleth nodded noncommittally. She didn't much care what lurked in Terryn du Balafre's core.

Kephan turned as though ready to ride west, but again hesitated. Pressing his lips into a line, he looked at Ayleth closely again. "I don't remember much of these last few weeks. But since learning about the girl . . . Nilly . . . a few things have come back to me. They're hazy, like dreams more than anything. But . . ." He bowed his head and seemed to be considering his next words carefully. "Nane received confirmation from the castra that the child was inborn. I saw the letter myself. They gave him sanction to . . . do what was necessary. I told him he couldn't do it. I told him he mustn't. I told him I would stop him if he tried. We argued, viciously. And he set out alone for Elsinoe Shrinehouse to find the girl, to fulfill his duty."

Ayleth listened, her chest tight, not even daring to ask the many questions piling up on her tongue.

"I gathered myself at last and followed Nane. Again, I don't remember much, but . . . I believe we fought. Violently this time. And I took the girl from him and fled with her, took her to the Great Barrier. I was half mad with grief, with horror that the man I . . . that someone I respected so deeply would even consider building a pyre for a child."

He held up a hand as though expecting protests. "I know the law. I know the teachings of our saint. And I'm telling you now, di Ferosa, I would rather be burned alive myself than be the one to strike that blaze."

He didn't continue right away. Ayleth, her hands clutching the pommel of her saddle, waited. Her mind filled in what Kephan did not say: He'd sent Nilly through the Great Barrier in a bid to save her. Then Nane went in after her, also intent upon her rescue, though of a different sort. How exactly things had played out from there, she couldn't guess and doubted she would ever learn, not completely.

"I don't remember trying to repair the Great Barrier," Kephan continued. "I don't remember meeting the Warpwitch. I don't remember anything really. But I think . . . I think I saw Nane die. I don't know for certain, but there's an image in my brain, a picture of him standing just beyond the Barrier, the opening widening as he played the song spell. Then a dark form swooping down from above, striking him. He falls and . . . I want to go to him . . . Perhaps I did. Perhaps that's where the Warpwitch found me."

Perhaps it was the Warpwitch who had commanded Kephan to forget his efforts to close the Barrier. Perhaps it was the Warpwitch who commanded him to forget his final moments with Nane. Perhaps she had taken Nane's logbook to prevent others from learning about the presence of a Seer in Wodechran. Perhaps . . . perhaps . . .

Kephan looked up, meeting Ayleth's gaze. For the first time since meeting him, Ayleth saw no hardness in his face, no sardonic twist to his lip. There was nothing but open, honest heartbreak.

"We are not what we think we are," he said. "None of us." He swallowed hard and looked away, off to the western horizon, the direction in which Castra Breçar lay. "In the end, I fear we may discover that we were the true monsters all along."

Ayleth didn't know what to say. She pried one hand from her pommel, half wanting to reach out to the other venator. To tell him she understood. To tell him that she would have attacked Terryn to save Nilly's life. But it wasn't the same. Terryn wasn't even her hunt brother, not really. It wasn't the same at all.

Kephan drew himself upright in the saddle and gave his head a short shake. "Goddess go with you, Venatrix di Ferosa," he said.

"Goddess go with you, Venator du Tam," she answered, saluting him solemnly, her fist pressed to her heart. "I hope you find the healing you seek at Castra Breçar."

Kephan nodded and saluted her in return. Without another word, he spurred his mount into motion and set off along the west road, making for the borders of Wodechran Borough. Ayleth watched him go for some while. He looked defeated somehow, despite the set of his shoulders and his upright posture in the saddle.

For a moment it seemed as though she could almost discern the ghost of a second rider at his side—another hooded hunter, never far from Kephan's thoughts, even now that his soul was lost.

What a lonely existence it was to serve in the Order of Evander! Ayleth turned back to the east road, nudging Chestibor into a brisk walk. Hollis's face flashed across her mind's eye, and her heart thudded a single sharp beat in response. She'd never fully understood why her mistress refused to let her go. It had seemed unfair, arbitrary, even cruel.

Now, she wondered if the older venatrix had simply dreaded the solitude that must follow the loss of her apprentice.

"*Laranta*," she whispered, reaching inward for some sense of her shade. But only the hum of suppressing spell songs answered her. She faced the long ride back to Milisendis alone.

Or so she thought until, cresting a rise in the road, she saw Terryn up ahead, his red mare pawing the ground impatiently as he held her in check. His rigid back was to her, his gaze fixed on the eastern horizon. But he didn't ride on. Was he waiting for her to catch up?

Haunts damn it. Though a moment before she'd been sighing over her lack of companionship, this was *not* the solution she'd had in mind. But Kephan was gone now. For better or worse, Terryn was her hunt brother for the next several weeks, possibly months.

Clucking to Chestibor, Ayleth trotted her horse up alongside Terryn. He, without a glance her way, urged his horse back into motion, and they progressed side by side for some while without speaking as the sun set at their backs. Ayleth's heart pounded uncomfortably. Why had he waited to ride with her? Simply to emphasize his disapproval with this frosty silence?

"What?" she demanded at last, a simple, sharp bark of a word. She turned in her saddle to face the venator, her brow tightening in a deep scowl.

Terryn swallowed, the muscles of his throat visibly constricting. "I realized something," he said.

Ayleth raised an eyebrow, waiting.

"I realized that I never thanked you. For saving my life."

He could have knocked her out of her saddle with a breath.

Ayleth gave her head a shake, convinced she must have heard wrong.

He looked her way, the briefest of sidelong glances. "From the curse," he said. "Nane's curse at the gate. I would have died before ever setting foot inside Milisendis if not for your quick action. So, thank you."

"That was . . . that was days ago," Ayleth said. It felt like longer. It felt like years.

"Yes."

"I . . . Why do you think you should . . .? I mean, what could you possibly . . .?" She scratched the back of her neck under her long braid, turning her gaze to study the landscape between Chestibor's ears. Then, after a huff of a sigh, she said, "You're welcome."

Another silence followed for the next mile. Several times Ayleth considered spurring Chestibor on ahead, determined to escape the oppressive presence of the venator. But something held her back. A question burned in her mind, a question she had to ask. A question to which she must know the answer before she could bear to spend another moment in this man's company.

"What would you have done?"

Another flashing sidelong glance. And silence.

Ayleth tried again, tried to frame her question more directly. "If I'd walked away last night. In the forest. If I'd left you with Nilly. Would you have killed her?"

He didn't answer at once. But there was something in his silence, some quality she scarcely dared define. Something . . .

The truth came to her, as clearly as though he'd spoken it out loud. She could almost see it, like a vision—she could see him watching until she had passed out of sight, out of hearing. She could see him take Nilly by the hand and walk with her into the darkness of the fringe forest, making for the Barrier.

She could see him sending the girl through.

She knew it. She knew it with more certainty than she knew what she herself would have done in his place. Something in the rhythm of that soul riding beside her told her the truth: Venator Terryn would not have killed the child.

"We are servants of Evander," he said at last. "By the will of the Goddess we serve. We have a duty to the souls of this world. We must honor that duty, no matter the cost."

A good answer. A venator's answer.

But it wasn't the truth. And she knew it.

Ayleth looked at him, hard. After a long moment of fighting with himself, he met her gaze, his face like ice-crusted stone. But there was something in his eye—a kind of desperation. She saw in his gaze the same question she had asked of herself.

If we are not loyal to the law of Evander . . . what are we?

Heretics. Witches.

Damned.

Ayleth reined in Chestibor until Terryn's red mare had walked well ahead. She then let the horse amble along the winding circuit road, slowly, leisurely, until the venator rounded a bend and passed beyond sight ahead of her.

Only then did she fully release the breath she'd been holding. Her chest hurt, and she pressed a hand to her heart, as though to somehow make it calm its frantic beating. For a while she could do nothing but breathe, driving out the tumultuous thoughts inside her head.

Laranta raised her head, pushing against her suppressions. *Mistress?* she asked, her voice barely audible above the song spells. *Mistress, we hunt?*

"*Not yet, my dear,*" Ayleth answered. "*Soon, I promise. Soon.*"

EPILOGUE

NILLY BURIED HER FACE IN THE WOMAN'S SHOULDER. She wept, her body shuddering with wave upon wave of terror. She longed for her mother, longed for her father, even longed for the comforting arms of the tall man who had held her in the forest. But there was only this woman who carried her now, her arms tight around Nilly's small body.

"Hush, sweet child," the woman kept murmuring. "Hush your tears now. Hush, for you are safe. I won't let anyone harm you, not a hair on your head. Not you, and not that beauty you carry inside you. Hush now, sweetness, hush."

The voice was harsh, but the rhythmic quality of her words was soothing. Nilly, exhausted, dozed off at last, her head lolling against that hard, bony shoulder. She slipped gratefully into a dream in which a ghostly figure appeared beside her. Like a bit of moonlight shaped into a dainty, cat-like being with delicate furred wings spreading from its shoulders. It wrapped those wings protectively around Nilly's soul, drawing her close and rocking her gently.

Don't worry, the being whispered. *Don't worry. You're not alone.*

"*Mama!*" Nilly cried, tears streaming down even her dream face.

Mama is gone now, the being answered. *But she loves you still.*

Nilly hiccupped on a sob, then pressed herself so close against the ghostly form, she almost disappeared inside those wings. "*Don't leave me,*" she begged.

Never. I will never leave you. They cannot take me away from you.

Nilly woke abruptly, startled out of the dream, startled out of the winged being's embrace. She was no longer carried in the witch's arms, no longer in the forest beneath the spreading canopy of trees. Instead, she looked around at the shadowy walls of a large, lonely room. Dawn light crept through broken, gaping windows to reveal ruinous furniture, rotten curtains, a half-burned rug upon a cold flagstone floor. One wall was partially caved in. Nilly herself sat in a sagging chair covered in threadbare brocade.

The woman was across the room, pushing her way through the fallen stones of the broken wall, rolling some back, heaving others aside. Nilly watched her uncertainly, afraid to speak, afraid to move. As she watched, the woman uncovered an old armoire. One of its sides was crushed, and when the woman opened the doors, Nilly saw the shelves inside all fallen, the contents shattered and spilled.

"Ruined," the woman muttered, picking up what looked like the top half of an old glass bottle. "A collection more than a century old—blood from hundreds of sources—all gone. Haunts damn those venators. But . . . ah!"

She dropped the broken vial. Her hand darted into the wreckage and came out with a small, unbroken bottle. Its black, faceted sides gleamed in the dawn light. "This will serve."

With those words, the woman drew a knife from her belt. Nilly pressed back deeper into her chair, but the woman didn't look her way. She held up the knife, the blade of which was stained with blood, and she began to speak in a strange, awful language. The stains of blood along the blade moved, shifted, rippled. The woman tilted the knife so that its tip was suspended over the lip of the bottle, still speaking her incantation. Fresh red blood poured in a stream down the steel edge, plopping daintily into the bottle, filling it halfway.

At last, with a sigh, the woman let the knife fall from her shaking hand. She clutched the bottle close to her chest, her stern face relaxing into a smile so joyful, it almost transformed her harsh features. "It is enough!" she said, then held the bottle up to peer inside, chewing her lip nervously. "It *must* be enough. Odile's own grace is with us still."

She turned to Nilly, and her smile grew so large, the girl could see every dark, blood-stained tooth.

"And now, sweet child," she said, "with your help, we will find our queen."

ABOUT THE AUTHOR

Sylvia Mercedes makes her home in the idyllic North Carolina countryside with her handsome husband, sweet baby-lady, and Gummy Bear, the Toothless Wonder Cat. When she's not writing she's . . . okay, let's be honest. When she's not writing, she's running around after her little girl, cleaning up glitter, trying to plan healthy-ish meals, and wondering where she left her phone. In between, she reads a steady diet of fantasy novels. But mostly she's writing.

After a short career in Traditional Publishing (under a different name), Sylvia decided to take the plunge into the Indie Publishing World and is enjoying every minute of it. The Venatrix Chronicles is her first series as an independent author, but she's got many more planned!

Don't miss the continuation of Ayleth's adventures in
Book 3 of The Venatrix Chronicles!

Poisoned. Trapped.
At the mercy of a bloodthirsty phantom.
She can handle this.

PATHS OF MALICE

Meanwhile don't miss Song of Shadows:

Visit www.SylviaMercedesBooks.com
to get your free copy.

www.ingramcontent.com/pod-product-compliance
Lightning Source LLC
Chambersburg PA
CBHW031054260626
47172CB00001B/60